George Horatio Derby, John Phœnix

Phœnixiana or Sketches and Burlesques

George Horatio Derby, John Phœnix

Phœnixiana or Sketches and Burlesques

ISBN/EAN: 9783743383326

Manufactured in Europe, USA, Canada, Australia, Japa

Cover: Foto ©Andreas Hilbeck / pixelio.de

Manufactured and distributed by brebook publishing software (www.brebook.com)

George Horatio Derby, John Phœnix

Phœnixiana or Sketches and Burlesques

Yours respectively
John P. Squibob

PHŒNIXIANA;

OR,

SKETCHES AND BURLESQUES

BY

JOHN PHŒNIX.

In the name of the Prophet — Figs."

TWELFTH EDITION.

NEW YORK:
D. APPLETON AND COMPANY,
549 & 551 BROADWAY.
1873.

TO

DR. CHARLES M. HITCHCOCK,

OF SAN FRANCISCO,

MY EARLIEST, KINDEST, AND MOST CONSTANT FRIEND,

𝕮𝖍𝖊𝖘𝖊 𝕾𝖐𝖊𝖙𝖈𝖍𝖊𝖘

ARE AFFECTIONATELY DEDICATED

BY

THE AUTHOR.

PREFACE.

——•••——

THIS book is merely a collection of sundry sketches, recently published in the newspapers and magazines of California. They were received with approval, separately, and it is to be hoped they may meet with it on their appearance in a collected form. When first published, the Author supposed he had seen and heard the last of them, but circumstances entirely beyond his control have led to their republication.

The Author does not flatter himself that he has made any very great addition to the literature of the age, by this performance ; but if his book turns out to be a very bad one, he will be consoled by the reflection that it is by no means the first, and probably will not be the last of that kind, that has been given to the Public. Meanwhile, this is, by the blessing of

Divine Providence, and through the exertions of the Immortal Washington, a free country ; and no man can be compelled to read any thing against his inclina tion. With unbounded respect for every body,

The Author remains,

JOHN PHŒNIX.

SAN FRANCISCO, July 15, 1855.

A WORD TO THE READER.

I<small>T</small> is proper to state, that while the following pages are collected with the permission of the Author, and thus presented in a book-form, he has yet himself not been consulted in any manner in relation to the order of arrangement of its contents; and it is quite probable, that his severer taste and better judgment might have operated to exclude some things which are here embraced. The Editor can only say, that preparing the volume hastily for the press, he has done the best he could in the premises; and only begs that the sin of omission or of commission that may be observable in these pages, should not be visited upon the head of the Author.

J. J. A.

S<small>AN</small> D<small>IEGO</small> C<small>AL</small>. October 1855.

CONTENTS.

———•◦•———

10 CONTENTS.

PHŒNIXIANA.

OFFICIAL REPORT

OF

PROFESSOR JOHN PHŒNIX, A. M.

*Of a Military Survey and Reconnoissance of the route from San Francisco to the Mission of Dolores, made with a view to ascertain the practicability of connecting those points by a Railroad.**

MISSION OF DOLORES, Feb. 15, 1855.

It having been definitely determined, that the great Rail· road, connecting the City of San Francisco with the head of navigation on Mission Creek, should be constructed without unnecessary delay, a large appropriation ($120,000) was granted, for the purpose of causing thorough military ex- aminations to be made of the proposed routes. The routes, which had principally attracted the attention of the public, were "the Northern," following the line of Brannan Street, "the Central," through Folsom Street, and "the extreme Southern," passing over the "Old Plank Road" to the Mis-

---

* The Mission Dolores is only 2½ miles from the City Hall of San Francisco, and a favorite suburban locality, lying within the limits of the City Survey. This fact noted for the benefit of distant readers of these sketches.

sion. Each of these proposed routes has many enthusiastic advocates; but "the Central" was, undoubtedly, the favorite of the public, it being more extensively used by emigrants from San Francisco to the Mission, and therefore more widely and favorably known than the others. It was to the examination of this route, that the Committee, feeling a confidence (eminently justified by the result of my labors) in my experience, judgment and skill as a Military Engineer, appointed me on the first instant. Having notified that Honorable Body of my acceptance of the important trust confided to me, in a letter, wherein I also took occasion to congratulate them on the good judgment they had evinced, I drew from the Treasurer the amount ($40,000) appropriated for my peculiar route, and having invested it securely in loans at three per cent a month (made, to avoid accident, in my own name), I proceeded to organize my party for the expedition.

In a few days my arrangements were completed, and my scientific corps organized, as follows :—

John Phœnix, A. M. . . .	Principal Engineer and Chief Astronomer.
Lieut. Minus Root . . .	Apocryphal Engineers. First Assistant Astronomer.
Lieut. Nonplus A. Zero . . .	Hypercritical Engineers. Second Assistant Astronomer.
Dr. Abraham Dunshunner .	Geologist.
Dr. Targee Heavystern . .	Naturalist.
Herr Von Der Weegates . .	Botanist.
Dr. Fogy L. Bigguns . . .	Ethnologist.
Dr. Tushmaker	Dentist.
Enry Halfred Jinkins, R. A. .	Draftsmen.
Adolphe Kraut	
Hi Fun	Interpreter.
James Phœnix, (my elder brother)	Treasurer.
Joseph Phœnix, ditto, . .	Quarter-Master.

WILLIAM PHŒNIX, (younger brother) . . . . . . Commissary.
PETER PHŒNIX, ditto, ... Clerk.
PAUL PHŒNIX, (my cousin) . . . . Sutler.
REUBEN PHŒNIX, ditto, ... Wagon-Master.
RICHARD PHŒNIX, (second cousin) . . . . . Assistant ditto.

These gentlemen, with one hundred and eighty-four laborers employed as teamsters, chainmen, rodmen, etc., made up the party. For instruments, we had 1 large Transit Instrument (8 inch acromatic lens), 1 Mural Circle, 1 Altitude and Azimuth Instrument (these instruments were permanently set up in a mule cart, which was backed into the plane of the true meridian, when required for use), 13 large Theodolites, 13 small ditto, 8 Transit Compasses, 17 Sextants, 34 Artificial Horizons, 1 Sidereal Clock, and 184 Solar Compasses. Each employee was furnished with a gold chronometer watch, and, by a singular mistake, a diamond pin and gold chain; for directions having been given, that they should be furnished with "*chains and pins*," —meaning of course such articles as are used in surveying —Lieut. Root, whose "zeal somewhat overran his discretion," incontinently procured for each man the above-named articles of jewelry, by mistake. They were purchased at Tucker's (where, it is needless to remark, "you can buy a diamond pin or ring)," and afterwards proved extremely useful in our intercourse with the natives of the Mission of Dolores, and indeed, along the route.

Every man was suitably armed, with four of Colt's revolvers, a Minie rifle, a copy of Col. Benton's speech on the Pacific Railroad, and a mountain howitzer. These last-named heavy articles required each man to be furnished with a wheelbarrow for their transportation, which was accordingly done; and these vehicles proved of great service on the survey, in transporting not only the arms but the baggage of the party, as well as the plunder derived from the natives. A squadron of dragoons, numbering 150 men, under Capt. Mc-Spadden, had been detailed as an escort. They accordingly left about a week before us, and we heard of them occasionally on the march.

On consulting with my assistants, I had determined to select, as a base for our operations, a line joining the summit of Telegraph Hill with the extremity of the wharf at Oakland, and two large iron thirty-two pounders were accordingly procured, and at great expense imbedded in the earth, one at each extremity of the line, to mark the initial points. On placing compasses over these points to determine the bearing of the base, we were extremely perplexed by the unaccountable local attraction that prevailed; and were compelled, in consequence, to select a new position. This we finally concluded to adopt between Fort Point and Saucelito ; but, on attempting to measure the base, we were deterred by the unexpected depth of the water intervening, which, to our surprise, was considerably over the chain bearers' heads. Disliking to abandon our new line, which had been selected with much care and at great expense, I determined to employ in its measurement a reflecting instrument, used very successfully by the United States Coast Survey. I therefore directed my assistants to procure me a " HELIOTROPE," but after being annoyed by having brought to me successively a sweet-smelling shrub of that name, and a box of " Lubin's Extract " to select from, it was finally ascertained, that no such instrument could be procured in California. In this extremity, I bethought myself of using as a substitute the flash of gunpowder. Wishing to satisfy myself of its practi- cability by an experiment, I placed Dr. Dunshunner at a dis- tance of forty paces from my Theodolite, with a flint-lock musket, carefully primed, and directed him to flash in the pan, when I should wave my hand. Having covered the Doctor with the Theodolite, and by a movement of the tan gent screw placed the intersection of the cross lines directly over the muzzle of the musket, I accordingly waved; when I was astounded by a tremendous report, a violent blow in the eye, and the instantaneous disappearance of the instrument.

Observing Dr. Dunshunner lying on his back in one direction, and my hat, which had been violently torn from my head, at about the same distance in another, I concluded that the musket had been accidentally loaded. Such proved to be the case; the marks of three buckshot were found in my hat, and a shower of screws, broken lenses and pieces of brass, which shortly fell around us, told where the ball had struck, and bore fearful testimony to the accuracy of Dr. Dunshunner's practice. Believing these experiments more curious than useful, I abandoned the use of the " Heliotrope" or its substitutes, and determined to reverse the usual pro cess, and arrive at the length of the base line by subsequent triangulation. I may as well state here, that this course was adopted and resulted to our entire satisfaction; the distance from Fort Point to Saucelito by the solution of a mean of 1,867,434,926,465 triangles, being determined to be exactly *three hundred and twenty-four feet*. This result differed very much from our preconceived ideas and from the popular opinion; the distance being generally supposed to be some ten miles; but I will stake my professional reputation on the accuracy of our work, and there can, of course, be no disputing the elucidations of science, or facts demonstrated by mathematical process, however incredible they may appear *per se*.

We had adopted an entire new system of triangulation, which I am proud to claim (though I hope with becoming modesty) as my own invention. It simply consists in placing one leg of a tripod on the initial point, and opening out the other legs as far as possible; the distance between the legs is then measured by a two-foot rule and noted down; and the tripod moved, so as to form a second triangle, connected with the first, and so on, until the country to be triangulated has been entirely gone over. By using a large number of tri-pods, it is easily seen with what rapidity the work may be carried on, and this was, in fact, the object of my requisition for so large a number of solar compasses, the tripod being in my opinion the only useful portion of that absurd instru-ment. Having given Lieut. Root charge of the triangula-tion, and detached Mr. Jinkins with a small party on hydro-graphical duty (to sound a man's well, on the upper part of Dupont Street, and report thereon), on the 5th of February I left the Plaza, with the *savans* and the remainder of my

party, to commence the examination and survey of KEARNY
STREET.

Besides the mules drawing the cart which carried the
transit instrument, I had procured two fine pack mules, each
of which carried two barrels of ale for the draftsmen. Fol·
lowing the tasteful example of that gallant gentleman—who
conducted the Dead Sea Expedition, and wishing likewise
to pay a compliment to the administration under which I
was employed, I named the mules " Fanny Pierce," and
" Fanny Bigler." Our *cortège* passing along Kearny Street
attracted much attention from the natives, and indeed, our
appearance was sufficiently imposing to excite interest even
in less untutored minds than those of these barbarians.

First came the cart, bearing our instruments; then a cart
containing Lieut Zero with a level, with which he constantly noted the changes of grade that might occur; then one
hundred and fifty men, four abreast, armed to the teeth, each
wheeling before him his personal property and a mountain
howitzer; then the *savans*, each with note-book and pencil,
constantly jotting down some object of interest (Doctor
Tushmaker was so zealous to do something, that he pulled a
tooth from an iron rake standing near a stable-door, and was
cursed therefor by the illiberal proprietor), and finally, the
Chief Professor, walking arm in arm with Dr. Dunshunner,
and gazing from side to side, with an air of ineffable bland-
ness and dignity, brought up the rear.

I had made arrangements to measure the length of Kearny Street by two methods; first, by chaining its sidewalks,

and secondly, by a little instrument of my invention called the " Go-it-ometer." This last consists of a straight rod of brass, firmly strapped to a man's leg and connected with a system of clock-work placed on his back, with which it performs, when he walks, the office of a *ballistic pendulum.* About one foot below the ornamental buttons on the man's back appears a dial-plate connected with the clock-work, on which is promptly registered, by an index, each step taken. Of course, the length of the step being known, the distance passed over in a day may be obtained by a very simple process.

We arrived at the end of Kearny Street, and encamped for the night about sundown, near a large brick building, inhabited by a class of people called " The Orphans," who, I am credibly informed, have no fathers or mothers ! After seeing the camp properly arranged, the wheelbarrows parked and a guard detailed, I sent for the chainmen and " Go-it-ometer " bearer, to ascertain the distance travelled during the day.

Judge of my surprise to find that the chainmen, having received no instructions, had simply drawn the chain after them through the streets, and had no idea of the distance whatever. Turning from them in displeasure, I took from the " Go-it-ometer " the number of paces marked, and on working the distance, found it to be four miles and a-half. Upon close questioning the bearer, William Boulder (called by his associates, " Slippery Bill"), I ascertained that he had been in a saloon in the vicinity, and after drinking five glasses of a beverage, known among the natives as " *Lager Bier,*" he had danced a little for their amusement. Feeling very much dissatisfied with the day's survey, I stepped out of the camp, and stopping an omnibus, asked the driver how far he thought it to the Plaza ?   He replied, " Half a-mile," which I accordingly noted down, and returned very much pleased at so easily obtaining so much valuable information.   It would appear, therefore, that " Slippery Bill," under the influence of five glasses (probably 2½ quarts) of " *Lager Bier*," had actually danced four miles in a few moments.

Kearny Street, of which I present above a spirited en-graving from a beautiful drawing by Mr. Kraut, is a pass, about fifty feet in width.   The soil is loose and sandy, about one inch in depth, below which Dr. Dunshunner discovered a stratum of white pine, three inches in thickness, and beneath this again, sand.

It is densely populated, and smells of horses.   Its surface is intersected with many pools of *sulphuretted protoxide of hydrogen*, and we found several specimens of a vegetable sub-stance, loosely distributed, which is classed by Mr. Wee-gates as the *stalkus cabbagiensis*.

It being late in the evening when our arrangements for encamping were completed, we saw but little of the natives until the next morning, when they gathered about our camp to the number of eighteen.

We were surprised to find them of diminutive stature, the tallest not exceeding three feet in height.   They were excesively mischievous, and disposed to steal such trifling things as they could carry away. Their countenances are of the color of dirt, and their hair white and glossy as the silk of maize. The one that we took to be their chief, was an exceedingly diminutive personage, but with a bald head which gave him a very venerable appearance. He was dressed in a dingy robe of jaconet, and was borne in the arms of one of his followers. On making them a speech, proposing a treaty, and assuring them of the protection of their great Father, Pierce, the chief was affected to tears, and on being comforted by his followers, repeatedly exclaimed, " da, da,—da, da; " which, we were informed by the interpreter, meant "father," and was intended as a respectful allusion to the President. We presented him afterwards with some beads, hawk-bells and other presents, which he immediately thrust into his mouth, saying " Goo," and crowing like a cock; which was rendered by the interpreter into an expression of high satisfaction. Having made presents to all his followers, they at length left us very well pleased, and we shortly after took up our line of march. From the notes of Dr. Bigguns, I transcribe the following description of one of this deeply interesting people :

" Kearney Street native ; name—Bill ;—height, two feet nine nches ;—hair, white ;—complexion, dirt color;—eyes, blue ;— no front teeth ;—opal at extremity of nose ;—dress, a basquine of bluish bombazine, with two gussets, ornamented down the front with *crotchet* work of molasses candy, three buttons on one side and eight button holes on the other—leggings of tow-cloth, fringed at the bottoms and permitting free ventilation behind—one shoe and one boot ;—occupation, erecting small

pyramids of dirt and water; when asked what they were, replied 'pies,' (word in Spanish meaning *feet ;* supposed they might
be the feet or foundation of some barbarian structure)—religious
belief, obscure ;—when asked who made him, replied 'PAR'
(supposed to be the name of one of their principal Deities)."

We broke up our encampment and moved North by com
pass across Market Street, on the morning of the 6th, and
about noon had completed the survey as far as the corner of
Second Street.

While crossing Market Street, being anxious to know the
exact time, I concluded to determine it by observation.
Having removed the Sidereal Clock from the cart, and put it
in the street, we placed the cart in the plane of the Meridian,
and I removed the eye and object-glass of the transit, for the
purpose of wiping them. While busily engaged in this manner, an individual, whom I have reason to believe is connected with a fire company, approached, and seeing the large
brazen tube of the transit pointed to the sky, mistook it for a
huge speaking trumpet. Misled by this delusion, he mounted
the cart, and in an awful tone of voice shouted through the
transit " *Wash her, Thirteen !* " but having miscalculated the
strength of his lungs, he was seized with a violent fit or
coughing, and before he could be removed had completely
coughed the vertical hairs out of the instrument. I was in
despair at this sudden destruction of the utility of our most
valuable instrument, but fortunately recollecting a gridiron,
that we had among our kitchen apparatus, I directed Dr.
Heavysterne to hold it up in the plane of the true Meridian.

and with an opera glass watched and noted by the clock the passage of the sun's centre across the five bars. Having made these observations, I requested the principal computer to work them out, as I wished to ascertain the time immediately; but he replying that it would take some three months to do it, I concluded not to wait, but sent a man into the grocery, corner of Market and Second, to inquire the time, who soon returned with the desired information. It may be thought singular, that with so many gold watches in our party, we should ever be found at a loss to ascertain the time ; but the fact was that I had directed every one of our employees to set his watch by Greenwich mean time, which, though excellent to give one the longitude, is for ordinary purposes the meanest time that can be found. A distressing casualty that befell Dr. Bigguns on this occasion may be found worthy of record. An omnibus, passing during the time of observation, was driven carelessly near our Sidereal Clock, with which it almost came into contact. Dr. Bigguns, with a slight smile, remarked that " the clock *was nearly run down*," and immediately fainted away. The pursuits of science cannot be delayed by accidents of this nature, two of the workmen removed our unfortunate friend, at once, to the Orphan Asylum, where, having rung the bell, they left him on the steps and departed, and we never saw him afterwards.

From the corner of Market to the corner of Second and Folsom Streets, the route presents no object of interest worthy of mention. We were forced to the conclusion, however, that little throwing of stones prevails near the latter point, as the inhabitants mostly live in glass houses. On the 8th we had brought the survey nearly up to Southwick's Pass on Folsom Street, and we commenced going through the Pass on the morning of the 9th. This pass consists of a rectangular ravine, about 10 feet in length, the sides lined with pine boards, with a white oak (*quercus albus*) bar, that at certain occasions forms across, entirely obstructing the whole route. We found no difficulty in getting through the Pass on foot, nor with the wheelbarrows; but the mule carts and the " two Fannies " were more troublesome, and we were finally unable to get them through without a considerable pecuniary disbursement, amounting in all to one dollar and fifty cents ($1.50). We understand that the City of San Francisco is desirous of effecting a safe and free passage through this celebrated cañon, but a large appropriation ($220,000) is required for the purpose.

The following passages relating to this portion of the route, transcribed from the Geological Notes of Dr. Dunshunner, though not directly connected with the objects of the survey, are extremely curious in a scientific point of view, and may be of interest to the general reader.

"The country in the vicinity of the route, after leaving Southwick's Pass, is very productive, and I observed with astonishment, that red-headed children appear to grow spontaneously. A building was pointed out to me, near our line of march, as the *locale* of a most astounding agricultural and architectural phenomenon, which illustrates the extreme fertility of the soil in a remarkable degree. A small pine wardrobe, which had been left standing by the side of the house (a frame cottage with a

2

piazza), at the commencement of the rainy season, took root, and in a few weeks grew to the prodigious height of thirty feet, and still preserving its proportions and characteristic appearance, extended in each direction, until it covered a space of ground some forty by twenty feet in measurement.

"This singular phenomenon was taken advantage of by the proprietors; doors and windows were cut in the wardrobe, a chimney erected, and it now answers every purpose of an addition to the original cottage, being two stories in height! This, doubtless, appears almost incredible, but fortunately the house and attached wardrobe may be seen any day, from the road, at a trifling expense of omnibus hire, by the sceptical. Some distance beyond, rises a noble structure, built entirely of cut-wood, called 'The Valley House, by Mrs. Hubbard." Not imagining that a venial species of profanity was conveyed by this legend, I concluded that Mrs. Hubbard was simply the proprietor. This brought to my mind the beautiful lines of a primitive poet, Spenser,* if I mistake not:

> 'Old Mother Hubbard went to the cupboard
> To get her poor dog a bone;
> But when she got there, the cupboard was bare,
> And so the poor dog got none.'

"Feeling curious to ascertain if this were, by any possibility, the ancient residence of the heroine of these lines, perchance an ancestress of the present proprietor, I ventured to call and inquire; and my antiquarian zeal was rewarded by the information that such was the case; and that, if I returned at a later hour during the evening, I could be allowed a sight of the closet, and a view of the skeleton of the original dog. Delighted with my success, I returned accordingly, and finding the door closed, ventured to knock; when a sudden shower of rain fell, lasting but about five seconds, but drenching me to the skin. Undeterred by this *contretemps*, I elevated my umbrella and knocked again, loudly, when a violent concussion upon the umbrella, ac-. companied by a thrill down the handle, which caused me to seal

---

* The Doctor is in error; the lines quoted are from Chaucer.   J. P.

myself precipitately in a bucket by the side of the door, convinced me that electrical phenomena of an unusual character
were prevalent, and decided me to return with all speed to our
encampment. Here I was astounded by discovering inverted on
the summit of my umbrella, a curious and deeply interesting
vase, of singularly antique shape, and composed, apparently, of
white porcelain. Whether this vase fell from the moon, a comet,
or a passing meteor, I have not yet decided; drawings of it are
being prepared, and the whole subject will receive my thorough
investigation at an early day.*

"I subsequently attempted to pursue my investigations at the
' Valley House,' but the curt manner of the proprietor led me to
suspect that the subject was distasteful, and I was reluctantly
compelled to abandon it.

"Near the ' Valley House,' I observed an advertisement of
' The Mountain View,' by P. Buckley; but the building in which
it is exhibited being closed, I had no opportunity to judge of the
merits of the painting, or the skill of Mr. Buckley as an artist.
A short distance further, I discovered a small house occupied by
a gentleman, who appeared engaged in some description of traf-
fic with the emigrants; and on watching his motions intently,
my surprise was great to find that his employment consisted in
selling them small pieces of pasteboard *at fifty cents apiece!*
Curious to know the nature of these valuable bits of paper, I
watched carefully the proprietor's motions through a window for
some hours; but being at length observed by him, I was requested to leave—and I left. This curious subject is, therefore,
I regret to say, enwrapped in mystery, and I reluctantly leave it
for the elucidation of some future *savant.* The beautiful idea,
originated by Col. Benton, that buffaloes and other wild animals
are the pioneer engineers, and that subsequent explorations can
discover no better roads than those selected by them, would appear to apply admirably to the Central Route. Many pigs, singly

---

* This curious antique, to which I have given the name of the "Dunshunner
Vase," has singularly the appearance of a *wash basin!* When the drawings are
completed, it is to be presented to the California Academy of Natural Sciences. J. I'

and in droves, met and passed me continually; and as the pig is unquestionably a more sagacious animal than the buffalo, their preference for this route is a most significant fact. I was, moreover, informed by the emigrants, that this route was 'the one followed by Col. Fremont when he lost his men.' This statement must be received *cum grano salis*, as, on my inquiry—'What men?' my informant replied 'A box of chessmen,' which answer, from its levity, threw an air of doubt over the whole piece of information, in my mind. There can be no question, however, that Lieut. Beale has frequently travelled this route, and that it was a favorite with him; indeed, I am informed that he took the first omnibus over it that ever left San Francisco for the Mission of Dolores.

" The climate in these latitudes is mild; snow appears to be unknown, and we saw but little ice; what there was being sold at twenty-five cents per lb.

" The geological formation of the country is not volcanic. I saw but one small specimen of trap during the march, which I observed at the ' Valley House,' with a mouse in it. From the vast accumulations of sand in these regions, I am led to adopt the opinions of the ethnologists of the ' California Academy of Natural Sciences,' and conclude that the original name of this territory was Sand Francisco, from which the final 'd' in the prefix has been lost by time, like the art of painting on glass.

" Considering the innumerable villages of pigs to be found located on the line of march, and the consequent effect produced on the atmosphere, I would respectfully suggest to the Chief Engineer the propriety of changing the name of the route by a slight alteration in the orthography, giving it the appropriate and euphonious title of the ' *Scent*ral R. R. Route.'

" Respectfully submitted,

" ABRAHAM DUNSHUNNER, LL. D.

" P. G. O. R. R. R. S."

From Southwick's Pass, the survey was continued with unabated ardor until the evening of the 10th instant, when we had arrived opposite Mrs. Freeman's " American Eagle,"

where we encamped. From this point a botanical party under Prof. Weegates was sent over the hills to the S. and W.
for exploration. They returned on the 11th, bringing a box
of sardines, a tin can of preserved whortleberries, and a bottle of whisky, as specimens of the products of the country
over which they had passed. They reported discovering on
the old plank road, an inn or hostel kept by a native American Irishman, whose sign exhibited the Harp of Ireland encircling the shield of the United States, with the mottoes

> " Erin go unum,
> E Pluribus Bragh."

On the 14th the party arrived in good health and excellent spirits at the "Nightingale," Mission of Dolores.

History informs us, that

> " The Nightingale club at the village was held,
> At the sign of the Cabbage and Shears."

It is interesting to the Antiquarian to look over the excellent
cabbage garden, still extant immediately opposite the Nightingale, and much more so to converse with Mr. Shears, the
respected and urbane proprietor.

The survey and *reconnoissance* being finished on our
arrival at the Mission, it may be expected that I should here
give a full and impartial statement as to the merits or de-
merits of the route, in connection with the proposed Railroad.

Some three months must elapse, however, before this can
be done, as the triangulation has yet to be perfectly com-
puted, the sub-reports examined and compiled, the observa

tions worked out, and the maps and drawings executed. Besides, I have received a letter from certain parties interested
in the Southern and Northern routes, informing me that if I
suspend my opinion on the "Great Central" for the present,
it will be greatly to my interest,—and as my interest is certainly my principal consideration, I shall undoubtedly com-
ply with their request, unless, indeed, greater inducement is
offered to the contrary.

Meanwhile I can assure the public, *that a great deal may
certainly be said in favor of the Central Route.* A full
report accompanied by maps, charts, sub-reports, diagrams,
calculations, tables and statistics, may shortly be expected.

Profiles of Prof. Heavysterne, Dr. Dunshunner and myself, executed in black court plaster by Mr. Jinkins, R. A.,
one of the Artists of the Expedition, in his unrivalled style
of elegance, may be seen for a short time at Messrs. LeCount
& Strong's—scale 1½ inch to 1 foot.

In conclusion I beg leave to return my thanks to the
Professors, Assistants, and Artists of the Expedition, for the
energy, fidelity and zeal, with which they have ever co-oper-
ated with me, and seconded my efforts ; and to assure them
that I shall be happy at any time to sit for my portrait for
them, or to accept the handsome service of plate, which I am
told they have prepared for me, but feel too much delicacy
to speak to me about.

I remain, with the highest respect and esteem for myself
and every body else,

JOHN PHŒNIX, A. M.,

Chief Engineer and Astronomer, S. F. A. M. D. C. R.

The annexed sketch of our route, prepared by Mr. Jinkins and Kraut, is respectfully submitted to the Public. It is not, of course, compiled with that accuracy, which will characterize our final maps, but for the ordinary purposes of travel, will be found sufficiently correct.

J. P., A. M. C. E. & C. A.

RECONNOISSANCE

OF THE

CENTRAL RAILROAD ROUTE,

FROM

SAN FRANCISCO TO THE MISSION OF DOLORES,

By Prof. John Phœnix, Esq., A. M. & C. A. & C. E.

DRAWN BY KRAUT AND JINKINS, R. A., ARTISTS TO THE EXPEDITION.

K E A R N Y   S T R E E T.

1   7   8   3   4   6   7   5   1

Plaza.

Orphans.

NOTE—The soundings are in fathoms, showing the depth of mud and water during the rainy season.

M A R K E T   S T R E E T.

(a)

(a) Represents a man walking down the street at the time of the passage of the Expedition.

S E C O N D   S T R E E T.

Glass House.

F O L S O M (a) **S T R E E T.**

Nightingale.

(a) Southwick's Pass.

E. Halfred Jinkins, Del.   *A. Kraut, Sculp.*

A NEW SYSTEM OF ENGLISH GRAMMAR

I HAVE often thought that the adjectives of the English lan
guage were not sufficiently definite for the purposes of de
scription. They have but three degrees of comparison—a
very insufficient number, certainly, when we consider that
they are to be applied to a thousand objects, which, though
of the same general class or quality, differ from each other by
a thousand different shades or degrees of the same peculiarity.
Thus, though there are three hundred and sixty-five days in a
year, all of which must, from the nature of things, differ from
each other in the matter of climate,—we have but half a
dozen expressions to convey to one another our ideas of this
inequality.   We say—"It is a fine day;" "It is a *very* fine
day;" "It is the *finest* day we have seen;" or, "It is an
unpleasant day;" "A *very* unpleasant day;" "The *most*
unpleasant day we ever saw."   But it is plain, that none of
these expressions give an *exact* idea of the nature of the day;
and the two superlative expressions are generally untrue. I

once heard a gentleman remark, on a rainy, snowy, windy and (in the ordinary English language) indescribable day, that it was " most preposterous weather." He came nearer to giving a correct idea of it, than he could have done by any ordinary mode of expression; but his description was not sufficiently definite.

Again :—we say of a lady—" She is beautiful; " " She is *very* beautiful," or " She is *perfectly* beautiful; "—descrip- tions, which, to one who never saw her, are no descriptions at all, for among thousands of women he has seen, probably no two are equally beautiful ; and as to a *perfectly* beautiful woman, he knows that no such being was ever created—un less by G. P. R. James, for one of the two horsemen to fall in love with, and marry at the end of the second volume.

If I meet Smith in the street, and ask him—as I am pretty sure to do—" How he does ? " he infallibly replies— " *Tolerable*, thank you "—which gives me no *exact* idea of Smith's health—for he has made the same reply to me on a hundred different occasions—on every one of which there *must* have been some slight shade of difference in his physi- cal economy, and of course a corresponding change in his feelings.

To a man of a mathematical turn of mind—to a student and lover of the exact sciences these inaccuracies of expres- sion—this inability to understand *exactly* how things are must be a constant source of annoyance ; and to one who like myself, unites this turn of mind to an ardent love of truth, for its own sake—the reflection that the English

language does not enable us to speak the truth with exact
ness, is peculiarly painful. For this reason I have, with
some trouble, made myself thoroughly acquainted with every
ancient and modern language, in the hope that I might find
some one of them that would enable me to express precisely
my ideas; but the same insufficiency of adjectives exist in
all except that of the Flathead Indians of Puget Sound,
which consists of but forty-six words, mostly nouns; but t:
the constant use of which exists the objection, that nobody
but that tribe can understand it. And as their literary and
scientific advancement is not such as to make a residenc:
among them, for a man of my disposition, desirable, I have
abandoned the use of their language, in the belief that for
me it is *hyas. cultus.*, or as the Spaniard hath it, *no me vale
nada.*

Despairing, therefore, of making new discoveries in
foreign languages, I have set myself seriously to work to
reform our own; and have, I think, made an important discovery, which, when developed into a system and universally
adopted, will give a precision of expression, and a consequent
clearness of idea, that will leave little to be desired, and will,
I modestly hope, immortalize my humble name as the pro-
mulgator of the truth and the benefactor of the human
race.

Before entering upon my system I will give you an account of its discovery (which, perhaps I might with more
modesty term an adaptation and enlargement of the idea of
another), which will surprise you by its simplicity, and like

the method of standing eggs on end, of Columbus, the inven-
tions of printing, gunpowder and the mariner's compass—
prove another exemplification of the truth of Hannah More's
beautifully expressed sentiment :

> " Large streams from little fountains flow,
> Large aches from little toe-corns grow."

During the past week my attention was attracted by a
large placard embellishing the corners of our streets, headed
in mighty capitals, with the word " PHRENOLOGY," and illustrated by a map of a man's head, closely shaven, and laid off
in lots, duly numbered from one to forty-seven. Beneath
this edifying illustration appeared a legend, informing the
inhabitants of San Diego and vicinity that Professor Dodge
had arrived, and taken rooms (which was inaccurate, as he
had but one room) at the Gyascutus House, where he would
be happy to examine and furnish them with a chart of their
heads, showing the moral and intellectual endowments, at
the low price of three dollars each.

Always gratified with an opportunity of spending my
money and making scientific researches, I immediately had
my hair cut and carefully combed, and hastened to present
myself and my head to the Professor's notice. I found him
a tall and thin Professor, in a suit of rusty, not to say seedy
black, with a closely buttoned vest, and no perceptible shirt-
collar or wristbands. His nose was red, his spectacles were
blue, and he wore a brown wig, beneath which, as I subsequently ascertained, his bald head was laid off in lots, marked

and numbered with Indian ink, after the manner of the diagram upon his advertisement. Upon a small table lay many little books with yellow covers, several of the placards, pen and ink, a pair of iron callipers with brass knobs, and six dollars in silver. Having explained the object of my visit, and increased the pile of silver by six half-dollars from my pocket—whereat he smiled, and I observed he wore false teeth—(scientific men always do; they love to encourage art) the Professor placed me in a chair, and rapidly manipulating my head, after the manner of a *sham pooh* (I am not certain as to the orthography of this expression), said that my temperament was "lymphatic, nervous, bilious." I remarked that "I thought myself dyspeptic," but he made no reply. Then seizing on the callipers, he embraced with them my head in various places, and made notes upon a small card that lay near him on the table. He then stated that my "hair was getting very thin on the top," placed in my hand one of the yellow-covered books, which I found to be an almanac containing anecdotes about the virtues of Dodge's Hair Invigorator, and recommending it to my perusal, he remarked that he was agent for the sale of this wonderful fluid, and urged me to purchase a bottle—price two dollars. Stating my willingness to do so, the Professor produced it from a hair trunk that stood in a corner of the room, which he stated, by the way, was originally an ordinary pine box, on which the hair had grown since "the Invigorator" had been placed in it—(a singular fact) and recommended me to be cautious in wearing gloves while rubbing it upon my head as unhappy accidents had occurred—the hair growing freely from the ends of the fingers, if used with the bare hand. He then seated himself at the table, and rapidly filling up what appeared to me a blank certificate, he soon handed over the following singular document.

"PHRENOLOGICAL CHART OF THE HEAD OF M. JOHN PHŒNIX, by FLATBROKE B. DODGE, Professor of Phrenology, and inventor and proprietor of Dodge's celebrated Hair Invigorator, Stimulator of the Conscience, and Arouser of the Mental Faculties:

Temperament,—*Lymphathic, Nervous, B'lious.*

Size of Head, 11.	Imitation, 11.
Amativeness, 11½.	Self-Esteem, ½.
Caution, 3.	Benevolence, 12.
Combativeness, 2¼.	Mirth, 1.
Credulity, 1.	Language, 12.
Causality, 12.	Firmness, 2.
Conscientiousness, 12.	Veneration, 12.
Destructiveness, 9.	Philoprogenitiveness, 0.
Hope, 10."	

Having gazed on this for a few moments in mute astonishment—during which the Professor took a glass of brandy and water, and afterwards a mouthful of tobacco—It turned to him and requested an explanation.

" Why," said he, " it's very simple; the number 12 is the maximum, 1 the minimum; for instance, you are as benevolent as a man can be—therefore I mark you, Benevolence, 12. You have little or no self-esteem—hence I place you, Self-esteem, ½. You've scarcely any credulity—don't you see?"

I did see! This was my discovery. I saw at a flash how the English language was susceptible of improvement, and, fired with the glorious idea, I rushed from the room and the house; heedless of the Pofessor's request that I would buy more of his Invigorator; heedless of his alarmed cry that I would pay for the bottle I'd got; heedless that I tripped on the last step of the Gyascutus House, and smashed there the precious fluid (the step has now a growth of four inches of hair on it, and the people use it as a door-mat); I rushed home, and never grew calm till with pen, ink and paper before me, I commenced the development of my system.

This system—shall I say this great system—is exceedingly simple, and easily explained in a few words. In the first place, "*figures won't lie.*" Let us then represent by the number 100, the maximum, the *ne plus ultra* of every human quality—grace, beauty, courage, strength, wisdom, learning— every thing. Let *perfection*, I say, be represented by 100, and an absolute minimum of all qualities by the number 1. Then by applying the numbers between, to the adjectives used in conversation, we shall be able to arrive at a very close approximation to the idea we wish to convey; in other words, we shall be enabled to speak the truth. Glorious, soul-inspiring idea! For instance, the most ordinary question asked of you is, " How do you do ? " To this, instead of replying, " Pretty well," " Very well," " Quite well," or the like absurdities—after running through your mind that *perfection* of health is 100, no health at all, 1—you say, with a graceful bow, " Thank you, I'm 52 to day ; " or, feeling poorly, " I'm 13, I'm obliged to you," or " I'm 68," or " 75," or ' 87½," as the case may be ! Do you see how very close in this way you may approximate to the truth; and how clearly your questioner will understand what he so anxiously wishes to arrive at—your *exact* state of health ?

Let this system be adopted into our elements of grammar, our conversation, our literature, and we become at once an exact, precise, mathematical, truth-telling people. It will apply to every thing but politics; there, truth being of no account, the system is useless. But in literature, how admirable! Take an example :

As a 19 young and 76 beautiful lady was 52 gaily tripping down the sidewalk of our 84 frequented street, she accidently come in contact—100 (this shows that she came in close contact) with a 73 fat, but 87 good-humored looking gentleman, who was 93 (i. e. intently) gazing into the window of a toy-shop. Gracefully 56 extricating herself, she received the excuses of the 96 embarrassed Falstaff with a 68 bland smile, and continued on her way. But hardly—7—had she reached the corner of the block, ere she was overtaken by a 24 young man, 32 poorly dressed, but of an 85 expression of countenance ; 91 hastily touching her 54 beautifully rounded arm, he said, to her 67 surprise—

"Madam, at the window of the toy-shop yonder, you dropped this bracelet, which I had the 71 good fortune to observe, and now have the 94 happiness to hand to you." Of course the expression " 94 happiness " is merely the young man's polite hyperbole.)

Blushing with 76 modesty, the lovely (76, as before, of course), lady took the bracelet—which was a 24 magnificent diamond clasp—(24 *magnificent*, playfully sarcastic; it was probably *not* one of Tucker's) from the young man's hand, and 84 hesitatingly drew from her beautifully 38 embroidered reticule a 67 port-monnaie. The young man noticed the action, and 73 proudly drawing back, added—

" Do not thank me; the pleasure of gazing for an instant at those 100 eyes (perhaps too exaggerated a compliment), has already more than compensated me for any trouble that I might have had."

She thanked him, however, and with a 67 deep blush and a 48 pensive air, turned from him, and pursued with a 33 slow step her promenade.

Of course you see that this is but the commencement of a pretty little tale, which I might throw off, if I had a mind to, showing in two volumes, or forty-eight chapters of thrilling interest, how the young man sought the girl's acquaintance, how the interest first excited, deepened into love, how they suffered much from the opposition of parents (her parents of course), and how, after much trouble, annoyance, and many perilous adventures, they were finally married— their happiness, of course, being represented by 100. But I trust that I have said enough to recommend my system to the good and truthful of the literary world; and besides, just at present I have something of more immediate importance to attend to.

You would hardly believe it, but that everlasting (100) scamp of a Professor has brought a suit against me for stealing a bottle of his disgusting Invigorator; and as the suit comes off before a Justice of the Peace, whose only principle of law is to find guilty and fine any accused person whom he thinks has any money—(because if he don't he has to take his costs in County Scrip,) it behooves me to " take time by the fore-lock." So, for the present, adieu. Should my system succeed to the extent of my hopes and expectations, I shall publish my new grammar early in the ensuing month, with suitable dedication and preface; and should you, with your well known liberality, publish my prospectus, and give me a handsome literary notice, I shall be pleased to furnish a presentation copy to each of the little Pioneer children.

P. S. I regret to add that having just read this article to Mrs. Phœnix, and asked her opinion thereon, she replied, that " if a first-rate magazine article were represented by 100, she should judge this to be about 13; or if the quintessence of stupidity were 100, she should take this to be in the neighborhood of 96." This, as a criticism, is perhaps a little discouraging, but as an exemplification of the merits of my system it is exceedingly flattering. How could she, I should like to know, in ordinary language, have given so *exact* and truthful an idea—how expressed so forcibly her opinion (which, of course, differs from mine) on the subject?

As Dr. Samuel Johnson learnedly remarked to James Boswell, Laird of Auchinleck, on a certain occasion—

' Sir, the proof of the pudding is in the eating thereof."

MUSICAL REVIEW EXTRAORDINARY.

SAN DIEGO, July 10th, 1854.

As your valuable work is not supposed to be so entirely identified with San Franciscan interests, as to be careless what takes place in other portions of this great *kedntry*, and as it is received and read in San Diego with great interest (I have loaned my copy to over *four* different literary gentlemen, most of whom have read some of it), I have thought it not improbable that a few critical notices of the musical performances and the drama of this place might be acceptable to you, and interest your readers. I have been, moreover, encouraged to this task by the perusal of your interesting musical and theatrical critiques on San Francisco performers and performances; as I feel convinced that, if you devote so much space to them, you will not allow any little feeling of rivalry between the two great cities to prevent your noticing ours, which, without the slightest feeling of prejudice, I must consider as infinitely superior. I propose this month to call your attention to the two great events in our theatrical and musical world—the appearance of the talented Miss PELICAN; and the production of Tarbox's celebrated " Ode Symphonie " of " The Plains."

The critiques on the former are from the columns of *The Vallecetos Sentinel*, to which they were originally contributed by me, appearing on the respective dates of June 1st and June 31st.

From the Vallecetos Sentinel, June 1st.

MISS PELICAN.—Never during our dramatic experience, has a more exciting event occurred than the sudden bursting upon our theatrical firmament, full, blazing, unparalleled, of the bright, resplendent and particular star, whose honored name shines refulgent at the head of this article. Coming among us unheralded, almost unknown, without claptrap, in a wagon drawn by oxen across the plains, with no agent to get up a counterfeit enthusiasm in her favor, she appeared before us for the first time at the San Diego Lyceum, last evening, in the trying and difficult character of Ingomar, or the Tame Savage. We are at a loss to describe our sensations, our admiration, at her magnificent, her superhuman efforts. We do not hesitate to say that she is by far the superior of any living actress; and, as we believe hers to be the perfection of acting, we cannot be wrong in the belief that no one hereafter will ever be found to approach her. Her conception of the character of Ingomar was perfection itself; her playful and ingenuous manner, her light girlish laughter, in the scene with Sir Peter, showed an appreciation of the savage character, which nothing but the most arduous study, the most elaborate training could produce ; while her awful change to the stern, unyielding, uncompromising father in the tragic scene of Duncan's murder, was indeed nature itself. Miss Pelican is about seventeen years of age, of miraculous beauty, and most thrilling voice. It is needless to say she dresses admirably, as in fact we have said all we can say when we called her most truthfully, perfection. Mr. John Boots took the part of Par thenia very creditably, etc., etc.

From the Vallecetos Sentinel, June 31st.

MISS PELICAN.—As this lady is about to leave us to com- mence an engagement on the San Francisco stage, we should regret exceedingly if any thing we have said about her, should send with her a *prestige* which might be found undeserved or. trial. The fact is, Miss Pelican is a very ordinary actress ; in- deed, one of the most indifferent ones we ever happened to see. She came here from the Museum at Fort Laramie, and we praised her so injudiciously that she became completely spoiled. She has performed a round of characters during the last week, very miserably, though we are bound to confess that her performance of King Lear last evening, was superior to any thing of the kind we ever saw. Miss Pelican is about forty-three years of age, singularly plain in her personal appearance, awkward and em- barrassed, with a cracked and squeaking voice, and really dresses quite outrageously. *She has much to learn—poor thing !*

I take it the above notices are rather ingenious. The fact is, I'm no judge of acting, and don't know how Miss Pelican will turn out. If well, why there's my notice of June the 1st; if ill, then June 31st comes in play, and, as there is but one copy of the *Sentinel* printed, it's an easy matter to destroy the incorrect one ; *both can't be wrong*; so I've made a sure thing of it in any event. Here follows my musical critique, which I flatter myself is of rather superior order:

THE PLAINS. ODE SYMPHONIE PAR JABEZ TARBOX.— This glorious composition was produced at the San Diego Odeon, on the 31st of June, ult., for the first time in this or any other country, by a very full orchestra (the performance taking place immediately after supper), and a chorus composed of the entire " Sauer Kraut-Verein," the Wee Gates Association," and choice selections from the "Gyascutus" and "Pikeharmonic " societies. The solos were rendered by Her Tuden Links, the recitations by Herr Von Hyden Schnapps, both performers being assisted by Messrs. John Smith and Joseph Brown, who held their coats, fanned them, and furnished water during the more overpowering passages.

" The Plains " we consider the greatest musical achievement that has been presented to an enraptured public. Like Waterloo among battles ; Napoleon among warriors ; Niagara among falls, and Peck among senators, this magnificent composition stands among Oratorios, Operas, Musical Melodramas and performances of Ethiopian Serenaders, peerless and unrivalled. *Il frappe toute chose parfaitment froid.*

" It does not depend for its success " upon its plot, its theme, its school or its master, for it has very little if any of them, but upon its soul-subduing, all-absorbing, high-faluting effect upon the audience, every member of which it causes to experience the most singular and exquisite sensations. Its strains at times remind us of those of the old master of the steamer McKim, who never went to sea without being unpleasantly affected ;—a straining after effect he use to term it. Blair in his lecture on beauty, and Mills in his treatise on logic, (p. 31,) have alluded to the feeling which might be produced in the human mind, by something of this transcendentally sublime description, but it has remained for M. Tarbox, in the production of The Plains, to call this feeling forth

The symphonie opens upon the wide and boundless plains, in longitude 115° W., latitude 35° 21′ 03″ N., and about sixty miles from the west bank of Pitt River. These data are beautifully and clearly expressed by a long (topographically) drawn note from an E flat clarionet. The sandy nature of the soil, sparsely dotted with bunches of cactus and artemisia, the extended view, flat and unbroken to the horizon, save by the rising smoke in the extreme verge, denoting the vicinity of a Pi Utah village, are represented by the bass drum. A few notes on the piccolo, calls the attention to a solitary antelope, picking up mescal beans in the foreground. The sun having an altitude of 36° 27′, blazes down upon the scene in indescribable majesty. "Gradually the sounds roll forth in a song" of rejoicing to the God of Day.

> "Of thy intensity
> And great immensity
> Now then we sing;
> Beholding in gratitude
> Thee in this latitude,
> Curious thing."

Which swells out into "Hey Jim along, Jim along Josey," then *decrescendo, mas o menos, poco pocita,* dies away and dries up.

Suddenly we hear approaching a train from Pike County, consisting of seven families, with forty-six wagons, each drawn by thirteen oxen; each family consists of a man in butternut-colored clothing driving the oxen; a wife in butternut-colored clothing riding in the wagon, holding a butter

nut baby, and seventeen butternut children running promis-
cuously about the establishment; all are barefooted, dusty,
and smell unpleasantly- (All these circumstances are expressed by pretty rapid fiddling for some minutes, winding
up with a puff from the orpheclide played by an intoxicated
Teuton with an atrocious breath—it is impossible to mis-
understand the description.) Now rises o'er the plains in
mellifluous accents, the grand Pike County Chorus.

> " Oh we'll soon be thar
> In the land of gold,
> Through the forest old,
> O'er the mounting cold,
> With spirits bold—
> Oh, we come, we come,
> And we'll soon be thar.
> Gee up Dolly ! whoo, up, whoo haw !

The train now encamp. The unpacking of the kettles
and mess-pans, the unyoking of the oxen, the gathering about
the various camp-fires, the frizzling of the pork, are so clearly
expressed by the music, that the most untutored savage could
readily comprehend it. Indeed, so vivid and lifelike was the
representation, that a lady sitting near us, involuntarily exclaimed aloud, at a certain passage, " *Thar, that pork's
burning !* " and it was truly interesting to watch the gratified
expression of her face when, by a few notes of the guitar,
the pan was removed from the fire, and the blazing pork ex
tinguished.

This is followed by the beautiful *aria :*—

> "O ! marm, I want a pancake ! "

Followed by that touching *recitative :*—

> " Shet up, or I will spank you ! "

To which succeeds a grand *crescendo* movement, representing the flight of the child, with the pancake, the pursuit
of the mother, and the final arrest and summary punishment
of the former, represented by the rapid and successive strokes
of the castanet.

The turning in for the night follows; and the deep and
stertorous breathing of the encampment, is well given by the
bassoon, while the sufferings and trials of an unhappy father
with an unpleasant infant, are touchingly set forth by the
cornet à piston.

Part Second—The night attack of the Pi Utahs; the
fearful cries of the demoniac Indians; the shrieks of the
females and children; the rapid and effective fire of the rifles;
the stampede of the oxen; their recovery and the final re-
pulse; the Pi Utahs being routed after a loss of thirty-six
killed and wounded, while the Pikes lose but one scalp (from
an old fellow who wore a wig, and lost it in the scuffle), are
faithfully given, and excite the most intense interest in the
minds of the hearers; the emotions of fear, admiration and
delight, succeeding each other in their minds, with almost
painful rapidity.   Then follows the grand chorus :

> " Oh ! we gin them fits,
> The Ingen Utahs.
> With our six-shooters—
> We gin 'em pertickuler fits."

After which, we have the charming recitative of Herr Tuden Links, to the infant, which is really one of the most charming gems in the performance :

" Now, dern your skin, *can't* you be easy ? "

Morning succeeds.   The sun rises magnificently (octavo flute)—breakfast is eaten,—in a rapid movement on three sharps; the oxen are caught and yoked up—with a small drum and triangle; the watches, purses, and other valuables of the conquered Pi Utahs, are stored away in a camp-kettle, to a small movement on the piccolo, and the train moves on, with the grand chorus :—

> " We'll soon be thar,
>   Gee up Bolly ! Whoo hup ! whoo haw ! "

The whole concludes with the grand hymn and chorus :—

> " When we die we'll go to Benton,
>   Whup ! Whoo, haw !
>   The greatest man that e'er land saw,
>   Gee !
>   Who this little airth was sent on
>   Whup ! Whoo, haw !
>   To tell a ' hawk from a hand-saw ! '
>   Gee ! "

The immense expense attending the production of this magnificent work; the length of time required to prepare the chorus; the incredible number of instruments destroyed at each rehearsal, have hitherto prevented M. Tarbox from placing it before the American public, and it has remained for San Diego to show herself superior to her sister cities of

3

the Union, in musical taste and appreciation, and in high souled liberality, by patronizing this immortal prodigy, and enabling its author to bring it forth in accordance with his wishes and its capabilities. We trust every citizen of San Diego and Vallecetos will listen to it ere it is withdrawn; and if there yet lingers in San Francisco one spark of musical fervor, or a remnant of taste for pure harmony, we can only say that the Southerner sails from that place once a fortnight, and that the passage money is but forty-five dollars.

LECTURES ON ASTRONOMY.

INTRODUCTORY.

THE following pages were originally prepared in the form of a course of Lectures to be delivered before the Lowell Institute, of Boston, Mass., but, owing to the unexpected circumstance of the author's receiving no invitation to lecture before that institution, they were laid aside shortly after their completion.

Receiving an invitation from the trustees of the Vallecetos Literary and Scientific Institute, during the present summer, to deliver a course of Lectures on any popular subject, the author withdrew his manuscript from the dusty shelf on which it had long lain neglected, and, having somewhat revised and enlarged it, to suit the capacity of the eminent scholars before whom it was to be displayed, repaired to Vallecetos. But, on arriving at that place, he learned with deep regret, that the only inhabitant had left a few days previous, having availed himself of the opportunity presented by a passing emigrant's horse,—and that, in consequence, the opening of the Institute was indefinitely postponed. Under these circumstances, and yielding with reluctance to the earnest solicitations of many eminent scientific friends, he has been induced to place the Lectures before the public in their present form. Should they meet with that success which his sanguine friends prognosticate, the author may be induced subsequently to publish them in the form of a text-book, for the use of the higher schools and universities; it being his greatest ambition to render himself useful in his day and generation, by widely disseminating the information he has acquired among those who, less fortunate, are yet willing to receive instruction.

JOHN PHŒNIX.

SAN DIEGO OBSERVATORY, September 1, 1854.

LECTURES ON ASTRONOMY.—PART I.

CHAPTER I.

The term Astronomy is derived from two Latin words,-Astra, a star, and onomy, a science; and literally means the science of the stars. "It is a science," to quote our friend Dick (who was no relation at all of Big Dick, though the latter occasionally caused individuals to see stars), " which has, in all ages, engaged the attention of the poet, the philosopher, and the divine, and been the subject of their study and admiration."

By the wondrous discoveries of the improved telescopes of modern times, we ascertain that upwards of several hundred millions of stars exist, that are invisible to the naked eye—the nearest of which is millions of millions of miles from the Earth; and as we have every reason to suppose that every one of this inconceivable number of worlds is peopled like our own, a consideration of this fact—and that we are undoubtedly as superior to these beings, as we are to the rest of mankind—is calculated to fill the mind of the American with a due sense of his own importance in the scale of animated creation.

It is supposed that each of the stars we see in the Heavens in a cloudless night, is a sun shining upon its own curvilinear, with light of its own manufacture; and as it would be absurd to suppose its light and heat were made to be diffused for nothing, it is presumed farther, that each sun, like an old hen, is provided with a parcel of little chickens, in the way of planets, which, shining but feebly by its reflected light, are to us invisible. To this opinion we are led, also, by reasoning from analogy, on considering our own Solar System.

THE SOLAR SYSTEM is so called, not because we believe it to be the sole system of the kind in existence, but from its principal body the Sun; the Latin name of which is *Sol*. (Thus we read of Sol Smith, literally meaning the *son* of Old Smith.) On a close examination of the Heavens we perceive

numerous brilliant stars which shine with a steady light
(differing from those which surround them, which are always
twinkling like a dew-drop on a cucumber-vine), and which,
moreover, do not preserve constantly the same relative distance from the stars near which they are first discovered.
These are the planets of the SOLAR SYSTEM, which have no
light of their own—of which the Earth, on which we reside,
is one,—which shine by light reflected from the Sun,—and
which regularly move around that body at different intervals
of time and through different ranges in space.   Up to the
time of a gentleman named Copernicus, who flourished about
the middle of the Fifteenth Century, it was supposed by our
stupid ancestors that the Earth was the centre of all creation,
being a large flat body, resting on a rock which rested on
another rock, and so on " all the way down;" and that the
Sun, planets and immovable stars all revolved about it once
in twenty-four hours.

This reminds us of the simplicity of a child we once saw
in a railroad-car, who fancied itself perfectly stationary, and
thought the fences, houses and fields were tearing past it at
the rate of thirty miles an hour;—and poking out its head,
to see where on earth they went to, had its hat —a very nice
one with pink ribbons—knocked off and irrecoverably lost.
But Copernicus (who was a son of Daniel Pernicus, of the
firm of Pernicus & Co., wool-dealers, and who was named Co.
Pernicus, out of respect to his father's partners) soon set this
matter to rights, and started the idea of the present Solar
System, which, greatly improved since his day, is occasionally

led the Copernican system. By this system we learn that the Sun is stationed at one *focus* (not hocus, as it is rendered, without authority by the philosopher Partington) of an ellipse, where it slowly grinds on for ever about its own axis, while the planets, turning about their axes, revolve in elliptical orbits of various dimensions and different planes of inclination around it.

The demonstration of this system in all its perfection was left to Isaac Newton, an English Philosopher, who, seeing an apple tumble down from a tree, was led to think thereon with such gravity, that he finally discovered the attraction of gravitation, which proved to be the great law of Nature that keeps every thing in its place. Thus we see that as an apple originally brought sin and ignorance into the world, the same fruit proved thereafter the cause of vast knowledge and enlightenment;—and indeed we may doubt whether any other fruit but an apple, and a sour one at that, would have produced these great results;—for, had the fallen fruit been a pear, an orange, or a peach, there is little doubt that Newton would have eaten it up and thought no more on the subject.

As in this world you will hardly ever find a man so small but that he has some one else smaller than he, to look up to and revolve around him, so in the Solar System we find that the majority of the planets have one or more smaller planets revolving about them. These small bodies are termed secondaries, moons or satellites—the planets themselves being called primaries.

We know at present of eighteen primaries, viz : Mercury Venus, the Earth, Mars, Flora, Vesta, Iris, Metis, Hebe, Astrea, Juno, Ceres, Pallas, Hygeia, Jupiter, Saturn, Herschel, Neptune, and another, yet unnamed. There are distributed among these, nineteen secondaries, all of which except our Moon, are invisible to the naked eye.

We shall now proceed to consider, separately, the different bodies composing the Solar System, and to make known what little information, comparatively speaking, science has collected regarding them. And, first in order, as in place, we come to

THE SUN.

This glorious orb may be seen almost any clear day, by looking intently in its direction, through a piece of smoked glass. Through this medium it appears about the size of a large orange, and of much the same color. It is, however, somewhat larger, being, in fact 887,000 miles in diameter, and containing a volume of matter equal to fourteen hundred thousand globes of the size of the Earth, which is certainly a matter of no small importance. Through the telescope it appears like an enormous globe of fire, with many spots upon its surface, which, unlike those of the leopard, are continually changing. These spots were first discovered by a gentleman named Galileo, in the year 1611. Though the Sun is usually termed and considered the luminary of day, it may not be uninteresting to our readers to know that it certainly has been seen in the night. A scientific friend of ours from New England (Mr. R. W. Emerson) while traveling through the northern part of Norway, with a cargo of tinware, on the 21st of June, 1836, distinctly saw the Sun in all its majesty, shining at midnight!—in fact, shining *all* night! Emerson is not what you would call a superstitious man, by any means—but, he left! Since that time many persons have observed its nocturnal appearance in that part of the country, at the same time of the year. This phenomenon has never been witnessed in the latitude of San Diego, however, and it is very improbable that it ever will be. Sacred history informs us that a distinguished military man, named Joshua, once caused the Sun to " stand still ; " how he did it, is not mentioned. There can, of course, be no doubt of the fact, that he arrested its progress, and possibly caused it to "stand *still ;*" —but translators are not always perfectly accurate, and we are inclined to the opinion that it might have wiggled a very little, when Joshua was not looking directly at it. The statement, however, does not appear so very incredible, when we reflect that seafaring men are in the habit of actually *bringing the Sun down* to the horizon every day at 12 Meridian. This they effect by means of a tool made of brass, glass and silver, called a sextant. The composition of the Sun has long been a matter of dispute.

By close and accurate observation with an excellent opera-glass, we have arrived at the conclusion that its entire surface is covered with water to a very great depth; which water, being composed by a process known at present only to the Creator of the Universe and Mr. Paine of Worcester Massachusetts, generates carburetted hydrogen gas, which, being

3*

inflamed, surrounds the entire body with an ocean of fire, from which we, and the other planets, receive our light and heat. The spots upon its surface are glimpses of water, obtained through the fire; and we call the attention of our old friend and former schoolmate, Mr. Agassiz, to this fact; as by closely observing one of these spots with a strong refracting telescope, he may discover a new species of fish, with little fishes inside of them. It is possible that the Sun may burn out after awhile, which would leave this world in a state of darkness quite uncomfortable to contemplate; but even under these circumstances it is pleasant to reflect, that courting and love-making would probably increase to an indefinite ex-tent, and that many persons would make large fortunes by the sudden rise in value of coal, wood, candles, and gas, which would go to illustrate the truth of the old proverb, " It's an ill wind that blows nobody any good."

Upon the whole, the Sun is a glorious creation; pleasing to gaze upon (through smoked glass), elevating to think upon, and exceedingly comfortable to every created being on a cold day; it is the largest, the brightest, and may be considered by far the most magnificent object in the celestial sphere; though with all these attributes it must be confessed that it is occasionally entirely eclipsed by the moon.

CHAPTER II.

We shall now proceed to the consideration of the several planets.

MERCURY.

This planet, with the exception of the asteroids, is the

smallest of the system. It is the nearest to the Sun, and, in consequence, cannot be seen (on account of the Sun's superior light), except at its greatest eastern and western elongations, which occur in March and April, August and September, when it may be seen for a short time immediately after sunset and shortly before sunrise. It then appears like a star of the first magnitude, having a white twinkling light, and resembling somewhat the star Regulus in the constellation Leo. The day in Mercury is about ten minutes longer than ours, its year is about equal to three of our months. It receives six and a half times as much heat from the Sun as we do; from which we conclude that the climate must be very similar to that of Fort Yuma, on the Colorado River. The difficulty of communication with Mercury will probably prevent its ever being selected as a military post; though it possesses many advantages for that purpose, being extremely inaccessible, inconvenient, and, doubtless, singularly uncomfortable. It receives its name from the God, Mercury, in the Heathen Mythology, who is the patron and tutelary Divinity of San Diego County.

VENUS.

This beautiful planet may be seen either a little after sunset, or shortly before sunrise, according as it becomes the morning or the evening star, but never departing quite 48° from the Sun. Its day is about twenty-five minutes shorter than ours; its year seven and half months or thirty-two weeks. The diameter of Venus is 7,700 miles, and she receives from the Sun thrice as much light and heat as the Earth.

An old Dutchman named Schroeter spent more than ten years in observations on this planet, and finally discovered a mountain on it twenty-two miles in height, but he never could discover any thing on the mountain, not even a mouse, and finally died about as wise as when he commenced his studies.

Venus, in Mythology, was a Goddess of singular beauty, who became the wife of Vulcan, the blacksmith, and we regret to add, behaved in the most immoral manner after her marriage. The celebrated case of Vulcan *vs.* Mars, and the consequent scandal, is probably still fresh in the minds of our readers. By a large portion of society, however, she was considered an ill-used and persecuted lady, against whose high tone of morals, and strictly virtuous conduct not a shadow of suspicion could be cast; Vulcan, by the same parties, was considered a horrid brute, and they all agreed that it served him right when he lost his case and had to pay the costs of court. Venus still remains the Goddess of Beauty, and not a few of her *protégés* may be found in California.

THE EARTH.

The Earth, or as the Latins called it, Tellus (from which originated the expression, " do tell us)," is the third planet in the Solar System, and the one on which we subsist, with all our important joys and sorrows. The *San Diego Herald* is published weekly on this planet, for five dollars per annum, payable invariably in advance. As the Earth is by no means the most important planet in the system, there is no reason to suppose that it is particularly distinguished from the others by being inhabited. It is reasonable, therefore, to conclude, that all the other planets of the system are filled with living, moving and sentient beings; and as some of them are superior to the Earth in size and position, it is not improbable that their inhabitants may be superior to us in physical and mental organization.

But if this were a demonstrable fact, instead of a mere hypothesis, it would be found a very difficult matter to persuade us of its truth. To the inhabitants of Venus the Earth appears like a brilliant star, very much, in fact, as Venus appears to us; and, reasoning from analogy, we are led to believe that the election of Mr. Pierce, the European war, or the split in the great Democratic party produced but very little excitement among them.

To the inhabitants of Jupiter, our important globe appears like a small star of the fourth or fifth magnitude. We recollect some years ago gazing with astonishment upon the inhabitants of a drop of water, developed by the Solar Microscope, and secretly wondering whether they were or not reasoning beings, with souls to be saved. It is not altogether a pleasant reflection that a highly scientific inhabitant of Jupiter, armed with a telescope of (to us) inconceivable form, may be pursuing a similar course of inquiry, and indulging in similar speculations regarding our Earth and its inhabitants. Gazing with curious eye, his attention is sud denly attracted by the movements of a grand celebration of Fourth of July in New York, or a mighty convention in Baltimore. "God bless my soul," he exclaims, "I declare they're alive, these little creatures, do see them wriggle!" To an inhabitant of the Sun, however, he of Jupiter is probably quite as insignificant, and the Sun man is possibly a mere atom in the opinion of a dweller in Sirius. A little reflection on these subjects leads to the opinion, that the death of an individual man on this Earth, though perhaps as important an event as can occur to himself, is calculated to cause no great convulsion of Nature or disturb particularly the great aggregate of created beings.

The Earth moves round the sun from west to east in a year, and turns on its axis in a day; thus moving at the rate of 68,000 miles an hour in its orbit, and rolling around at the tolerably rapid rate of 1,040 miles per hour. As our readers may have seen that when a man is galloping a horse violently over a smooth road, if the horse from viciousness or other cause suddenly stops, the man keeps on at the same rate over the animal's head; so we, supposing the Earth to be suddenly arrested on its axis, men, women children, horses, cattle and sheep, donkeys, editors and members of Congress, with all our goods and chattels, would be thrown off into the air at a speed of 173 miles a minute, every mother's son of us describing the arc of a parabola which is probably the only description we should ever be able to give of the affair.

This catastrophe, to one sufficiently collected to enjoy it would, doubtless, be exceedingly amusing; but as there would probably be no time for laughing, we pray that it may not occur until after our demise; when, should it take place, our monument will probably accompany the movement. It is a singular fact, that if a man travel round the Earth in an eastwardly direction, he will find, on returning to the place of departure, he has gained one whole day; the reverse of this proposition being true also, it follows that the Yankees who are constantly travelling to the West, do not live as long by a day or two as they would if they had staid at home; and supposing each Yankee's time to be worth $1.50 per day, it may be easily shown that a considerable amount of money is annually lost by their roving dispositions.

Science is yet but in its infancy; with its growth, new discoveries of an astounding nature will doubtless be made among which, probably, will be some method by which the course of the Earth may be altered and it be steered with the same ease and regularity through space and among the stars, as a steamboat is now directed through the water. It will be a very interesting spectacle to see the Earth "rounding to," with her head to the air, off Jupiter, while the Moon is sent off laden with mails and passengers for that planet, to bring back the return mails and a large party of rowdy Jupiterians going to attend a grand prize fight in the ring of Saturn.

Well, Christopher Columbus would have been just as much astonished at a revelation of the steamboat, and the lo

comotive engine, as we should be to witness the above per
formance, which our intelligent posterity during the ensuing
year, A. D. 2,000, will possibly look upon as a very ordinary
and common-place affair.

Only three days ago we asked a medium, where Sir John
Franklin was at that time; to which he replied, he was cruis-
ing about (officers and crew all well) on the interior of the
Earth, to which he had obtained entrance through SYMMES
HOLE!

With a few remarks upon the Earth's Satellite, we conclude the first Lecture on Astronomy; the remainder of the
course being contained in a second Lecture, treating of the
planets, Mars, Jupiter, Saturn and Neptune, the Asteroids,
and the fixed stars, which last, being " fixings," are, according to Mr. Charles Dickens, American property.

THE MOON.

This resplendent luminary, like a youth on the 4th of
July, has its first quarter; like a ruined spendthrift its last
quarter, and like an omnibus, is occasionally full and new.
The evenings on which it appears between these last stages
are beautifully illumined by its clear, mellow light.

The Moon revolves in an elliptical orbit about the Earth
in twenty-nine days twelve hours forty-four minutes and three
seconds, the time which elapses between one new Moon and
another. It was supposed by the ancient philosophers that
the Moon was made of green cheese, an opinion still entertained by the credulous and ignorant. Kepler and Tyco
Brahe, however, held to the opinion that it was composed of

Charlotte Russe, the dark portions of its surface being sponge cake, the light *blanc mange*. Modern advances in science and the use of Lord Rosse's famous telescope, have demonstrated the absurdity of all these speculations by proving conclusively that the Moon is mainly composed of the *Ferro—sesqui—cyanuret, of the cyanide of potassium!* Up to the latest dates from the Atlantic States, no one has succeeded in reaching the Moon. Should any one do so hereafter, it will probably be a woman, as the sex will never cease making an exertion for that purpose as long as there is a man in it.

Upon the whole, we may consider the Moon an excellent institution, among the many we enjoy under a free, republican form of government, and it is a blessed thing to reflect that the President of the United States cannot *veto* it, no matter how strong an inclination he may feel, from principle or habit, to do so.

It has been ascertained beyond a doubt that the Moon has no air. Consequently, the common expressions, " the Moon was gazing down with an air of benevolence," or with " an air of complacency," or with " an air of calm superiority," are incorrect and objectionable, the fact being that the Moon has no air at all.

The existence of the celebrated " Man in the Moon " has been frequently questioned by modern philosophers. The whole subject is involved in doubt and obscurity. The only authority we have for believing that such an individual exists, and has been seen and spoken with, is a fragment of an old poem composed by an ancient Astronomer of the name of Goose, which has been handed down to us as follows:

> "The man in the Moon, came down too soon
> To inquire the way to Norwich;
> The man in the South, he burned his mouth,
> Eating cold, hot porridge."

The evidence conveyed in this distich is however rejected by the sceptical, among modern Astronomers, who consider the passage an allegory. "The man in the South," being supposed typical of the late John C. Calhoun, and the "cold, hot porridge," alluded to the project of nullifcation.

END OF LECTURE FIRST.

NOTE BY THE AUTHOR.—Itinerant Lecturers are cautioned against making use of the above production, without obtaining the necessary authority from the proprietors of the Pioneer Magazine. To those who may obtain such authority, it may be well to state, that at the close of the Lecture it was the intention of the author to exhibit and explain to the audience an orrery, accompanying and interspersing his remarks by a choice selection of popular airs on the hand-organ.

An economical orrery may be constructed by attaching eighteen wires of graduated lengths to the shaft of a candlestick, apples of different sizes being placed at their extremities to represent the Planets, and a central orange resting on the candlestick, representing the Sun.

An orrery of this description is however liable to the objection, that if handed around among the audience for examination, it is seldom returned uninjured. The author has known an instance in which a child four years of age, on an occasion of this kind, devoured in succession the planets Jupiter and Herschel, and bit a large spot out of the Sun before he could be arrested.

J. P.

PISTOL SHOOTING—A COUNTER CHALLENGE.

San Diego, Cal., *Sept.* 1, 1854.

I copy the following paragraph from the *Spirit of the Times*, for July 15th :

" PISTOL SHOOTING—A CHALLENGE.

Owing to the frequent and urgent solicitations of many of my friends, I am induced to make the following propositions:

1. I will fit a dollar to the end of a twig two inches long, and while a second person will hold the other end in his mouth, so as to bring the coin within an inch and a half of his face, I engage to strike the dollar, three times out of five, at the distance of ten paces, or thirty feet. I will add in explanation, that there are several persons willing and ready to hold the twig or stick described above, when required.

2. I will hit a dollar, tossed in the air, or any other object of the same size, three times out of five *on a wheel and fire.*

3. At the word, I will split three balls out of five, on a knife blade, placed at the distance of thirty feet.

4. I will hit three birds out of five, sprung from the trap, standing thirty feet from the trap when shooting.

5. I will break, at the word, five common clay pipe stems out of seven, at the distance of thirty feet.

6. I engage to prove, by fair trial, that no pistol-shot can be produced who will shoot an apple off a man's head, at the distance of thirty feet, oftener than I can. Moreover I will produce two persons willing and ready to hold the apple on their heads for me, when required to do so.

7. I will wager, lastly, that no person in the United States can be produced who will hit a quarter of a dollar at the distance of thirty feet, oftener than I can, *on a wheel and fire.*

I am willing to bet $5,000 on any of the above propositions, one fourth of that amount forfeit. So soon as any bet will be closed, the money shall be deposited in the Bank of the State of Missouri, until paid over by the judges, or withdrawn, less forfeit. I will give the best and most satisfactory references that my share will be forthcoming when any of my propositions are taken up. Any one desiring to take up any of my propositions must address me by letter, through the St. Louis Post Office, as the advertisements or notices of newspapers might not meet my eye. Propositions will be received until the first of September next.

EDMUND W. PAUL,

140 Sixth Street, between Franklin Avenue and Morgan Street, St. Louis, Missouri.

I am unable to see any thing very extraordinary in the above propositions, by Mr. Edmund W. Paul. Any person, acquainted with the merest rudiments of the pistol, could certainly execute any or all of the proposed feats without the slightest difficulty.

"Owing" to my entertaining these opinions, "without solicitation from friends, and unbiassed by unworthy motives," *I* am induced to make the following propositions :—

1. I will suspend *two* dollars by a ring from a second person's nose, so as to bring the coins within three fourths of an inch from his face, and with a double barrelled shot-

gun, at a distance of thirty feet, will blow dollars, nose and man at least thirty feet further, four times out of five. I will add, in explanation, that, San Diego containing a rather intelligent community, I can find, at present, no one here willing or ready to have his nose blown in this manner; but I have no manner of doubt I could obtain such a person from St. Louis, by Adams &. Co.'s Express, in due season.

2. I will hit a dollar, or any thing else that has been tossed in the air (of the same size), on a wheel, *on a pole or axletree, or on the ground*, every time out of five.

3. At the word, I will place five balls on the blade of a penknife, and split them all!

4. I will hit three men out of five, sprung from obscure parentage, and stand within ten feet of a steel-trap (properly set) while shooting!

5. I will break at the word, a whole box of common clay pipes, with a single brick, at a distance of thirty feet.

6. I engage to prove by a fair trial, that no pistol-shot (or other person) can be produced, who will throw more apples at a man's head than I can. Moreover, I can produce in this town more than sixty persons willing and ready to hold an apple on their heads for me, provided they are allowed to eat the apple subsequently.

7. I will wager, lastly, that no person in the United States can be produced, who, with a double barrelled shotgun, while throwing a back-handed summerset, can hit

oftener, a dollar and a half, on the perimeter of a *revolving* wheel, *in rapid motion*, than I can.

Any one desiring to take up any of my propositions, will address me through the columns of *The Pioneer Magazine*. Propositions will be received on the first of April next.

JOHN PHŒNIX.

1334 Seventeenth Street, Vallecitos.
" *Se compra oro aqui*, up stairs."

P. S. Satisfactory references given and required. A bet from a steady, industrious person, who will be apt to pay if he loses, will meet with prompt attention.   J. P.

ANTIDOTE FOR FLEAS.

THE following recipe from the writings of Miss Hannah More, may be found useful to your readers:

In a climate where the attacks of fleas are a constant source of annoyance, any method which will alleviate them becomes a *desideratum.* It is, therefore, with pleasure I make known the following recipe, which I am assured has been tried with efficacy.

Boil a quart of tar until it becomes quite thin. Remove the clothing, and before the tar becomes perfectly cool, with a broad flat brush, apply a thin, smooth coating to the entire surface of the body and limbs. While the tar remains soft, the flea becomes entangled in its tenacious folds, and is rendered perfectly harmless; but it will soon form a hard, smooth coating, entirely impervious to his bite. Should the coating crack at the knee or elbow joints, it is merely necessary to retouch it slightly at those places. The whole coat should be renewed every three or four weeks. This remedy is sure, and having the advantage of simplicity and economy, should be generally known.

So much for Miss More. A still simpler method of preventing the attacks of these little pests, is one which I have lately discovered myself;—in theory only—I have not yet put it into practice. On feeling the bite of a flea, thrust the part bitten immediately into boiling water. The heat of the water destroys the insect and instantly removes the pain of the bite.

.   You have probably heard of old Parry Dox. I met him here a few days since, in a sadly seedy condition. He told me that he was still extravagantly fond of whisky, though he was constantly "running it down." I inquired after his wife. " She is dead, poor creature," said he, " and is probably far better off than ever she was here. She was a seamstress, and her greatest enjoyment of happiness in this world was only so, so."

PHŒNIX AT THE MISSION DOLORES.

Mission of Dolores, 15th January, 1855.

It was my intention to furnish you, this month, with an elaborate article on a deeply interesting subject, but a serious domestic calamity has prevented. I allude to the loss of my stove-pipe, in the terrific gale of the 31st December.

There are few residents of this city whose business or inclination has called them to the Mission of Dolores, that have not seen and admired that stove-pipe. Rising above the kitchen chimney to the noble altitude of nearly twelve feet, it pointed to a better world, and was pleasantly suggestive of hot cakes for breakfast. From the window of my back porch, I have gazed for hours upon that noble structure ; and watching its rotary cap, shifting with every breeze, and pouring forth clouds of gas and vapor, I have mused on politics, and fancied myself a Politician. It was an accomplished stove-pipe. The melody accompanying its movements, inaptly termed creaking by the soulless, gave evidence of its taste for Music, and its proficiency in Drawing was the wonder and delight of our family circle. It had no bad habits—it did not even smoke.

I fondly hoped to enjoy its society for years, but one by one our dearest treasures are snatched from us : the soot fell, and the stove-pipe has followed soot. On the night of the 31st of Dec., a gale arose, perfectly unexampled in its terrific violence. Houses shook as with tertian ague, trees were uprooted, roofs blown off, and ships foundered at the docks. A stove-pipe is not a pyramid—what resistance could mine oppose to such a storm ? One by one its protecting wires were severed ; and as it bowed its devoted head to the fury of the blast, shrieks of more than mortal agony attested the desperate nature of its situation. At length the Storm Spirit fell upon the feeble and reeling structure in its wrath, and whirling it madly in the air with resistless force, breaking several tenpenny nails, and loosening many of the upper bricks of the chimney, dashed it down to earth. But why harrow up the feelings of your readers by a continuation of the distressing narrative. The suffering that we have endured, the tears that have been shed since this loss will be understood, and commiserated, when I add—the next morning the kitchen chimney smoked, and has been doing it intermittently ever since !

Since my last, scarcely a gleam of fun has come to illumine the usual dull monotony of the Mission of Dolores,—

"The days have been dark and dreary
It rains, and the wind is never weary."

A little occurrence at the toll-gate, the other day, is worthy of notice, perhaps, as betokening "the good time a-coming." A well-known gentleman of your city, who frequently drives forth on the Plank Road, perched on one of those little gigs that somebody compares to a tea-tray on wheels, with the reins hanging down behind, like unfastened suspenders, in an absent frame of mind, drove slowly past the Rubicon without bifurcating the customary half-dollar. Out rushed the enthusiastic toll-gatherers, shouting, "Toll, sir, toll! you've forgot the toll!" "Oh! don't bother me, gentlemen," replied the absent one, in a lachrymose tone, and with a most woful expression, "*I'm an orphan boy!*" This appeal to the sympathies of the toll-men was effective; their hearts were touched, and the orphan went on his way rejoicing.

It is amusing to observe the shifts a maker of Poetry will resort to, when compelled to make use of an irrelevant subject to eke out his rhyme to convince himself and his readers that the *faux pas* was quite intentional, the result of study, and should be admired rather than criticised. In a poem called "Al Aaraaf," by Edgar A. Poe, who, when living, thought himself, in all seriousness, the *only* living original Poet, and that all other manufacturers of Poetry were mere copyists, continually infringing on his patent—occurs the following passage, in which may be found a singular instance of the kind alluded to :

'Ligeia! Ligeia!
My beautiful one!
Whose harshest idea
Will to melody run:

Oh is it thy will,
On the breezes to toss ;
Or capriciously still,
Like the lone Albatross,
Incumbent on Night,
(As she on the air),
To keep watch with delight
On the harmony there ? ”

Observe that note : “ *The Albatross is said to sleep on the wing.*” Who said so ? I should like to know. Buffon didn't mention it; neither does Audubon. Coleridge, who made the habits of that rare bird a study, never found it out; and the undersigned, who has gazed on many Albatrosses, and had much discourse with ancient mariners concerning them, never suspected the circumstance, or heard it elsewhere remarked upon.

I am inclined to believe that it never occurred to Mr. Poe, until having become embarrassed by that unfortunate word “ toss,” he was obliged to bring in either a *hoss*, or an albatross; and preferring the bird as the more poetical, invented the extraordinary fact to explain his appearance.

The above lines, I am told, have been much admired; but if they are true poetry, so are the following :

Highflier! Highflier!
My long-legged one!
Whose mildest idea
Is to kick up and run :
Oh, is it thy will
Thy switch-tail to toss ;
Or caper viciously still,
Like an old sorrel horse, [*pron.* “ *hoss,*”]

> Incumbent on thee,
> As on him, to rear, [*pron.* "*rare*,"]
> And though sprung in the knee,
> With thy heels in the air?

A note for me, and the man waiting for an answer, said ye? Now, by the shade of Shadrach, and the chimney of Nebuchadnezzar's fiery furnace! 'tis the bill for the new chimney! Bills, bills, bills! How *can* a man name his child William? The horrid idea of the partner of his joys, and sorrows, presenting him with a *Bill !*—and to have that Bill continually in the house—constantly running up and down stairs—always unsettled,—Distraction's in the thought! Tell that man, Bridget, I'm sick; and, lucky thought, say it's the smallpox; and ask him to call again when I've got better, and gone to San Diego for my health.——He's gone. I see him from a hole in the window curtain, flying off in a zigzag direction, and looking back timorously, like a jacksnipe, with his long bill. I shall write no more; like that bill, I feel unsettled. Adieu!

SQUIBOB IN BENICIA.

BENICIA, October 1st, 1850.

LEAVING the metropolis last evening by the gradually-in-creasing-in-popularity steamer, "West Point," I 'skeeted' up Pablo Bay with the intention of spending a few days at the world-renowned seaport of Benicia. Our Captain (a very pleasant and gentlemanly little fellow by the way) was named Swift, our passengers were emphatically a fast set, the wind blew like well-watered rose bushes, and the tide was strong in our favor. All these circumstances tended to impress me with the idea, that we were to make a wonderfully quick passage, but alas, "the race is not always to the Swift," the "Senator" passed us ten miles from the wharf, and it was nine o'clock and very dark at that, when we were roped in by the side of the "ancient and fishlike" smelling hulk that forms the broad wharf of Benicia. As I shouldered my carpet bag, and stepped upon the wharf among the dense crowd of four individuals that were there assembled, and gazing upon the mighty city whose glimmering lights, feebly discernible through the Benician darkness, extended over an area of five acres, an overpowering sense of the grandeur and majesty of the great rival of San Francisco, affected me.—I felt my own extreme insignificance, and was fain to lean upon a pile of water melons for support. " Boy ! " said I, addressing an intelligent specimen of humanity who formed an integral portion of the above mentioned crowd, " Boy ! can you direct me to the best hotel in this city ? "—" Aint but one," responded the youth, " Winn keeps it ; right up the hill thar." Decidedly, thought I, I will go in to Winn, and reshouldering my carpet bag, I blundered down the ladder, upon a plank foot-path leading over an extensive morass in the direction indicated, not noticing, in my abstraction, that I had inadvertently retained within my grasp the melon upon which my hand had rested " *Saw yer !*" resounded from the wharf as I retired—" *Saw yer !* " repeated several individuals upon the foot-path.   For an instant my heart beat with violence at the idea of being seen accidentally appropriating so contemptible an affair as a water-melon ; but hearing a man with a small white hat, and large white moustache, shout "hello ! " and immediately rush with frantic violence up the ladder, I comprehended that Sawyer was his proper name, and by no means alluded to me or my proceedings ; so slipping the melon in my carpet bag, I tranquilly resumed my journey.   A short walk brought me to the portal of the best and only hotel in the city, a large two-story building dignified by the title of the " Solano Hotel," where I was graciously received by mine host, who welcomed me to Benicia in the

most *winning* manner. After slightly refreshing my innei
man with a feeble stimulant, and undergoing an introduction
to the oldest inhabitant, I calmly seated myself in the bar-room,
and contemplated with intense interest the progress of a game
of billiards between two enterprising citizens; but finding after
a lapse of two hours, that there was no earthly probability of its
ever being concluded, I seized a candlestick and retired to my
room.   Here I discussed my melon with intense relish, and
then seeking my couch, essayed to sleep.—But, oh ! the fleas !
skipping, hopping, crawling, biting ! " Won't some one establish an agency for the sale of D. L. Charles & Co's. Flea
bane, in Benicia ?" I agonizingly shouted, and echo answered
through the reverberating halls of the " Solano Hotel," " Yes,
they won't ! " What a night ! But every thing must have an
end (circles and California gold excepted), and day at last
broke over Benicia.   Magnificent place ! I gazed upon it
from the attic window of the " Solano Hotel," with feelings
too deep for utterance.   The sun was rising in its majesty,
gilding the red wood shingles of the U. S. Storehouses in the
distance; seven deserted hulks were riding majestically at
anchor in the bay; clothes-lines, with their burdens, were
flapping in the morning breeze; a man with a wheelbarrow
was coming down the street !—Every thing, in short, spoke of
the life, activity, business, and bustle of a great city. But in
the midst of the excitement of this scene, an odoriferous
smell of beef-steak came, like a holy calm, across my olfacto-
ries, and hastily drawing in my *cabeza,* I descended to breakfast.   This operation concluded, I took a stroll in company

with the oldest inhabitant, from whom I obtained much valuable information (which I hasten to present), and who
cheerfully volunteered to accompany me as a guide, to the
lions of the city.   There are no less than forty-two wooden
houses, many of them two stories in height, in this great
place—and nearly twelve hundred inhabitants, men, women
and children !   There are six grocery, provision, drygoods,
auction, commission, and where-you-can-get-almost-any-little-
thing-you-want-stores, one hotel, one school-house—which is
also a *brevet* church—three billiard tables, a post-office—from
which I actually saw a man get a letter—and a ten-pin-alley,
where I am told a man once rolled a whole game, paid $1.50
for it, and walked off chuckling.—Then there is a " monte
bank "—a Common Council, and a Mayor, whom my guide
informed me, was called " *Carne*," from a singular habit he
has of eating roast beef for dinner.—But there isn't a tree
in all Benicia.   " There was one," said the guide, " last year
—only four miles from here, but they chopped it down for
firewood for the ' post.'   Alas ! why didn't the woodman spare
that tree ? "   The dwelling of one individual pleased me indescribably—he had painted it a vivid green !   Imaginative
being.   He had evidently tried to fancy it a tree, and in the
enjoyment of this sweet illusion, had reclined beneath its
grateful shade, secured from the rays of the burning sun, and
in the full enjoyment of rural felicity even among the crowded
streets of this great metropolis.   How pretty is the map of
Benicia !   We went to see that, too.   It's all laid off in
squares and streets, for ever so far, and you can see the pegs
4*

stuck in the ground at every corner, only they are not exactly in a line, sometimes; and there is Aspinwall's wharf, where
they are building a steamer of iron, that looks like a large pan,
and Semple Slip, all divided on the map by lines and dots, into
little lots, of incredible value; but just now they are all under
water, so no one can tell what they are actually worth. Oh !
decidedly Benicia is a great place. " And how much, my dear
sir," I modestly inquired of the gentlemanly recorder who
displayed the map ; "how much may this lot be worth ? " and
I pointed with my finger at lot No. 97, block 16,496—situated as per map, in the very centre of the swamp. " That, sir,"
replied he with much suavity, " ah ! it would be held at about
three thousand dollars, I suppose."—I shuddered—and retired.　The history of Benicia is singular.　The origin of its
name as related by the oldest inhabitant is remarkable.　I put
it right down in my note-book as he spoke, and believe it
religiously, every word. " Many years ago," said that aged
man, " this property was owned by two gentlemen, one of
whom, from the extreme candor and ingenuousness of his
character, we will call Simple; the other being distinguished
for waggery, and a disposition for practical joking, I shall
call, as in fact he was familiarly termed in those days—Larkin.　While walking over these grounds in company, on one
occasion, and being naturally struck by its natural advantages, said Simple to Larkin, ' Why not make a city here, my
boy ? have it surveyed into squares, bring up ships, build
houses, make it a port of entry, establish depots, sell lots, and
knock the centre out of Yerba Buena straight.' (Yerba

Buena is now San Francisco, reader.) 'Ah!' quoth Larkin with a pleasant grin diffusing itself over his agreeable countenance 'that would be nice, hey?'" Need we say that the plan was adopted—carried out—proved successful—and Larkin's memorable remark "*be nice, hey,*" being adopted as the name of the growing city, gradually became altered and vulgarized into its present form Benicia! A curious history this, which would have delighted Horne Took beyond measure. Having visited the Masonic Hall, which is really a large and beautiful building, reflecting credit alike on the Architect and the fraternity, being by far the best and most convenient hall in the country, I returned to the Solano Hotel, where I was accosted by a gentleman in a blue coat with many buttons, and a sanguinary streak down the leg of his trowsers, whom I almost immediately recognized as my old friend, Captain George P. Jambs, of the U. S. Artillery, a thorough-going *adobe*, as the Spaniard has it, and a member in high and regular standing of the Dumfudgin Club. He lives in a delightful little cottage, about a quarter of a mile from the centre of the city—being on duty at the Post—which is some mile, mile and a half or two miles from that metropolis—and pressed me so earnestly to partake of his hospitality during my short sojourn, that I was at last fain to pack up my property, including the remains of the abstracted melon, and in spite of the blandishments of my kind host of the Solano, accompany him to his domicile, which he very appropriately names "Mischief Hall." So here I am installed for a few days, at the expiration of which I shall make a rambling excursion to Sonoma, Napa and the like, and from whence perhaps you may hear from me.   As I set here looking from my airy chamber, upon the crowds of two or three persons, thronging the streets of the great city ; as I gaze upon that man carrying home a pound and a half of fresh beef for his dinner; as I listen to the bell of the Mary (a Napa steam packet of four cat power) ringing for departure, while her captain in a hoarse voice of authority, requests the passengers to " step over the other side, as the larboard paddle-box is under water;" as I view all these unmistakable signs of the growth and prosperity of Benicia, I cannot but wonder at the infatuation of the people of your village, who will persist in their absurd belief that San Francisco will become a *place*, and do not hesitate to advance the imbecile idea that it may become a successful rival of this city.   Nonsense !—Oh Lord ! at this instant there passed by my window the—prettiest—little—I can't write any more this week; if this takes, I'll try it again.

Yours for ever

SQUIBOB

SQUIBOB IN SONOMA.

Sonoma, October 10, 1350.

I ARRIVED at this place some days since, but have been
so entirely occupied during the interval, in racing over the
adjacent hills in pursuit of unhappy partridges, wandering
along the banks of the beautiful creek, whipping its tranquil
surface for speckled trout, or cramming myself with grapes
at the vineyard, that I have not, until this moment, found
time to fulfil my promise of a continuation of my travelling
adventures.   I left Benicia with satisfaction.   Ungrateful
people   I had expected, after the very handsome manner in
which I had spoken of their city ; the glowing description of
its magnitude, prosperity and resources that I had given, the
consequent rise in property that had taken place ; the mani-
fest effect that my letter would produce upon the action of
Congress in making Benicia a port of entry; in view of all
these circumstances I had, indeed, expected some trifling
compliment—a public dinner, possibly, or peradventure a deli-
cate present of a lot or two—the deeds inclosed in a neat and

appropriate letter from the Town Council. But no!—the
name of Squibob remains unhonored and unsung, and, what is
far worse, unrecorded and untaxed in magnificent Benicia.
" How sharper than a serpent's thanks it is to have a toothless
child," as Pope beautifully remarks in his Paradise Lost.
One individual characterized my letter as "a d—d burlesque."
I pity that person, and forgive him.

For the last few days of my stay in Benicia, that city
was in a perfect whirl of excitement. The election was
rapidly approaching, and Herr Rossiter was exhibiting feats
of legerdemain at the California House. Individuals were
rushing about the streets proffering election tickets of all
shapes and sizes, and tickets for the exhibition were on sale
at all the principal hotels. One man conjured you to take a
ticket, while another asked you to take a ticket to see the
man conjured, so that what, with the wire-pulling by day,
and the slack wire performance by night, you stood an excellent chance for getting slightly bewildered. Public meetings
were held, where multitudes of fifty excited individuals surrounded the steps of the " El Dorado," listening with breath-
less interest to a speech in favor of McDaniels, and abusive to
Bradford, or in favor of somebody else and everlastingly condemnatory of both. Election meetings, any where, are always exciting and interesting spectacles, but the moral effect
produced by the last which I attended in Benicia, when (after
some little creature named Frisbie had made a speech, declar-
ing his readiness to wrap himself in the Star-spangled Banner, fire off a pistol, and die like a son of——Liberty, for

the Union) Dr. Simple slowly unfolded himself to
his utmost height, and with one hand resting upon the
chimney of the "El Dorado," and the other holding his
serape up to Heaven, denounced such sentiments, and declar-
ing that California had made him, and he should go his
length for California, right or wrong, union or disunion.
The moral effect, I say, produced, was something more than
exciting; it was sublime; it was tremendous! "That's a
right-down good speech," said my fair companion; "but my!
how the General gave it to him! didn't he, Mr. Squibob?"
"He did so," said I. The candidates were all Democrats, I
believe, and all but one entertained the same political sentiments. This gentleman (a candidate for the Senate), however, in the elucidation of his political principles, declared
that he "went in altogether for John C. Calhoun, and
nothing shorter." Now I'm no politician, and have no wish
to engage in a controversy on the subject; but, God forgive
me if I am in error, I thought Calhoun had been dead for
some months. Well, I suppose some one is elected by this
time, and the waves of political excitement have become
calm, but Benicia was a stormy place during the election, I
assure you. I succeeded in borrowing one dollar at ten per
cent. a month (with security on a corner lot in Kearney
street, San Francisco), purchased a ticket, and went to see
Herr Rossiter. Gracious! how he balanced tobacco pipes,
and tossed knives in the air, and jumped on a wire, and sat
down on it, and rolled over it, and made it swing to and fro
while he threw little brass balls from one hand to the other

The applause was tremendous, and when, after a solo by the orchestra (which consisted of one seedy violin, played by an individual in such a state of hopeless inebriation that his very fiddle seemed to hiccough), he threw a back-handed summerset, and falling in a graceful attitude, informed the audience that " he should appear again to-morrow evening with a change of performance." We enthusiastically cheered, and my friend, the man in the red vest, who had sat during the whole evening in a state of rapt admiration, observed with a profound ejaculation, " that it went ahead of any thing he had ever seen in his life, except the Falls of Niagara! " I made many friends in Benicia. I don't like the place much, but I do like the people ; and among my acquaintances, from Dr. Simple to my friend Mr. Sawyer, which two gentlemen may be termed the long and short of the place ;—I have never met with more kindness, more genuine hospitality than from the gentlemen of Benicia. The ladies are pretty, too; but, to use an entirely original metaphor, which, I presume, none of your readers ever heard before or will hear again : they are " like angels' visits, few and far between." There isn't a more moral place on the face of the earth than Benicia. Ephesus, where the stupid people, a few years since, used to worship Diana, wasn't a circumstance to it.

Sonoma is twelve miles from Napa, and is—but I shall defer my description until next week, for I have scarcely made up my mind with regard to it, and my waning paper warns me I have said enough at present. Yours for ever.

SQUIBOB IN SAN FRANCISCO.

October 15th, 185(.

Time! At the word Squibob comes cheerfully up to the scratch, and gracefully smiling upon his friends and supporters, lets fly his one, two, as follows ;—

Sonoma *is* a nice place. As my Sabbath school instructor (peace to his memory) used to add, by way of a clincher to his dictum—Piety is the foundation of all Religion—" thar can't be no doubt on't." Situated in the midst of the delightful and fertile valley which bears its name, within three miles of the beautiful creek upon whose " sil very tide, where whilom sported the *tule* boats of the un pleasant Indians, the magnificent (ly little) steamer *Georgina* now puffs and wheezes tri-weekly from San Fransicso ; enjoying an unvaryingly salubrious climate, neither too warm nor too cold. With little wind, few fleas, and a sky of that peculiarly blue description, that Fremont terms the Italian, it may well be called, as by the sentimentally struck travelling snob it frequently is, the Garden of California. I re

mained there ten whole days—somewhat of a marvel for so
determined a gad-about as myself—and don't remember of
ever passing ten days more pleasantly.   It is useless for me
to occupy time, and trespass upon your patience by a lengthy
description of Sonoma.   If any of your readers would know
the exact number of houses it contains, the names of the
people who dwell therein, the botanical applications of the
plants growing in its vicinity, or any thing else about it that
would be of any mortal use to any one, without being positively amusing, let them purchase Revere, or some other
equally scientific work on California, and inform themselves;
suffice it to say that there is delightful society, beautiful
women, brave men, and most luscious grapes to be found
there ; and the best thing one can possibly do, if a tired and
ennuyeed resident of San Francisco, Benicia, or any other
great city of all work and no play, is to take the Georgina
some pleasant afternoon and go up there for a change.   He'll
find it !   General Smith and his staff reside at Sonoma, and
a small detachment of troops have their station and quarters
there.   I saw a trooper in the street one day; he wore a
coat with a singularly brief tail, and a nose of a remarkably
vivid tinge of redness.   I thought he might have just returned
from *the* expedition, for his limbs were evidently weakened
by toil and privation, and his course along the street slow in
movement and serpentine in direction.   I would have asked
him to proceed to the Sink of Mary's River, and recover an
odd boot that I left there last fall, but he looked scarcely fit
to make the journey.   I feared he might be Jenkins, and

forbore. But it's a glorious thing to reflect that we have an army at our disposal in this country, and a blessed reflection, that should we lose any old clothing in the wilderness, we can get Mr. Crawford to get that branch of the service to pick it up.

Tired at last of monotony, even in beautiful Sonoma, I packed up my carpet bag, and taking the two-mule stage, passed through pretty little " Napa " again, and found myself, one evening, once more at Benicia. It had increased somewhat since I had left it. I observed several new clothes poles had been erected, and noticed a hand cart at the corner of a street, that I had never seen before. But I had little time for observation, for the " New World " came puffing up to the hulks as I arrived, and I hastily stepped on board. Here I met my ancient crony, and distinguished friend Le Baron Vieux, who was on his way from Sacramento to the metropolis. The Baron is a good fellow and a funny man. You have frequently laughed over his drolleries in the " True Delta," and in his usually unimpeachably " good style," he showed me about the boat, introduced me to the captain, pointed out the " model artists " who were on board, and finally capped the climax of his polite attention by requesting me to take a drink. I didn't refuse, particularly—and we descended to the bar. And " what," said the Baron with a pleasant and hospitable smile, "what, my dear fellow, will you drink ?" I chose *Bine* and *Witters*,—the Baron himself drinking *Bin* and *Gitters*. We hob-a-nobbed, tossed off our glasses, without winking, and, for an instant gazed at each other in gasping, unspeakable astonishment. "Turpentine and aqua fortis !" shuddered I. "Friend !" said the Baron, in an awful voice, to the bar-keeper, "that drink is fifty cents, but I will with pleasure give you a dollar to tell us *what* it was we drank." "We call it," replied that imperturbable man, "Sherry Wine, but I don't know as I ever saw any one drink it before." Quoth the Baron, who by this time had partially recovered his circulation and the conse-quent flow of his ideas : "I think, my friend, you'll never see it drank before or behind, hereafter." The New World is an excellent and, for California, an elegant boat. Her Cap-tain (who don't know Wakeman ?) is a pleasant gentleman. Her accommodations are unequalled—but, and I say this expressly for the benefit of my brethren of the "Dumfudgin Club," never call for "wine and bitters" at her bar. Ascend-ing to the cabin on the upper deck, I had the satisfaction of a formal presentation to Dr. Collyer and his interesting family. Sober, high-toned, moral and well-conducted citi-zens may sneer if they please ; rowdies may visit, and with no other than the prurient ideas arising from their own ob-scene imaginations, may indorse the same opinions more forcibly by loud ejaculations and vulgar remarks ; but I pretend to say that no right-minded man, with any thing like the commencement of a taste for the beautiful and artistic, can attend one of these "Model Artist" exhibitions without feeling astonished, gratified, and, if an enthusiast, delighted. As our gallant boat, dashing the spray from her bow, bore us safely and rapidly onward through the lovely bay of San

Pablo, the moon tipping with its silvery rays each curling wave around us, and shedding a flood of yellow light upon -our upper deck, " I walked with Sappho." And " oh, beautiful being," said I, somewhat excited by the inspiring nature of the scene, and possibly, the least thought, by the turpentine I had imbibed, " do you never feel, when in the pride of your matchless charms you stand before us, the living, breathing representation of the lovely, poetic, and ill-fated Sappho; do you never feel an inspiration of the moment, and entering into the character, imagine yourself in mind, as in form, her beauteous illustration ? "   " Well—yes," said she, with the slightest possible indication of a yawn, " I don't know but I do, but it's *dreadful tearing on the legs !* "

Hem ! a steamer's motion always made me feel unpleasantly, and the waves of San Pablo Bay ran high that evening. The Baron and I took more turpentine immediately. We landed in your metropolis shortly after, and succeeding in obtaining a man to carry my valise a couple of squares, for which service, being late, he charged me but thirty-two dollars, I repaired to, and registered my name at, the St. Francis Hotel, which being deciphered with an almost imperceptible grin by my own and every other traveller's agreeable and gentlemanly friend, Campbell, I received the key of No. 12, and incontinently retired to rest. What I have seen in San Francisco I reserve for another occasion. I leave for San Diego this evening, from which place, I will take an early opportunity of addressing you. I regret that I cannot remain to be a participant in the coming celebration, but my cousin Skewball, a resident of the city, who writes with a keen if not a " caustic pen," has promised to furnish you an elaborate account of the affair, which, if you print, I trust you will send me. Write me by the post orifice. *Au reservoir.*

PHŒNIX INSTALLED EDITOR OF THE SAN DIEGO HERALD.*

"*Facilis decensus Averni,*" which may be liberally, not literally translated, it is easy to go to San Francisco. Ames has gone; departed in the "Goliah." During his absence, which I trust will not exceed two weeks, I am to remain in charge of the 'Herald,' the literary part thereof—I would beg to be understood—the *responsible* portion of the editoral duties falling upon my friend Johnny, who has, in the kindest manner, undertaken "the fighting department," and to whom I hereby refer any pugnacious or bellicose individual who may take offence at the tone of any of my leaders. The public at large, therefore, will understand that I stand upon "Josh

---

* [On the —— of —— 33, the Editor of the San Diego Herald, a democratic organ, committed his paper to the hands of the writer of these Sketches to be publish: d as usual, weekly, during the Editor's temporary absence in San Francisco. On his return, shortly after the fall election, he found the Herald still in regular order of publication, but owing to his having neglected to charge his proxy with the particular keeping of his political principles, *or some other cause*, the Herald, which had been an uncompromising ally of the Democracy was now no less vehement and active on the other side.

Haven's platform," which that gentleman defined some years since to be the liberty of saying any thing he pleased about any body, without considering himself at all responsible. It is an exceedingly free and independent position, and rather agreeable than otherwise; but I have no disposition whatever to abuse it.

It will be perceived that I have not availed myself of the editorial privilege of using the plural pronoun in referring to myself. This is simply because I consider it a ridiculous affectation. I am a "lone, lorn man," unmarried (the Lord be praised for his infinite mercy), and though blessed with a consuming appetite "which causes the keepers of the house where I board to tremble," I do not think I have a tape worm, therefore I have no claim whatever to call myself "we," and I shall by no means fall into that editorial absurdity.

San Diego has been usually dull during the past week, and a summary of the news may be summarily disposed of. There have been no births, no marriages, no arrivals, no departures, no earthquakes, nothing but the usual number of drinks taken, and an occasional "small chunk of a fight" (in which no lives have been lost), to vary the monotony of our existence. Placidly sat our village worthies in the arm-chairs in front of the "Exchange," puffing their short clay pipes, and enjoying their "*otium cum dignitate*," a week ago, and placidly they sit there still.

*   *   *   *   *   *   *

The only topic of interest now discussed among us is the

approaching election, and on this subject I desire to say a few words:

*   *   *   *   *   *   *

To those old soldiers who were with us before the adoption of the Constitution, and, in consequence, are entitled to vote, I would say: remember, my lads, that the duty of a good soldier in time of peace is to be an estimable citizen, and, as such, to assist in the election of good men to office. The man who seeks your vote for any office by furnishing you with whiskey, gratis, and credit at his little shop (if he happens to keep one), is by no means calculated to be either a good maker or dispenser of the laws. Drink his whiskey, by all means, if you like it, and he invites you, but make him no pledges, and on the day of election vote any other ticket than that he gives you. You know well enough, oh! my soldiers, how much he cares for you, and can appreciate his professions of attachment. They amount to precisely the same as those of Jacob, who bought the birthright of Esau for a mess of pottage. Don't barter yours for a little whiskey, and make for the county a worse mess than Esau could ever have concocted.

Should any gentleman, differing with me in opinion, feel anxious " to give utterance to the thought," I can only say, my dear sir, the " *Herald* " is an Independent paper, and while I have charge of it, its light shall shine for all ; express yourself, therefore, fully, but concisely, in an ably written article; hand it to me, and I will, with pleasure, present it to the world, through the columns of this wide-spread journal, merely reserving for myself the privilege of using you up, as

5

I shall infallibly do, and to a fearful extent, if facts are facts, reason is reasonable, and "I know myself intimately," of which, at present, I have no manner of doubt.

And thus having said my say, in a plain, straightforward manner, I shall close, for the present, with the assurance to the public, that I remain their very obedient, and particularly humble servant.

———

Mr. Kerren drove the Chaplain to the Mission from Old Town last Sunday, after the performance of the afternoon service—

> "With four gray horses, and two on the lead,
> They made tracts for the other side of Jordan."

The rattling 2.40 pace at which they tore along, was rather too much for the worthy preacher.

"Kerren," gasped his anxious reverence, as he held firmly by the back seat, after a flying leap over a stone of unusually large dimensions, "do you know why you are like the Pharisees?" "No, sir," said Kerren, touching up his off leader. "Why," rejoined the good old man, "ye appear unto men *too* fast."

Kerren gave a deep groan, and the horses struck a religious walk, which they adhered to until their arrival at the Mission.

" The Squire's Story."—" Oh!" says the squire, " I wish't I was married and well of it, *I dread it powerful*—I'd like to marry a widow—I allers liked widows since I knowed one down in Georgia that suited my ideas, adzactly.

" About a week after her husband died, she started down to the grave-yard whar they'd planted of him, as she said, to read the prescription onto his monument. When she got there, she stood a minute a looking at the stones which was put at each end of the grave, with an epithet on 'em that the minister had writ for her. Then she bust out, ' Oh! boo hoo,' says she, ' Jones—he was one of the best of men ; I remember how the last time he come home, about a week ago, he brought down from town some sugar, and a little tea, and some store goods for me, and lots of little necessaries, and a little painted hoss for Jeems, which that blessed child got his mouth all yaller with sucking of it, and then he kissed the children all round, and took down that good old fiddle of his'n and played up that good old tune,

" Rake her down, Sal, oh rang dang diddle,
Oh rang, dang diddle dang, dang dang da."

" Here," says the Squire, " she begin to dance, and I just thought she was the greatest woman ever I see."

" The Squire " always gives a short laugh, after telling this anecdote, and then filling and lighting his pipe, subsides into an arm-chair in front of the " Exchange," and indulges in calm and dreamy reflection.

WANTED.—Back numbers of the Democratic Review speeches and writings of Jefferson, Coffroth, Calhoun, Bigler Van Buren and others. Copies of the San Joaquin Republican (with George's daguerreotype), Files of the Times and Transcript (a few at a time), and a diagram representing the construction of the old United States Bank for the use of a young man desirous of turning Democrat.—Apply at this office (by firing a gun, or punching on the ceiling, he being deeply engaged in study in the garret), to

J. PHŒNIX.

THE COMEDY OF ERRORS.—We have been accused, with great injustice, of a " reckless propensity to lampoon." We disclaim, with indignation, any such propensity. On the contrary, such has been our anxiety to avoid personalities, or unpleasant allusions, that we have actually suppressed some of the very funniest things we have ever heard—little drolleries over which we have laughed, ourselves, in the sanctity of the sanctum, until the " arm-chair " has cracked again, and wondering men in the billiard room below, have poked up against the ceiling with their cues (that they might take their cue from us), simply because the mention of some name, Jones, Brown or Muggins, has rendered us unable to present them to the public. The conductor of a public journal is responsible for every thing that he presents, and he should never indulge in personalities, however humorous they may appear, or however much they may amuse himself, or be calculated to amuse his readers.

It is for this reason that we forbear publishing the following capital thing, dramatized expressly for our paper, and which we are solemnly assured, occurred very nearly, if not exactly, as represented.

SCENE.—*The interior of the City Post Office at San Francisco, Gov. B ——. discovered, sitting, holding a copy of the San Francisco Herald at arms-length, in a pair of tongs, and reading it with every mark of scorn and deep disgust. Enter Judge A. from the South, Editor of the San Diego Herald.*

Judge A. Ah! Governor, your most obedient; how do you do, sir?

Governor B. (Putting the Herald in a bucket of water, and laying down the tongs). How do you do, A., how d'ye do? Well, how are matters going on in San Diego county?

Judge A. Oh! admirably; you may depend on the unanimous support of that county, sir, the Herald has an immense, a commanding influence there, it will be felt, sir. I have left the paper in the charge of an able literary friend there, sir, Mr. Phœnix, probably you may have heard of him, a man of great ability; I expect an admirable paper from him this week, sir.

Governor B. (With a bland smile).—Ah! thorough Democrat, eh?

Judge A. Oh! certainly; I never thought to ask him, but—oh, of course, certainly he is a Democrat.

Governor B. Oh! certainly; I shall be glad to see his paper, Mr. A., ah! very glad, sir.

Here the mail is opened, the Judge eagerly receives a bundle of the first Phœnix Herald, hastily tears off the envelop, hands one copy to the Governor, and takes another himself. Each put on spectacles and glance at the first column, where appears in fatal capitals the respectable name of William Waldo. *Grand Tableau ! ! !* The Governor and the Judge gaze at each other over the tops of their respective papers, the one, with wrathful and indignant glance, the other, with the most concentrated expression of horror and misery of which the human countenance is capable.

[*Here the Ghost of old Squibob himself (ought to have been) seen rising, and hovering for an instant over the pair in an attitude of benediction, murmuring, " Bless ye, my children," larfs and disappears in a " sweet scented " cloud.*]

We forbear to give the conversation that ensued—this is a Christian community in which we live, and the introduction of excessive profanity in the columns of a public journal even as a quotation, would not and ought not to be tolerated.

We have received by the Goliah, an affecting letter from Judge Ames, beseeching us to return to the fold of Democracy from which he is inclined to intimate we have been straying. Is it possible that we have been laboring under a delusion—and that Waldo is a Whig ! Why ! lor ! How singular ! But anxious to atone for our past errors, willing to please the taste of the Editor, and above all, ever soli-citous to be on the strong side, we gladly abjure our former opinions, embrace Democracy with ardor, slap her on the back, declare ourselves in favor of erecting a statue of Andrew Jackson in the Plaza, and to prove our sincerity, run up to-day at the head of our columns, a Democratic ticket for 1855, which we hope will please the most fastidious. Being rather hard up for principles for our political faith, we have commenced the study of the back numbers of the Democratic Review, and finding therein that "DEMOCRACY IS THE SUPREMACY OF MAN OVER HIS ACCIDENTS," we hereby express our contempt for a man with a sprained ankle, and unmitigated scorn for any body who may be kicked by a mule or a woman. That's Democratic, ain't it? Oh, we understand these things.—Bless your soul, Judge, we're a Democrat.

LATE—Passing by one of our doggeries about 3 A. M., the other morning, from which proceeded " a sound of revelry by night," a hapless stranger on his homeward way paused to obtain a slight refreshment, and to the host he said, " It appears to me your visitors are rather late to-night." " Oh no," replied the worthy landlord, " the boys of San Diego generally run for forty-eight hours, stranger; *it's a little late for night before last*, but for to-night! why, it's just in the shank of the evening." Volumes could not have said more.

WANTED—By the subscriber, a serious young man, with fixed principles of integrity and sobriety, to make beds, sweep a room, black boots and bring water. For a youth of religious principles, to whom a large salary is not of so much object as a knowledge of the business, an eligible situation is here offered.

The best of references given and required.

J. PHŒNIX.

N. B. No female in disguise need apply.

AN APT QUOTATION.—His Reverence coming into the Colorado House last Sunday afternoon, was invited by the urbane proprietor to *irrigate*. Being in an arid state, he consented to take a glass of lemonade, but accidentally took a brandy cocktail which had been mixed for Mr. Mariatowskie, and drank it off without noticing his mistake. " Why, Doctor," said Frank, when he observed the disappearance of his sustenance, " that was my horn you drank." Ah, my young friend, quoth the good old man, with a benevolent smile and a smack of his lips, while the moisture stood on the inside of his venerable spectacles—" Ah, my young friend, *the horn of the ungodly shall be put down.*" Psalms 75 : 10

FOR SALE.—A valuable Law Library, lately the property of a distinguished legal gentleman of San Francisco, who has given up practice and removed to the Farralone Islands. It consists of one volume of " Hoyle's Games," complete, and may be seen at this office.

Our friend Charley Poole was complaining bitterly the other morning of the muddy quality of the water brought him for his daily ablutions, when he was consoled by a remark of " Phœnix," that he was probably a descendant of old Pool of Bethesda, mentioned in the Scriptures, and that, the angel that used to " come down and trouble " his ancestor's water, still continued his attentions to the family.

———

" THERE'S MANY A SLIP 'TWEEN THE CUP AND THE LIP." Proverbs 53 : 14.—It was my intention to have devoted about two columns of this journal, this week, to an exposition of the nefarious scheme of the " Water Front Extension," at San Francisco, and the abuse of the gubernatorial power that has been exercised in the matter of the "State Printing," during the past year.

But I have been deterred from doing all this by two good and sufficient reasons. In the first place, I can find but one man in the county who ever intended to vote for Bigler, and I have labored with him to prove the errors of opinion into which he has fallen, to that extent, that partly from the effects of the Fiesta, at San Luis Rey (where, as a matter of course, he became excessively inebriated), and partly from agitation of mind produced by my arguments, he has fallen into a violent fit of sickness, from which his physician thinks he cannot possibly recover before the day of election. And, secondly, I have a horrible misgiving that the editor *de facto* will return before this edition has gone to press, in which case, coming down on me from San Francisco "like a young giant refreshed with new wine," and finding (what he would consider) such abominable heresy in his columns, he would doubtless knock the whole matter into *pi*, and perhaps, in the extremity of his wrath, inflict some grievous bodily injury on me, all of which would be intensely disagreeable. Moved by these considerations, therefore, I shall let John Bigler entirely alone, and in case of his re-election, shall make a great merit of having done so, and apply to him immediately for a commission as Notary Public.

The great event of the past week has been the FIESTA at San Luis Rey.—Many of our citizens attended, and a very large number of native Californians and Indians collected from the various ranchos in the vicinity. High mass was celebrated in the old church on Thursday morning, an Indian baby was baptized, another nearly killed by being run over by an excited individual on an excited horse, and that day and the following, were passed in witnessing the absurd efforts of some twenty natives to annoy a number of tame bulls, with the tips of their horns cut off. This great national amusement, ironically termed bull-fighting, consists in waving a *serape*, or handkerchief, in front of the bull until he is sufficiently annoyed to run after his tormentor, when that individual gets out of his way, with great precipitation. The nights were passed in an equally intellectual manner.

*   *   *   *   *   *

The "Phœnix Ticket" *generally*, appears to give general satisfaction. It was merely put forward suggestively, and not being the result of a clique or convention, the public are at perfect liberty to make such alterations or erasures as they may think proper. I hope it may meet with a strong support on the day of election; but should it meet with defeat, I shall endeavor to bear the inevitable mortification that must result, with my usual equanimity.

Like unto the great Napoleon after the battle of Water-loo, or the magnanimous Boggs after his defeat, in the gubernatorial campaign of Missouri, I shall fold my arms with tranquillity, and say either " *C'est fini*," or *Oh shaw, I know'd it!* "

Though this is but my second bow to a San Diego audience, I presume it to be my last appearance and valedictory, for the editor will doubtless arrive before another week elapses—the gun will be removed from my trembling grasp, and the *Herald* will resume its great aims, and heavy firing, and I hope will discharge its debt to the public with accuracy, and precision. Meanwhile "The Lord be with you." "BE VIR-TUOUS AND YOU WILL BE HAPPY."

———

☞ We have received for publication, an article signed "LEONIDAS," from the pen of an old and esteemed friend of ours, intended to counteract the effect of our leader last week, which we should publish were it not for its length, and the rather strong style in which it is written. Many of

the principal points of " Leonidas' " opposition are removed
in this issue of the paper, and we doubt if it would serve
any useful purpose to publish extracts from his letter, or if
he would be pleased with our doing so.

He winds up by exhorting the Democrats "to keep together" (we hope they will, it would give us unfeigned regret to see *any* man explode or fall to pieces), and by calling us, indirectly, "*a rabid Whig.*"

In this, "Leonidas," you are mistaken. Our ideas on
political matters are precisely those of the lamented Joseph
Bowers, who when running for the office of —— in the state
of —— was asked by the —— committee, "Mr. Bowers, what
are your politics?" To which he replied, "Gentle*men*, I
. have no politics "—" What," exclaimed the committee in
surprise,—" no politics." " No, gentle*men*," rejoined the
imperturbable Joseph, " not a d—d politic."

He was elected unanimously, as many of our readers
from —— will doubtless remember, and we hope, should it
ever come to pass, that we are a candidate for public office,
we may meet with the like good fortune.

So farewell, oh Leonidas, we trust you are not yet " boiling with indignation;" but if unhappily that is the case, we
can only placidly remark—"*Boil on.*"

———

As an incident of the election we are told that late
in the afternoon an elderly gentleman, much overcome by
excitement and spirituous potations, was found like Peter

' weeping bitterly," as he reclined on the cold cold ground, behind the Court House. " I'm an old man, gentle-*men*," sobbed he, " and a poor old man, and a d—d *ugly* old man, and I've gone and voted for Bigler !" " Well, you *have* done it," remarked one of the crowd, and with this expression of sympathy, the unhappy old fellow was left to the stings of his conscience. A melancholy instance of misplaced attachment.

A GAME OF POKER.—An Eastern paper mentions the case of an individual in Terre Haute, Ind., who attacked his wife with a poker, and was arrested by a gentleman attracted by the lady's screams. Ah, the gentleman *passed*, the lady saw him and *called*.

☞ We carelessly threw a bucket of water from our office door the other day, the most of which fell upon an astonished Spaniard, sitting upon his horse, before the Colorado House. He made the brief remark " *Carajo*," meaning that we were courageous, and on observing his stalwart form, and the ferocity of his expression and moustaches, we thought we were.

A SYLLOGISM.—David was a Jew—Hence, " the Harp of David " was a Jewsharp. Question—How the deuce did he sing his Psalms and play on it the same time ?

We recommend this difficult question to " Dismal Jeems '
for solution, the answer to be left at Barry and Patten's
directed to " Phœnix."   .

———•♦•———

RETURN OF THE EDITOR.

' *Te Deum Laudamus.*"—Judge Ames has returned !
With the completion of this article my labors are ended;
and wiping my pen on my coat-tail, and placing it behind
my sinister ear, with a graceful bow and bland smile for my
honored admirers, and a wink of intense meaning for my
enemies, I shall abdicate, with dignity, the " Arm-Chair," in
favor of its legitimate proprietor.

By the way, this " Arm-Chair " is but a pleasant fiction
of " the Judge's,"—the only seat in the Herald Office being
the empty nail keg, which I have occupied while writing my
leaders upon the inverted sugar box, that answers the purpose of a table. But such is life. Divested of its poetry
and romance, the objects of our highest admiration become
mere common-places, like the Herald's chair and table.
Many ideas which we have learned to love and reverence,
from the poetry of imagination, as tables, become old sugar
boxes on close inspection, and more intimate acquaintance.
' Sic—but I forbear that sickening and hackneyed quotation.

During the period in which I have had control over the Herald. I have endeavored to the best of my ability to amuse and interest its readers, and I cannot but hope that my good humored efforts have proved successful. If I have given offence to any by the tone of my remarks, I assure them that it has been quite unintentional, and to prove that I bear no malice, I hereby accept their apologies. Certainly no one can complain of a lack of versatility in the last six numbers. Commencing as an Independent Journal, I have gradually passed through all the stages of incipient Whiggery, decided Conservatism, dignified Recantation, budding Democracy and rampant Radicalism, and I now close the series with an entirely literary number, in which, I have carefully abstained from the mention of Baldo and Wigler, I mean, Wagler and Bildo, no—never mind—as Toodles says, I haven't mentioned *any of 'em*, but been careful to preserve a perfect armed neutrality

The paper this week will be found particularly stupid. This is the result of deep design on my part; had I attempted any thing remarkably brilliant, you would all have detected it, and said, probably with truth;—Ah, this is Phœnix's last appearance, he has tried to be very funny, and has made a miserable failure of it. Hee! hee! hee! Oh! no, my Public, an ancient weasel may not be detected in the act of slumber, in that manner. I was well aware of all this, and have been as dull and prosy as possible to avoid it. Very little news will be found in the Herald this week: the fact is, there never is much news in it, and it is very well that it is so; the climate here is so delightful, that residents, in the enjoyment of their *dolce far niente*, care very little about what is going on elsewhere, and residents in other places, care very little about what is going on in San Diego, so all parties are likely to be gratified with the little paper, " and long may it wave."

In conclusion, I am gratified to be able to state that Johnny's office (the fighting department), for the last six weeks, has been a sinecure, and with the exception of the atrocious conduct of one miscreant, who was detected very early one morning, in the act of chalking A S S on our office door, and who was dismissed with a harmless kick, and a gentle admonition that he should not write his name on other persons' property, our course has been peaceful, and undisturbed by any expression of an unpleasant nature.

So, farewell Public, I hope you will do well; I do, upon my soul. This leader is ended, and if there be any man among you who thinks he could write a better one, let him try it, and if he succeeds, I shall merely remark, that I could have done it myself if I had tried. Adios!

Respectably Yours.

———•••———

INTERVIEW BETWEEN THE EDITOR AND PHŒNIX.

The Thomas Hunt had arrived, she lay at the wharf at New Town, and a rumor had reached our ears that "the

"Judge" was on board. Public anxiety had been excited to the highest pitch to witness the result of the meeting between us. It had been stated publicly that "the Judge" would whip us the moment he arrived; but though we thought a conflict probable, we had never been very sanguine as to its terminating in this manner. Coolly we gazed from the window of the Office upon the New Town road ; we descried a cloud of dust in the distance ; high above it waved a whip lash, and we said, " the Judge " cometh, and "his driving is like that of Jehu the son of Nimshi, for he driveth furiously."

Calmly we seated ourselves in the " arm chair," and continued our labors upon our magnificent Pictorial. Anon, a step, a heavy step, was heard upon the stairs, and "the Judge " stood before us.

" In shape and gesture proudly eminent, stood like a tower: . . . . . . but his face deep scars of thunder had intrenched, and care sat on his faded cheek; but under brows of dauntless courage and considerate pride, waiting revenge."

We rose, and with an unfaltering voice said : "Well, Judge, how do you do?" He made no reply, but commenced taking off his coat.

We removed ours, also our cravat.

*   *   *   *   *   *   *   *

*   *   *   *   *   *   *   *

The sixth and last round, is described by the pressman and compositors, as having been fearfully scientific. We held "the Judge" down over the Press by our nose (which we had inserted between his teeth for that purpose), and while our hair was employed in holding one of his hands, we held the other in our left, and with the "sheep's foot" brandished above our head, shouted to him, "say Waldo," Never! he gasped—

Oh! my Bigler he would have muttered,
But that he 'dried up,' ere the word was uttered.

At this moment, we discovered that we had been laboring under a "misunderstanding," and through the amicable intervention of the pressman, who thrust a roller between our faces (which gave the whole affair a very different complexion), the *matter* was finally settled on the most friendly terms—"and without prejudice to the honor of either party." We write this while sitting without any clothing, except our left stocking, and the rim of our hat encircling our neck like a 'ruff' of the Elizabethan era—that article of dress having been knocked over our head at an early stage of the proceedings, and the crown subsequently torn off, while the Judge is sopping his eye with cold water, in the next room, a small boy standing beside the sufferer with a basin, and glancing with interest over the advertisements on the second page of the San Diego Herald, a fair copy of which was struck off upon the back of his shirt, at the time we held him over the Press. Thus ends our description of this long anticipated personal collision, of which the public can believe precisely as much as they please if they disbelieve the whole of it, we shall not be at all offended, but can simply quote as much to the point, what might have been the commencement of our epitaph, had we fallen in the conflict,

" HERE LIES PHŒNIX.

ILLUSTRATED NEWSPAPERS.

A YEAR or two since a weekly paper was started in London, called the "*Illustrated News.*" It was filled with tolerably executed wood cuts, representing scenes of popular interest, and though perhaps better calculated for the nursery than the reading room, it took very well in England, where few can read, but all can understand pictures, and soon attained an immense circulation. As when the inimitable London Punch attained its world-wide celebrity, supported by such writers as Thackeray, Jerrold and Hood, would-be funny men on this side of the Atlantic—attempted absurd imitations—the "Yankee Doodle"—the "John Donkey,' &c., which as a matter of course proved miserable failures; so did the success of this Illustrated affair inspire our money-loving publishers with hopes of dollars, and soon appeared from Boston, New York and other places, Pictorial and Illustrated Newspapers, teeming with execrable and silly effusions, and filled with the most fearful wood engravings, "got up regardless of expense " or any thing else; the contemplation of which was enough to make an artist tear his hair and rend his garments. A Yankee named Gleason, of Boston, published the first, we believe, calling it "Gleason's Pictorial (it should have been Gleason's Pickpocket) and Drawing Room Companion." In this he presented to his unhappy subscribers, views of his house in the country, and his garden, and for aught we know, of "his ox and his ass, and the stranger within his gates." A detestable invention for transferring Daguerreotypes to plates for engraving, having come into notice about this time, was eagerly seized upon by Gleason, for farther embellishing his catchpenny publication, duplicates and uncalled for pictures were easily obtained, and many a man has gazed in horror-stricken astonishment on the likeness of a respected friend, as a "Portrait of Monroe Edwards," or that of his deceased grandmother, in the character of "One of the Signers of the Declaration of Independence." They love pictures in Yankeedom; every tin peddler has one on his wagon, and an itinerant lecturer can always obtain an audience by sticking up a likeness of some unhappy female, with her ribs laid open in an impossible manner, for public inspection, or a hairless gentleman, with the surface of his head laid out in eligible lots, duly marked and numbered. The factory girls of Lowell, the Professors of Harvard all bought the new Pictorial. (Professor Webster was reading one, when Dr. Parkman called on him on the morning of the murder.) Gleason's speculation was crowned with success, and he bought himself a new cooking stove and erected an out-building on his estate, with both of which he favored the public in a new wood cut im mediately.

Inspired by his success, old Feejee-Mermaid-Tom-Thumb-Woolly-horse-Joyce-Heth-Barnum, forthwith got out another Illustrated Weekly, with pictures far more extensive, letter-press still sillier, and engravings more miserable, if possible, than Yankee Gleason's. And then we were bored and buf-feted by having incredible likenesses of Santa Anna, Queen Victoria and poor old Webster, thrust beneath our nose, to that degree that we wished the respected originals had never existed, or that the art of wood engraving had perished with that of painting on glass.

It was, therefore, with the most intense delight that we saw a notice the other day of the failure and stoppage of Barnum's Illustrated News; we rejoiced thereat, greatly, and we hope that it will never be revived, and that Gleason will also fail as soon as he conveniently can, and that his trashy Pictorial will perish with it.

It must not be supposed from the tenor of these remarks that we are opposed to the publication of a properly conducted and creditably executed Illustrated paper. " On the contra-ry, quite the reverse." We are passionately fond of art our-selves, and we believe that nothing can have a stronger tendency to refinement in society, than presenting to the pub-lic, chaste and elaborate engravings, copies of works of high artistic merit, accompanied by graphic and well written essays. It was for the purpose of introducing a paper con-taining these features to our appreciative community, that we have made these introductory remarks, and for the purpose of challenging comparison, and defying competition, that we have criticised so severely the imbecile and ephemeral productions mentioned above. At a vast expenditure of money, time and labor, and after the most incredible and unheard of exertion, on our part, individually, we are at length able to present to the public an Illustrated publication of unprecedented merit, containing engravings of exceeding costliness and rare beauty of design, got up on an expensive scale, which never has been attempted before, in this or any other country.

We furnish our readers this week with the first number, merely promising that the immense expense attending its issue, will require a corresponding liberality of patronage on the part of the Public, to cause it to be continued.

PHŒNIX'S PICTORIAL,

And Second Story Front Room Companion.

Vol. I.]   San Diego, October 1, 1853.   [No. I.

Portrait of His Royal Highness Prince Albert.—Prince Albert, the son of a gentleman named Coburg, is the husband of Queen Victoria of England, and the father of many of her children. He is the inventor of the celebrated "Albert hat," which has been lately introduced with great effect in the U. S. Army. The Prince is of German extraction, his father being a Dutchman and his mother a Duchess.

Mansion of John Phœnix, Esq., San Diego, California.

House in which Shakespeare was born, in Stratford-on-Avon.

Abbotsford, the residence of Sir Walter Scott, author of Byron's Pilgrim's Progress, &c.

The Capitol at Washington.

Residence of Governor Bigler, at Benicia, California.

Battle of Lake Erie, (*see remarks*, p. 96.)

[Page 96.]

The Battle of Lake Erie, of which our Artist presents spirited engraving, copied from the original painting, by Hannibal Carracci, in the possession of J. P. Haven, Esq., was fought in 1836, on Chesapeake Bay, between the U. S. Frigates Constitution and Guerriere and the British Troops under General Putnam. Our glorious flag, there as everywhere was victorious, and " Long may it wave, o'er the land of the free, and the home of *the slave.*"

Fearful accident on the Camden & Amboy Railroad !! Terrible loss of life ! ! !

6

View of the City of San Diego, by Sir Benjamin West.

Interview between Mrs. Harriet Beecher Stowe and the Duchess of Sutherland, from a group of Statuary, by Clarke Mills.

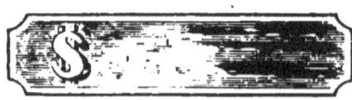

Bank Account of J. Phœnix, Esq., at Adams & Co. Bankers, San Francisco, California

Gas Works, San Diego Herald Office.

Steamer Goliah.

View of a California Ranch.—Landseer.

Shell of an Oyster once eaten by General Washington, showing the General's manner of opening Oysters.

There !—this is but a specimen of what we can do if liberally sustained. We wait with anxiety to hear the verdict of the Public, before proceeding to any farther and greater outlays.

Subscription, $5 per annum, payable invariably in advance.

INDUCEMENTS FOR CLUBBING.

Twenty Copies furnished for one year, for fifty cents. Address John Phœnix, Office of the San Diego Herald.

SANDYAGO—A SOLIQUY.

Oh my what a trying thing it is for a feller
To git kooped up in this ere little plais
Where the males dont run reglar no how
Nor the females nuther, cos there aint none.
But by the mails I mean the post orifices
By which we git our letters and sufforth
From the Atlantic States and the British Provinces.
But here there aint no kind of a chance
Except by the Sutherner or the leky Fremont
Which runs very seldom, and onst in the latter
I come to this plais, and wisht I was furder.
The natives is all sorts complected
Some white, some black, & some kinder speckled,
And about fourteen rowdy vagabonds
That gits drunk and goes round lickin every body.
And four stores to every white human
Which are kept by the children of Zion
Where they sell their goods bort at auction
At seven times more than they costed,
With a grand jury thats sittin forever
But dont never seem to indite nothin,
And if they do what comes on it
The petty ones finds em not guilty
And then they go off much in licker
And hit the fust feller they come to.
All night long in this sweet little village
You hear the soft note of the pistol
With the pleasant screak of the victim

Whose been shot prehaps in his gizzard.
And all day hosses is running
With drunken greasers astraddle
A hollerin and hoopin like demons
And playin at billiards and monte
Till they've nary red cent to ante
Having busted up all the money
Which they borryed at awful percentags
On ranches which they haint no title
To, and the U. S. board of commission
Will be derned if they ever approve it.
While the squire he goes round a walkin
And sasses all respectable persons
With his talk of pills he's invented
To give a spirit of resentment.
And persons fite duels on paper.
Oh its awful this here little plais is
And quick as my business is finished
I shall leave here you may depend on it
By the very first leky steambote,
Or if they are all of em busted
I'll hire a mule from some feller
And just put out to Santy Clara.

"THE JUDGE" looks melancholy!—He knows that this is Phœnix's Last, and that's exactly "where the shoe pinches." This squib is adapted to the comprehension of the meanest shoemaker.

FOURTH OF JULY CELEBRATION IN SAN DIEGO.

(Reported expressly for the San Diego Herald.)

TUESDAY last, the 4th of July, being the anniversary of the discovery of San Diego by the Hon. J. J. Warner, in 1846 as well as that of our National Independence ("long may it wave," &c.), was celebrated in this city with all that spirit and patriotism for which it has ever been distinguished.

Every citizen, with the exception of those who had retired in a state of intoxication, was aroused at 2 A. M. by the soul-stirring and tremendous report of the Plaza Artillery, which had been carefully loaded the previous evening with two pounds of powder, and half a bushel of public documents franked to this place by our late honorable representatives. Each citizen on being awakened in this manner (if he imitated the example of your respected reporter), reflected a moment with admiration on our glorious institutions; with pride on our great and increasing country, and with gratitude

on the efforts of those patriotic spirits who had thus aroused
him, and after murmuring some aspiration for their future
happiness, was about to sink again to sleep, when—Bang!
No. 2, more powder, more public documents, effectually
aroused him again, to go through the same train of thought,
murmur the same aspirations, a little warmer, perhaps, this
time, and again become sleepy in time for Bang! No. 3.   In
this agreeable manner the attention was occupied, and the
mind filled with patriotic ideas until just before daylight,
when the powder unfortunately gave out, though four bushels
of public documents still remained (but they wouldn't go off),
and the firing ceased.   At sunrise the National Banner would
have unfolded its "broad stripes and bright stars" to the
breeze, but for the unlucky circumstance of there being no
halliards to our flag-staff.   We are gratified to learn that a
new set will probably be furnished by the Board of Trustees
before the next anniversary.

At 8 A. M. a procession was formed, and moved to the
sound of an excellent military band, consisting of a gong and
a hand-bell, across the Plaza, where it separated into two
divisions, one proceeding to the Union House, the other to
the Colorado Hotel.   At each of these excellent establishments an elegant *dejeuner* was served up, of the sumptuous-
ness of which the following bill of fare will give some faint
idea :—

BREAKFAST BILL OF FARE.

Coffee.	Cafe, con sucre.
Bread.	Pan.
Butter.	Mantequilla.
Fried beefsteaks.	Carne.
Hash.	No sa.

At 9 A. M. precisely, the San Diego Light Infantry in full uniform, consisting of Brown's little boy in his shirt-tail, fired a National salute with a large bunch of fire crackers. This part of the celebration went off admirably; with the exception of the young gentleman having set fire to his shirt-tail, which was fortunately extinguished immediately, without accident.

At 12 M. an oration was delivered by a gentleman, in the Spanish language, in front of the Exchange, of which your reporter regrets to say he has been unable to remember but the concluding sentence, which, however, he is informed contains many fine ideas. It was nearly as follows :

"*Hoy es el dia de Santa Refugia ! Hic, Los Americanos son abajos, no vale nada ! (Hic,) nada, nada, nada, (hiccup.) Mira ! hombre, dar me poco de aguadiente Caramba.*"

This oration was remarkably well received, and shortly after, the band commencing its performance, the procession was again formed, and dividing as before, moved off to dinner.

The afternoon passed pleasantly away, in witnessing the performances of a gentleman who had been instituting a series of experiments to test the relative strength of various descriptions of spirituous liquor, and who becoming excited and enthusiastic thereby, walked round the Plaza and howled dismally.

Upon the whole, every thing passed off in the most creditable manner, and we can safely say that never in our recollection have we witnessed *such* a celebration of the glorious anniversary of our Nation s Independence.

MELANCHOLY ACCIDENT.—DEATH OF A YOUNG MAN.

Mr. Mudge has just arrived in San Diego from Arkansas; he brings with him four yoke of oxen, seventeen American cows, nine American children, and Mrs. Mudge. They have encamped in the rear of our office, pending the arrival of the next coasting steamer.

Mr. Mudge is about thirty-seven years of age, his hair is light, not a "sable silvered," but a *yaller*, gilded; you can see some of it sticking out of the top of his hat; his costume is the national costume of Arkansas, coat, waistcoat, and pantaloons of homespun cloth, dyed a brownish yellow, with a decoction of the bitter barked butternut—a pleasing alliteration; his countenance presents a determined, combined with a sanctimonious expression, and in his brightly gleaming eye —a red eye we think it is—we fancy a spark of poetic fervor may be distinguished.

Mr. Mudge called on us yesterday. We were eating
6*

watermelon. Perhaps the reader may have eaten watermelon, if so, he knows how difficult a thing it is to speak, when the mouth is filled with the luscious fruit, and the slippery seed and sweet though embarrassing juice is squizzling out all over the chin, and shirt-bosom.   So at first we said nothing, but waved with our case knife toward an unoccupied box, as who should say sit down.   Mr. Mudge accordingly seated himself, and removing his hat (whereat all his hair sprang up straight like a Jack in the box), turned that article of dress over and over in his hands, and contemplated its condition with alarming seriousness.

Take some melon, Mr. Mudge? said we, as with a sudden bolt we recovered our speech and took another slice ourself.   " No, I thank you," replied Mr. Mudge, " I wouldn't choose any, now."

There was a solemnity in Mr. Mudge's manner that arrested our attention; we paused, and holding a large slice of watermelon dripping in the air, listened to what he might have to say.

" Thar was a very serious accident happened to us," said Mr. Mudge, " as we wos crossin the plains. ' Twas on the bank of the Peacus river.   Thar was a young man named Jeames Hambrick along, and another young feller, he got to fooling with his pistil, and he shot Jeames. He was a good young man and hadn't a enemy in the company; we buried him thar on the Peacus river we did, and as we went off, these here lines sorter passed through my mind."   So saying, Mr. Mudge rose, drew from his pocket—his waistcoat pocket—a crumpled piece of paper, and handed it over.   Then he drew from his coat-tail pocket a large cotton handkerchief with a red ground and yellow figure, slowly unfolded it, blew his nose—an awful blast it was—wiped his eyes, and disappeared.   We publish Mr. Mudge's lines, with the remark, that any one who says they have no poets or poetry in Arkansas, would doubt the existence of William Shakspeare:

DIRGE ON THE DETH OF JEAMES HAMBRICK.

BY MR. ORION W. MUDGE, ESQ.

it was on June the tenth
our hearts were very sad
for it was by an awfull accident
we lost a fine young lad

Jeames Hambrick was his name
and alas it was his lot
to you I tell the same
he was accidently shot

on the peacus river side
the sun was very hot
and its there he fell aud died
where he was accidently shot

on the road his character good
without a stain or blot
and in our opinions growed
until he was accidently shot

a few words only he spoke
for moments he had not
and only then he seemed to choke
I was accidently shot

we wraped him in a blanket good
for coffin we had not
and then we buried him where he stood
when he was accidently shot

and as we stood around his grave
our tears the ground did blot
we prayed to god his soul to save
he was accidently shot

This is all, but I writ at the time a epitaff which I think is
short and would do to go over his grave :—

EPITAFF.

here lies the body of Jeames Hambrick
who was accidently shot
on the bank of the peacus river
by a young man

he was accidently shot with one of the large size colt's revolver
with no stopper for the cock to rest on it was one of the old
fashion kind brass mounted and of such is the kingdom of heaven.
truly yourn
ORION W MUDGE ESQ

SECOND EDITION!

Such has been the demand for the back numbers of the "Phœnix" Herald, that our editions have been entirely exhausted, and we have at last concluded to have the whole of them stereotyped. We have now seven hundred and eighty-two Indians employed night and day in mixing adobe for the type moulds, and as no suitable metal is to be found in San Diego, to cast the stereotypes, we have engaged 324,000 ball cartridges, from the Mission, for the sake of the lead. A very serious accident came near occurring in our office this morning, owing to the ignition of a cartridge, caused by friction, resulting from the rapid manner in which it was unrolled, but fortunately we escaped, with slight loss, one of our compositors having had his leg fractured just above the knee joint. The injured member was promptly and neatly taken off by "Phœnix," with a broad-axe in 2.46, and the sufferer is now doing well and engaged in setting type with his teeth. Our steam roller presses having failed to arrive (owing to the non arrival of the Goliah, as a matter of course), we have been obliged to work off the Pictorial Herald on our solitary Power Press.

"The Press is a tremendous engine." We have two tremendous Indians working at ours. Four men remove the papers as fast as printed, and forming a line to the outer door, four boys distribute them from the gallery to the excited crowd below.

Nothing is heard but the monotonous *houp! hank!* of the Indians, as in a cloud of steam of their own manufacture they strike off the paper. Nothing can be seen without but a shower of quarters, bits, and dimes darkening the air as they are thrown from the purchasers. Fourteen bushels and three pecks of silver have been received since we commenced distribution, and the cry is still they come.

THIRD EDITION!!

Fatal Accident!

A MELANCHOLY accident has just taken place. A fleshy gentleman had received a copy of the "Pictorial," and retired to the foot of the Flag-staff to peruse it. He had glanced over the first column, when he was observed to grow black in the face. A bystander hastened to seize him by the collar, but it was too late! Exploding with mirth, he was scattered into a thousand fragments, one of which striking him, probably inflicted some fatal injury, as he immediately expired, having barely time to remove his hat, and say in a feeble voice, "Give this to Phœnix." A large back tooth lies on the table before us, driven through the side of the office with fearful violence at the time of the explosion. We have enclosed it to his widow with a letter of condolence. The name of the unfortunate man was MUGGINS!

FOURTH EDITION!!!

The Very Latest!!!!

Mrs. Muggins has just been picking up the fragments of the deceased in a hand-basket. We omitted to state that the tooth had been filled by Dr. R. E. Cole, Dentist, whose advertisement may be found in another column! In her frantic agony the bereaved widow has accused us of purloining the gold. A terrible scene has ensued in our office, in consequence—after much recrimination between us, we have been atrociously " clapper-clawed " by Mrs. Muggins!

A LITTLE MORE FOR THE VERY LAST!!

After great exertion the fragments have been put together by Dr. H——, and the Muggins family have retired to their home, each bearing a copy of the "Pictorial," in triumph before them. Old Muggins has presented us with the tooth, and it may be seen at our office.

SAN FRANCISCO ANTIQUARIAN SOCIETY,

AND

CALIFORNIA ACADEMY OF ARTS AND SCIENCES.

PURSUANT to notice, a large and respectable number of those of our citizens interested in the advancement of the arts and sciences in California, assembled in the large hall over the Union Hotel, at 8 o'clock on Thursday evening, the 31st of June ult.

The meeting having come to order, was organized by our distinguished fellow-citizen, Dr. Keensarvey, being called to the chair, and the appointment of A. Cove, Esq. as Secretary

The chairman then rose, and in that lucid style which ever characterizes his public Addresses, briefly explained the object of the meeting :—It had been urged, he said. and he feared with too much justice, by our scientific friends in the Eastern States, that the inhabitants of California, residing in a country which opens to the Geologist, the Ethnologist, the Mineralogist, the Botanist, the Taxidermist, the Antiquarian, the Historian, the Philosopher and, in short, the Savant, the richest and most unexampled field on the face of the globe, or elsewhere, for their labors, were entirely regardless of their privileges in this respect, utterly absorbed in the pursuit of gain, and while excavating from the bowels of the earth its auriferous deposits in sufficient quantity, they cared not, to use a forcible illustration, the execration of a tinker, for those sciences in the pursuit of which they could alone find a rational manner of expending their accumulated wealth.

Was it possible that this could be the case? Had we not among us men of science, of liberality, of intelligence? (Cries of " Yes, Yes! " from the meeting, and " Si Señor " from a Castilian Savant in a glazed hat and judicious state of spiritual elevation.) Had we not in our midst many who, having acquired a sufficiency of worldly wealth, now wished to find among the treasures of science, that calm satisfaction which the possession of no amount of " dinero " can possibly afford? (Tumultuous shouts of " Yes, yes! Seguro! Si Señor," and a voice, " Whar is he? ")—Yes, gentlemen, it was the pride and pleasure of the Chairman to believe that such was the case; and it was in the hope of being able to hurl back the aspersions of the Savants of the east, that this meeting was called together; it was with the hope of forming a permanent, scientific, California Association, composed of such material as cannot be found elsewhere, and whose researches and transactions should be read with mingled emotions of astonishment, delight and envy, by every enlightened lover of science, from the eastern end of the North Farralocne Island, proceeding easterly, to the western end of the same. (Loud applause—cries of "Good! bon! bueno!" broke from the meeting, and a deep moan of acquiescence from the Castilian Savant, who, with the glazed hat partially shrouding his massive intellectual developments, had become slightly somnolent.)

The applause consequent upon this beautiful effort of the Chairman having subsided, Mr. B. S. Bags rose toad dress the Chair :—

He had not the advantage of an early education—not much, he hadn't; but he read a good deal, and liked it; and he dare say now, that if the truth had been found out, he knowed a great deal more than some of those filosifers at the east. He wanted to see science go on in California. He had a considerable interest in the place, and expected to spend his days thar. He was now fifty-three years old; he come out here twenty-three years ago as Steward of a Whale ship, and he run away and turned Doctor. (Laughter; cries of "Hush, hush!") But he married a Californy widder, with a large ranch; and he had, when the gold mines broke out, made his "pile"—he had over three hundred thousand dollars, and he didn't care who knowed it. He meant to devote the interest of the same to learning science. (Uproarious applause —cries of "Go it! that's the pint!" and "Carrambas!") He had three daughters, and he meant each on em should be a scientific man (loud applause); one of em wore green specs now, (immense applause accompanied by a cry of "Hep --ah!"

from a person in a white hat and blue blanket coat, who having evidently mistaken his place, was requested by the Chair
to leave at once—but he didn't do it). Order being restored,
Mr. Bags went on to say, that he had money enough, and
had gin up trading stock, and began to study science for itself. He had bought a "Mahomedon," and could tell how
hot it was any time; he had examined the "Ah teasing"
well in the square, and knew something about Hydrocianics
from a contemplation of scientific structures. By reading the
papers daily, particularly the "Alta California," he found all
sorts of new matters which he supposed give him considerable idea of "New Mattix;" but above all, having seen in the
papers from the States an account of the "Bosilist pendulum"
and its application to the Bunker Hill Monument, by which
it showed how the earth turned round from east to west, he
had ever since for three hours each day, watched the Flag-
staff on the Plaza, and he could assure the meeting that when
the flag was trailed it always flew out to the West, and when
it was histed the rope always bent out to the East—(" Hear!
Hear!)—Gentlemen might say it was the wind that did
it, but what made the wind? If any gentleman here had
ever rid out to the Mission on a calm day ("Hear!" from a
Savant who kept a Livery Stable in Kearney Street), he must
have felt a breeze blowing in his face. Well! *he* made that
wind, he did, agoing! and it was the earth that made the
wind by turning around in just the same way. (Deep impression produced: low remarks, "we must examine this! Bags is
a trump, &c.")

Mr. Bags concluded that he had took up a good deal of time, but he hoped that a society would be formed, and that he would pay his share towards it (applause), and more too (loud applause) ; he hoped he would be able to do more :—he was now reading a paper in Silliman's Journal on the " Horizontal Paralysis " with its effects on the " Cellular system," and he hoped to get some ideas out of it which he would adapt to California; and if he should, the society should have the benefit of it.   Mr. Bags here sat down amid prolonged and continued cheering.

Barney Braglagan was now loudly called for, but not appearing, the meeting was addressed by several of our most scientific citizens, the tendency of whose remarks was entirely and unreservedly in favor of the formation of a permanent society; and the meeting being wound up to the highest state of scientific excitement, it was unanimously—*Resolved* : That this meeting resolve itself into a permanent scientific association, to be known as the " San Francisco Antiquarian Society and California Academy of Arts and Sciences," and immediately enter into correspondence with all learned and scientific associations on the face of the earth.

Immediately after the passage of the above resolution, a committee, consisting of Dr. Keensarvey, A. Cove, and James Calomel, M. D., were appointed to prepare a constitution for the society.   Leaving the hall, they immediately repaired to the saloon of the California Exchange; when returning in seven minutes and five seconds (mean solar time), they submitted the following draft of a constitution, which was adopted by acclamation :

ARTICLE I. The officers of this Society shall consist of a President, Corresponding Secretary, Recording Secretary, Treasurer and Librarian, who shall be elected annually, by ballot.

ARTICLE II. The objects of this Society shall comprise inquiries into every thing in the remotest degree scientific or artful.

ARTICLE III. The Society shall consist of members, corresponding members and honorary members. The first to be persons residing in California; the two last to include both persons and residents of any other place on the face of the globe, or elsewhere.

ARTICLE IV. There shall be an annual payment of one hundred dollars, in City, County, or State scrip, by each member residing in the City of San Franscisco, or its vicinity.

The Society now proceeded to the election of officers for the ensuing year, with the following result : President, Dr. Keensarvey; Vice-President, M. Quelque Chose; Corresponding Secretary, G. Squibob ; Recording Secretary, A. Cove; Treasurer, Buck S. Bags; Librarian, the Consul for Ireland, *ex-off.*

On motion, the Treasurer received permission from the Society to apply to the City Council for liberty to stack the scrip forming the funds of the association upon the Plaza under cover of a Tarpaulin.

On motion, committees were appointed to report at the first meeting of the Society, on the following subjects namely: 1st. Antiquity; 2d. Geology; 3d. Toxicology; 4th. Ethnology; all as applicable to California.

On motion the proceedings of this meeting, and the future transactions of the Society shall be published in the San Francisco Daily Alta Californian, Silliman's Journal, the Boston Olive Branch, and the extra documents accompanying the President's annual message.

On motion, the Society adjourned to hold its first regular meeting on Thursday evening, July 15, in the remains of the old Adobe building anciently standing on the north-west corner of the Plaza.

Immediately on adjournment the several committees entered with zeal upon their various duties:

The Committee on Antiquities left at once, in the night boat, for Vallejo, the residence of their Chairman, who had informed them of the existence at that place of some speci- mens of a substance termed " Old Monongahela " lately dis- covered by a scientific gentleman residing at the Capitol; —the Committee on Geology were seen eagerly inquiring for the omnibus for Yerba Buena Island; that on Ethnology appointed a sub-committee for the City of San Francisco, and made arrangements for the departure of its main body to the upper counties of the State, for the purpose of holding interviews with the primitive inhabitants, while the Castilian savant in the glazed hat, who had been appointed Chairman of the Committee on Toxicology, repaired incontinently to a drinking saloon, where he commenced a series of experiments in hydrostatics, with the endeavor to ascertain the quantity of fluid possible to be raised from a glass in a given time, by a straw applied to his mouth, which resulted so much to his satisfaction that he was seen to emerge therefrom at four o'clock on the following morning, in a high state of pleasurable excitement, chanting huskily as he meandered down the street, that highly refreshing Mexican anthem—

"Castro viene—en poco tiempo
Cuidado los Americanos."

A. COVE,

Sec'y pro tem.

G. SQUIBOB,

Cor. Sec. S. F. A. S. and C. A. A. S.

San Francisco July 10, 1851

7

THE LADIES RELIEF SOCIETY.

EDITOR OF THE ——

SAN FRANCISCO, July 12.

LEARNING that a meeting of the "Ladies' Relief Society" was to be held this morning, at Pine Church, on Baptist Street, your Reporter, actuated by a desire to discharge his duty to the public by collecting valuable information, and incited by a laudable curiosity to ascertain what on earth the ladies desired to be relieved from (on which last point he obtained the most complete satisfaction, as will appear), re-paired to that sacred edifice, and ensconsing himself in a pew conveniently situated, in case of a sudden retreat be-coming expedient, near the door, patiently awaited the com-mencement of the proceedings.

At half past nine, A. M. precisely, as I ascertained by reference to the magnificent silver watch, valued at $18, which I did *not* draw in Tobin and Duncan's grand raffle, yesterday but which, "on the contrary, quite the reverse," was bestowed on me by my deceased Grandmother (excuse the digression ; I am approaching a painful subject and like to do it gradually), the ladies began to assemble in their beauty, and, I regret to add, their strength. From the somewhat inconvenient position which, from motives of delicacy and a desire to avoid the appearance of intrusion, I had assumed on the floor of the pew, I counted fifty-two of the "sweeten-ers of our cup of human happiness," of every age, figure and appearance. There was the maid of blushing sixteen, and there was the widow of sixty, dressed in all imaginable styles of colors—white hats, red shawls, chip bonnets, green aprons and pink colored boots.

The Pine Church looked like a conservatory, and as I lay *perdue,* like an innocent (green) snake among the flowers, listening to the merry laugh and innocent playful gurglings of delight that fell from their hundred and four lips."—How'd do, dear ? " My ! what a love of a bonnet ! " " What did you draw, Fanny ? " " Is Lizzy going to marry that fellow ? " &c., I thought that "my lines were cast in very pleasant places, and that I had a goodly heritage." How painfully was I undeceived; how totally was I engulfed ! (a prefer-able mode of expression—that 'engulfed'—to the common but indelicate one of "sucked in)." but I will not anticipate

As the town clock struck ten, the doors were closed, and a lady of mature age and benign though unyielding expres-sion (I do you justice, Madam, though you havn't used me well), ascended the steps of the pulpit, and taking from the

desk a fireman's speaking trumpet that laid thereon, she
smote an awful blow upon a copy of the sacred scriptures,
and vociferated through the brazen instrument, " *Order !* "
Conversation ceased, laughter was hushed, and with the exception of an irrepressible murmur and a subdued snicker
from your reporter, as some charming being exclaimed, *sotto
voce*, "don't pinch me," silence reigned profound. "Ladies,"
said the President, "you are aware of the object of this meeting.   Tied down by the absurd prejudices of society; tram-
melled by the shackles of custom and unworthy superstition;
we have found it necessary to form ourselves into a society,
where, free from the intrusion of execrable man; aloof from
his jealous scrutiny, whether as father, brother, or that still
more objectionable character of husband, we may throw off
restraint, exert our natural liberty, and *seek relief* from the
tedious and odious routine of duty imposed upon us in our
daily walk of life.   Any motion is in order."

At this instant, while my wondering gaze was attracted by
an elderly female in a Tuscan bonnet and green veil, who,
drawing a black pint bottle from the pocket of her dress,
proceeded to take a "snifter" therefrom, with vast appa-
rent satisfaction, and then tendered it to the lady that sat next
(a sweet little thing in a Dunstable, with cherry-colored ribbons), a lady rose and said—"Mrs. President: I move that
a committee of one be appointed to send a servant to Batty
and Parrens, for fifty-two *brandy smashes.*"   A thrill of horror ran through my veins ; I rose mechanically to my feet ;
exclaimed "gracious goodness!" and fell, in a fainting con-

dition, against the back of the pew. *It was my Susan!!*
You remember the instant that intervenes between the flash
of the lightning and the ensuing thunder clap:—for an instant there was silence, dead silence—you might have heard
a paper of pins fall—then "at once there rose so wild a yell,"
"a man! a man!" they cried, and a scene of hubbub and
confusion ensued that beggars description. The venerable
female in the Tuscan shyed the pint bottle at my head—the
little thing in the Dunstable gave me a back-handed wipe
with a parasol, and for an instant my life was in positive
danger from the shower of fans, hymn-books and other missiles
that fell around me. "Put him out, Martha," said an old
lady to a lovely being in a blue dress in an adjacent pew—
"I shan't," was the reply, "I haven't been introduced to him."
"Wretched creature," said the President in an awful voice,
"who are you?" "Reporter for the *Alta*" rose to my throat,
but my lips refused their utterance. "What do you want?"
she continued,—"I want to go home," I feebly articulated.
"Put him out!" she rejoined; and before I could think, much
less expostulate, I was pounced upon by two strong-minded
women, and found myself walking rapidly down Baptist street,
with the impression of a number three gaiter boot on my clothing about ten inches below the two ornamental buttons upon
the small of my back. From this latter circumstance, I have
formed the impression that the little thing with the Dunstable and cherry-colored ribbons assisted at my elimination.

And now, Mr. Editor, what are we to think of this?
Does it not give rise to very serious reflections, that a society

should exist in our very midst of so nefarious———but indignation is useless. " I cannot do justice to the subject."
Ruffled in disposition, wounded to the heart in the best and
most sacred feelings of my common nature, I can only subscribe
myself,   Your outraged Reporter,

INAUGURATION OF THE NEW COLLEC-
TOR!—TREMENDOUS EXCITEMENT.!!

ORIENTAL HOTEL, SAN FRANCISCO.

PASSING up Montgomery street yesterday afternoon, between 3 and 4 o'clock, my attention was attracted by a little gentleman with a small moustache, who rushed hastily past me, and turning down Commercial street sought to escape observation by plunging among the crowd of drays that perpetually tangle up Long Wharf. Though slightly lame, he had passed me with a speed that may have been equalled, but for a man of his size could never have been excelled; and his look of frantic terror—his countenance, wild, pallid with apprehension, as I caught for an instant his horror-stricken gaze, I shall never forget. I had turned partly around to watch his flight, when with a sudden shock I was borne hurriedly along, and in an instant found myself struggling and plunging in the midst of a mighty crowd who were evidently in hot pursuit. There were old men young men and maidens,—at least I presume they were maidens, but it was no time for close scrutiny;—there were Frenchmen, Englishmen, China-men, and every other description of men; gentlemen with spectacles and gentlemen who were spectacles to behold; men with hats and men without hats; an angry sea of moustaches, coat-tails and hickory shirts, with here and there a dash of foam in the way of a petticoat; and all pouring and rushing down Long Wharf with me in the midst, like a bewildered gander in a mill race.

There was no shouting—a look of stern and gloomy de-termination sat on the countenance of each individual; and save an occasional muttered ejaculation of " There he goes! " " I see him! " we rushed on in horrid silence.

A sickly feeling came over me as the conviction that I was in the midst of the far-famed and dreaded Vigilance Committee, settled on my mind; here was I, borne along with them, an involuntary and unwilling member—I, a life member of the Anti-Capital Punishment Scociety, and author of the little work called " Peace, or Directions for the use of the Sword as a Pruning Hook," who never killed a fly in my life—here I was, probably about to countenance, by my presence, the summary execution of the unhappy little cul-prit with the small moustache, who, for aught I knew to the contrary, might be as immaculate as Brigham Young him-self

What would Brother Greeley say to see me now? But it was no time for reflection. " Onward we drove in dreadful race, pursuers and pursued," over boxes, bales, drays and

horses; the Jews screamed and shut their doors as they saw
us coming; there was a shower of many-bladed knives,
German silver pencils, and impracticable pistols, as the show-
cases flew wildly in the air.   It was a dreadful scene.   I am
not a fleshy man—that is, not particularly fleshy—but an
old villain with a bald head and spectacles, punched me in
the abdomen; I lost my breath, closed my eyes, and remember nothing further.   On recovering my faculties, I found
myself jammed up flat against a sugar box, like a hoe cake,
with my head protruding over the top in the most uncomfortable manner, and apparently the weight of the whole crowd
(amounting by this time to some six thousand) pressed against
me, keeping me inextricably in my position.   Here for an
instant I caught a glimpse of a Stockton boat just leaving the
wharf;—then every thing was obscured by a sudden shower
of something white, and then burst from the mob a deep and
melancholy howl, prolonged, terrific, hideous.   I wrenched
myself violently from the sugar box, and confronted a seedy-
looking individual with a battered hat; in his hand he held a
crumpled paper, and on his countenance sat the gloom of despair.   " In the name of heaven," I gasped, " what is this ? "
" He has escaped," he replied, with a deep groan.   " What
has he done ? " said I ; " who is the criminal ? "   " Done,"
said he of the seedy garments, turning moodily away, " nothing—*it is the new Collector ! ! !*   He's off to Stockton."   The
crowd dispersed; slowly and sadly they all walked off.   I
looked over the side of the wharf.   I am not given to exag-
geration.   You will believe me when I tell you that the sea
7*

was white with letters that had been thrown by that crowd
for miles it was white with them, and far out in the stream her
wheels filled with letter paper, her shafts clogged with dissolv
ing wafers, lay the Stockton boat.   On her upper deck, in a
frenzied agony, danced the Pilot, his hand grasping his shattered jaw.   An office-seeker had thrown a letter attached to
a stone, which had dislodged four of his front teeth!   As I
gazed, the steamer's wheels began to move.   At her after-
cabin window appeared a nose above a small moustache, a
thumb and fingers twinkled for an instant in the sun-light,
and she was gone.   I walked up the wharf, and gazed rue-
fully on my torn clothing and shattered boots, which had
suffered much in this struggle of democracy.   "Thank God!
Oh, Squibob," said I, "that you are a fool, or what amounts
to the same thing in these times—a Whig—and have no offices to dispense, and none to seek for.   Verily, the aphorism
of Scripture is erroneous: It should read, *It is equally
cursed to give as to receive.*"

I repaired to my own room at the Oriental.   Passing the
chamber of the Collector, I espied within, the chambermaid,
an interesting colored person named Nancy.   Now I used to
have an unworthy prejudice against the colored race; but
since reading that delightful and truthful work, "Uncle
Stowe's Log," my sympathies are with them, and I have
rather encouraged a Platonic attachment for Nancy, which
had been engendered between us by numerous acts of civility
on my part and amiability on hers.   So I naturally stopped
to speak to her.   *She stood up to her middle in unopened*

.etters. There must have been on the floor of that room eighteen thousand unopened letters. The monthly mail from the East would be nothing to it. "Mr. Squibob," said Nancy, with a sweet smile, "is you got airy shovel?" "No, Nancy," said I; "why do you want a shovel?" "To clar out dese yere letters," said she; "de Collecker said I muss frow dem all away; he don't want no such trash about him." A thought struck me. I hastened to my room, seized a slop-pail, returned and filled it with letters, opened them, read them, and selected a few, which strike me as peculiarly deserving. If the Collector reads the *Herald*—and I know he "does nothing else"—these must attract his attention, and the object of the writers will be attained. Here they are. Of course, I suppress the dates and signatures; the authors will doubtless be recognized by their peculiar styles; and the time and place at which they were written is quite immaterial.

NO. I.

My Dear Friend :—I presume you will be perfectly surrounded this morning, as usual, by a crowd of heartless office-seekers; I therefore take this method of addressing you. I thank God, I want no office for myself or others. You have known me for years, and have never known me to do a mean or dishonorable action. I saw W—— up at Stockton the other day, and he is very anxious that I should be appointed Inspector of Steamboats. He said that I needed it, and deserved it, and that he hoped you would give it to me; but I told him I was no office-seeker—I should never ask you for any office.   He said he would write to you about it.   Please write to me as soon as you receive this, care of Parry & Batten.

Your affectionate friend

P. S.—My friend John Smith, who you know is a true Pierce & King man, is anxious to get the appointment of Weigher and Guager of Macaroni.   He is an excellent fellow, and a true friend of yours.   I hope, whether you can spare an Inspectorship for me or not, you will give Smith a chance.

NO. II.

MY DEAR SIR:—Allow me to congratulate you on your success in obtaining your wishes.   I have called twice to see you, but have not been able to find you in.   You were kind enough to assure me, before leaving for Washington, that I might depend upon your friendship.   I think it very improbable that I shall be re-nominated.   The water-front Extension project has not been received with that favor that I expected, and what with Roman and the Whigs and that d——d *Herald*, I feel very doubtful.   You will oblige me by retaining in your possession, until after the Convention, the office of —— to the Custom House.   I must look about me to

command the means of subsistence.   I will see you again on
this subject.

Very truly yours,

P. S.—My young friend, Mr. John Brown, wishes to be
made Inspector of Vermicelli.   He is a pure Democrat
dyed in the wool, and I trust in making your appointments
you will not overlook his claims.   Brown tells me he con-
siders himself almost a relative of yours.   His aunt used to
go to school with your father.   She frequently writes to him,
and always speaks of you with great esteem.

NO. III.

Mon Amie:—I ave been ver malade since that I hav arrive, I ver muche thank you for you civilite on la vapor which
we come ici, juntos.   The peoples here do say to me, you si
pued give to me the littel offices in you customs house.   I
wish if si usted gustan you me shall make to be Inspectors
de cigarritos.   Je l entends muy bien.   Come to me see.

Countess de ——

Mister José Jones he say wish to be entree clerky.   You
mucho me oblige by make him do it.

NO. IV.

The following was evidently dictated by some belligerent old Democrat to an amanuensis, who appears not to have got precisely the ideas intended :

SIR :—I have been a dimocrat of the Jackson School thank God for twenty years. If you sir had been erected to an orifice by the pusillanimous sufferings of the people as I was onst I would have no clam but sir you are appointed by Pierce for whom I voted and King who is dead as Julia's sister and I expectorate the office for which my friends will ask you sir I am a plane man and wont the orifice of Prover and taster of Brandy and wish you write to me at the Niantic where I sick three days and have to write by a young gentleman or come to see me before eleven o'clock when I generally get sick   Yours

P. S. My young man mr. Peter Stokes I request may be made inspector of pipes.

NO. V.

Mr. Colected H——.   Detor
      Elizer Muggins
            fore dosen peaces . . . .$12. .
            Reccat pament.

Mister Colected My husban Mikel Muggins will wish me write you no matur for abuv if you make him inspector in yore custom hous, he always vote for Jackson and Scott and all the Dimocrats and he vote for Bugler and go for extension the waser works which I like very much. You will much oblige by call and settel this one way or other.

ELIZIR MUGGINS.

Mike wants Mr. Timothy flaherty, who was sergent in Pirces regiment and held Pirces hoss when he rared and throwed him to be a inspector too hes verry good man.

E. M.

NO. VI.

Sir :—I have held for the last four years the appointment of Surveyor of Shellfish in the Custom House, and have done my duty and understand it. I have been a Whig, but never interfered in politics, and should have voted for Pierce—it was my intention—but a friend by mistake gave me a wrong ballot, and I accidentally put it in, having been drinking a little. Dear sir, I hope you will not dismiss me ; no man in this city understands a clam as I do, and I shall be very much indebted to you to keep my office for the present though have much finer offers but don't wish at present to accept.

Very respectfully,

P. S.—My friend Mr. Thomas Styles wishes to keep his office. Dear sir, he is Inspector of Raccoon Oysters; he is an excellent gentleman, and though they call him a Whig I think dear sir, there is great doubt. I hope you'll keep us both; it's very hard to get good Inspectors who understand shell-fish.

So much for to-day. If any gentleman incited by a laudable curiosity wishes to peruse more of these productions, let him proceed to Telegraph Hill, and on the summit of the tower at the extremity of the starboard yard-arm, in the discharge of his duty will be found, always ready, attentive courteous and obliging,

SQUIBOB.

SQUIBOB ABHORS STREET INTRODUC-
TIONS.

No matter of local interest having occurred, worthy the pen of history, since the return of the "Congressional Rifles" from their target excursion at San Mateo, I propose to devote a few moments to the reprobation of an uncomfortable custom prevalent in this city, to an alarming extent, and which if persisted in, strikes me as calculated to destroy public confidence, and, to use an architectural metaphor, shake the framework of society to its very piles. I allude to the pernicious habit which every body seems to have adopted, of making general, indiscriminate and public introductions. You meet Brown on Montgomery street: "Good morning, Brown;" "How are you, Smith?" "Let me introduce you to Mr. Jones"—and you forthwith shake hands with a seedy individual, who has been boring Brown for the previous hour for a small loan probably—an individual you never saw be-

fore, never had the slightest desire to see, and never wish to
see again.   Being naturally of an arid disposition, and perhaps requiring irrigation at that particular moment, you
unguardedly invite Brown, and your new friend Jones of
course, to step over to Parry and Batten's, and imbibe.
What is the consequence ?   The miscreant Jones introduces
you to fifteen more equally desirable acquaintances, and in
two minutes from the first introduction there you are, with
seventeen newly formed friends, all of whom " take sugar in
their'n," at your expense.

This is invading a man's *quarters* with a vengeance.   But
this is not the worst of it.   Each gentleman to whom you
have been introduced, wherever you may meet thereafter, in
billiard room, tenpin alley, hot house or church, introduces
you to somebody else, and so the list increases in geometrical
progression, like the sum of money, which Colman in his
arithmetic informs us the gentleman paid for the horse, with
such a number of nails in his shoes—a story which in early
childhood I remember to have implicitly believed.   In this
manner you form a crowd of acquaintances, of the majority
of whom you recollect neither names nor faces, but being continually assailed by bows and smiles on all sides, from unknown gentlemen, you are forced, to avoid the appearance of
rudeness, to go bowing and smirking down the street, like a
distinguished character in a public procession, or one of those
graven images at Tobin & Duncan's, which are eternally
wagging their heads with no definite object in view.   This
custom is peculiarly embarrassing in other respects.   If you

are so unfortunate as to possess an indifferent memory for names, and a decided idiosyncrasy for forgetting faces, you are continually in trouble as to the amount of familiarity with which to receive the salutation of some unknown individual to whom you have been introduced, and who persists in remembering all about you, though you have utterly forgotten him.

Only the other day, at the Oriental Hotel, I met an elderly gentleman, who bowed to me in the most pleasant manner as I entered the bar-room. I wasn't quite sure, but I thought I had been introduced to him at Pat Hunt's; so, walking up, I seized him familiarly by one hand, and slapping him on the shoulder with the other, exclaimed, " How are you old cock?" I shall not soon forget his suspicious glance, as muttering, " Old Cock, sir!" he turned indignantly away; nor my confusion at learning shortly after, that I had thus irreverently addressed the Rev. Aminadab Sleek, Chairman of the " Society for Propagating the Heathen in California," to whom I had brought a letter of introduction from Mrs. Harriet Bitcher Stowe. On the same day I met and addressed, with a degree of distant respect almost amounting to veneration, an individual whom I afterwards ascertained to be the husband of my washerwoman—a discovery which I did not make until I had inquired most respectfully after his family, and promised to call at an early day to see them.

There are very few gentlemen in San Francisco, to whom I should dislike to be introduced, but it is not to gentlemen alone, unhappily, to whom this introduction mania is confined.

Everybody introduces everybody else; your tailor, your barber, and your shoemaker, deem it their duty to introduce you to all their numerous and by no means select circle of acquaintance. An unfortunate friend of mine, T——hf—l J——s, tells me that, stopping near the Union Hotel the other day to have his boots blacked by a Frenchman, he was introduced by that exile, during the operation, to thirty-eight of his compatriots, owing to which piece of civility he is now suffering with a cutaneous disorder, and has been *vi donc-ed*, *icid*, and g——d ever since, to that degree that he hates the sight of a French roll, and damns the memory of the great Napoleon.

My own circle of acquaintance is not large; but if I had a dollar for every introduction I have received during the last six weeks I should be able to back up the Baron in one of his magnificent schemes, or purchase the entire establishment of the *Herald* office.

But I have said quite enough to prove the absurdity of indiscriminate introductions. Hoping, therefore, that you will excuse my introduction of the subject, and that Winn won't make an advertisement out of this article,

I remain, as ever, yours faithfully.

SQUIBOB AT THE PLAY.

ANOTHER SQUIBOB IN THE FIELD.

SAN FRANCISCO, June 10, 1853.

THE sympathies of the community have been strongly excited within the last few days in favor of an unfortunate gentleman of the Hebrew persuasion, on whom the officers of the Golden Gate perpetrated a most inhuman atrocity, during her late trip from Panama. I gather from information of indignant passengers, and by contemplation of an affecting appeal to the public, posted in the form of a hand-bill at the corners of the streets, that this gentleman was forced, by threats and entreaties, to do violence to his feelings and constitution, by eating his way through a barrel (*not* a half barrel, as has been stated by interested individuals, anxious to palliate the atrocious deed) of clear pork! The hand-bill alluded to is headed by a graphic and well-executed sketch by Solomon Ben David, a distinguished artist of this city, and represents the unhappy sufferer as he emerged from the barrel after his oleaginous repast, in the act of asking, very naturally, for a drink of water. The offence alleged, I find from a hasty perusal of the resolutions contained in the hand-bill, was simply that this gentleman, whose name appears to have been Oliver, was heard inquiring for Colonel Moore, our well known and respected Ex-Postmaster. My friend Saul Isaacs, who keeps the " anything on this table for a quarter " stand, tells me that on ' doffing his cask," the miserable Oliver was found completely bunged up, and that he is now engaged in composing a pathetic ode, describing his sufferings, to be called " The Barrel," with a few staves of which he favored me on the spot. It was truly touching. But it is needless to ring the chimes farther on this subject. But one *side* of the story has yet been heard, and as the officers promise a full and complete explanation, it is to be hoped that public opinion may be suspended for a few months, till they can be heard from.

I attended the American Theatre last evening, and had the pleasure of seeing several admirable pieces capitally performed, by the largest and finest assemblage of dramatic talent ever collected on one stage in San Francisco. The occasion was the benefit of the Hebrew Benevolent Society, a very worthy and respectable charity, and the house was absolutely crammed from pit to dome. The aisles and lobbies were thronged with gentlemen who were unable to obtain seats, and who could obtain but hasty and imperfect glimpses of the stage from their uncomfortable positions. Through the kindness of the box-keeper I was furnished with a chair, from which, planted in the middle aisle of the parquette, I had an admirable view of the audience and the drop-curtain. The dress circle was crowded with the fair daughters of Zion and other localities, with silken hair darker than the driven charcoal, "and bright eyes that flashed on eyes that shone again." Above the second circle appeared a dense forest of black whiskers, and curvilinear proboscis; while from the gallery, that paradise of miners and minors, rang as from a dragoon stable the never-ceasing cry of *hay!* The curtain rose on San Francisco's Pet—the accomplished Caroline Chapman—who appeared in one of her favorite pieces, a pretty little burletta, called the " Actress of All Work," in which she sustained, it is needless to say, most admirably, five distinct characters. She was greeted on her first entrance with tremendous and long-continued applause, which followed her throughout the piece, at the conclusion of which she was called before the curtain, when with one of her sweet smiles she sufficiently rewarded the audience for their just appreciation of her talent, and her legion of admirers for the beautiful bouquets which fell around her. To say that she was the " bright particular star " of the evening's entertainment, would perhaps appear invidious; but for pure, fresh, natural acting, ever-graceful, sparkling, and all-pretty as she appeared, she certainly could not be excelled, in her peculiar line of character—and she wasn't. The audience admired thee, Caroline ! and the humble hat of Squibob is at thy disposal for ever ! Miss Chapman was assisted by Mr. Hamilton, a veteran and most worthy actor, who did himself much credit,

as he always does in any part he undertakes. Then came
Miska Hauser, who with his violin "went up higher, and
came down lower," and performed variations to that extent you
couldn't distinguish the original tune more bewilderingly, and
made it to squeal, and to bray, and to groan, and to whistle,
and to grunt, and looked fiercer at the audience while he was
doing it, than any concentrated number of musicians ever
collected by that regal lover of harmony, the convivial Cole,
could possibly have effected. He was received with roars of
applause by the audience, who made him do it all over again;
but as I am somewhat like a corn-field, with plenty of ears
but no particular idea of music, I was not perhaps as ecstati-
cally delighted as I ought to have been. Then Madame la
Comtesse de Landsfeldt appeared in the second act of the
pantomime of Yelva, in which she delighted the audience
with her artistic delineations of the character of an artless
and affectionate dumb girl, and was most enthusiastically
received and applauded. After which a comic song was given
and *encored* by W. B. Chapman, well known as a comic actor
of great celebrity, who enjoys a reputation in his style of performances only inferior to Burton and Placide. After this
Mr. and Mrs. Baker acted very admirably, a very singular
piece, neither farce or comedy, but rather suggestive of a
school dialogue, which though not deficient in wit, and abound-
ing in sparkling repartee, lacks adaptation to the stage, and
would perhaps have seemed tiresome, had it not been for the
talent of the performers. Mr. and Mrs. Baker were received
with a tempest of applause, and on being called before the

curtain at the conclusion of the dialogue, a large bouquet, or small conservatory of flowers, was thrown upon the stage, as a tribute of admiration and regard. The performance closed with the dance of "Le Olle" by the bewitching Lola, which she performed with inimitable grace and elasticity and very much to the satisfaction of the audience, if I may judge by the roars that rent the air as she appeared before the curtain in response to their call.

Thus finished the entertainment of the evening, with which I, murmuring a kind *ajew*, retired to my virtuous bed, perfectly satisfied, as I presume did the Hebrew Benevolent Society generally, as their receipts must have been between three and four thousand dollars, with which I hope they will do as much good as I should, if I had it. As I walked up the street on my return home, I noticed a lady who passed me in happy unconsciousness of a small placard adhering to what a sailor would call the *afterpart* of her shawl, on which, in capital letters, appeared the significant word—TAKEN. As she walked between two gentlemen, holding an arm of each, the notice was not altogether inappropriate. She had evidently sat upon one of the little placards so liberally distributed every night over the front seats at the American, and it had adhered to her dress.

Who is the witty individual that has adopted my time-honored signature in the *Evening Journal*. Funny beggar ! He certainly, he ! he ! he ! does get off, ha ! ha ! ha ! the drollest things, ho ! ho ! ho ! that I ever, ever heard. I was taking my dinner at the Oriental when that capital hit at the

8

Japan Expedition met my eye, and was borne from the room by two strong waiters, choking with half a glass of water imbibed the wrong way, kicking violently in the air with con- vulsions of laughter and delight, and exclaiming, oh ! d——n it; thus losing my repast, and forfeiting for ever the esteem of a grave and elderly gentleman with green spectacles, who sits opposite me, and has made strenuous efforts for my conver- sion, with great hope of ultimate success. Adopt another name, funny man, and do not continue to enhance thus unde- servedly, the literary reputation of

SQUIBOB.

THE PARABLE OF THE FOX AND ASS.

Editor of the ——

SAN FRANCISCO, June 12.

I would respectfully call the attention of the *Evening Journal* to the following fable, to be found in Esop's collec- tion, page 194 :

"THE FOX AND THE ASS."

" An ass, finding a Lion's skin, disguised himself therein, and ranged about in the forest. After he had diverted him- self for some time, he met a Fox, and being desirous to astonish him, he leaped at him with some fierceness, and endeavored to imitate the roaring of a Lion. 'Your humble servant, sir,' said the Fox, 'if you had held your tongue, I might have taken you for a Lion, as others did, but now you bray, *I know who you are.*'

" MORAL :

" We perceive from this fable how proper it is for those to hold their tongues who would not discover the shallowness of their understandings."

I rather think it would be " painting the lily " to attempt any improvement on this beautiful and instructive parable, by any crude remarks of my own.

SQUIBOB.

THE LITERARY CONTRIBUTION BOX.

LINES TO LOLA MONTES

SAN FRANCISCO, June 13th, 1853.

ON assuming the responsible position of poetical critic for the *Herald*, I applied to my friend Mr. Parry for permission to place in one corner of his San Francisco renowned establishment, a cigar-box, with a perforated sliding cover, for the reception of poetical contributions, a request which that gentleman most urbanely granted. Knowing that " Parry's " was the favorite resort of the wits, literati and savans of the city, I hoped and believed that this enterprise would be crowned with the success that it merited; but either our city poets are unable to find quarters in that establishment, or there is dearth of that description of talent at present; for with the exception of two or three contributions of " old soldiers " and a half-dollar deposited by an inebriated member of the last Legislature, on the representation of his friends that the box was placed there for the relief of distressed Chinese women, nothing has come of it.

Diurnally, after imbibing my morning glass of bimbo (a temperance drink, composed of "three parts of root beer and two of water-gruel, thickened with a little soft squash, and strained through a cane-bottomed chair)," have I gazed mournfully into that aching void, and have turned away to meet the sympathetic glance of Batten, who, being a literary man himself, feels for my disappointment, and shakes his head sadly as in reply to my mute inquiry, he utters the significant monosyllable " Nix." But this morning my exertions were rewarded: "I had a bite." In my box I found the following contribution, and feeling delighted at my success, and to encourage others who may dread criticism, I shall publish it without remark or annotation, merely premising that I know nothing whatever of M. W. but that he appears to be a worthy and impulsive young fellow, who, having become possessed of five dollars, invested it very properly in the purchase of a ticket at the American Theatre, where he incontinently fell in love with Mrs. Heald (as possibly others may have done before him) and where he hastily "threw off" the following lines, written doubtless on the back of a playbill, immediately after the conclusion of the Spider Dance, when he probably found himself in a sweet state, compounded of love, excitement and perspiration, caused by a great physical exertion, in producing the *encore*. Here it is:

"TO LOLA MONTES.

"FAIR LOLA!
"I cannot believe, as I gaze on thy face,
    And into thy soul-speaking eye,
There rests in thy bosom one lingering trace
    Of a spirit the world should decry.
        No, Lola, no!

I read in those eyes, and on that clear brow,
    A Spirit—a Will—it is true;
I trace there a Soul—kind, loving, e'en now;
    But it is not a wanton I view;
        No, Lola, No!

I will not believe thee cold, heartless and vain!
    Man's *victim* thou ever hast been!
With *thee* rests the sorrow, on *thee* hangs the chain.
    Then on thee should the world cast the sin ?
        No, Lola, no.
                                            M. W."

Now isn't this —— but I promised not to criticise.   Try
it again, M. W.—you'll do!   Winn, who is looking over my
shoulder, and is a connoisseur in this description of poetry
says it is very fair—but he will persist in inquiring " what
chain is alluded to in the last line but one ?"   He thinks
" there is a link wanting there to complete the connection.'
But never mind this, M. W.; he would be glad enough
to reward you liberally for a similar article laudatory
of buckwheat cakes and golden syrup.   Don't be dis-

heartened! Just you go on and fill the cigar box, confident of deserving the "smiles" of Parry, the "cheer" of Batten, and the appreciation, with a "first-rate notice,' of your admiring

SQUIBOB.

A VERY MOURNFUL CHAPTER.

DEATH AND SPIRIT RESURRECTION OF SQUIBOB.

[Reported by his friend Skewball.]

SAN FRANCISCO, June 15th, 1853.

EDITOR HERALD—It becomes my melancholy duty to inform you of the decease, under most painful circumstances,
of your friend and contributor, the unfortunate " SQUIBOB."
It has been evident to the public for some days past that his
faculties were becoming much impaired, and his friends had
noticed, with regret, growing evidences of imbecility, evinced
by a disposition to make unnecessary and inappropriate puns,
and a tendency to ridicule the Board of Aldermen, the code
of duelling, and other equally serious subjects and sacred
institutions. Hopes were still entertained of his rallying,
and many believed that he would yet be spared to us ; but,
on the 13th instant, he was seized with a violent attack of
the *Evening Journal*—a species of intermittent epidemic
which made its appearance regularly at four o'clock each

afternoon, and under the influence of which he rapidly sunk. He sent for me late yesterday evening, and I had the mournful satisfaction of being with him in his last moments, and of closing one of his eyes. I say one of his eyes, for the other persisted in remaining partly open, and his interesting countenance, even in death, preserves that ineffable wink of intelligence which so eminently characterized him while among the living. I found him suffering much from physical and mental prostration, but evidently well aware of his approaching end, and calm and resigned in the ˙ contemplation of that event. Some idea may be formed of his condition " from a remark that he made : " " I sent to the cook for a *broiled* pork chop," he feebly articulated, " and he sent me a *fried* one. It is satisfactory, in one's last moments thus to receive the consolations of religion from a *San Franciscan Friar.*" I could not resist an expression of horror at this sad evidence of the alarmingly low state to which he had been brought. He smiled sadly, and said, with ineffable sweetness, " Never mind—it's better so. My friends have all advised me to die, and it is my safest course. If I had continued in the papers, some bellicose individual would have ' called me *out*,' and the *Herald* would have been ' rifled of its sweets.' " He was here seized with an alarming paroxysm, during which his hands were extended in a right line from the tip of his nose, the fingers separated and " twiddling ' (if I may be allowed the expression) in a convulsive manner. On recovering, his eye fell on a copy of the *Evening Journal* He shuddered, and muttering, in an incoherent manner

8*

" I am done Brown," turned away. I then gave him a glass of " Bimbo," which appeared to arouse his energies, and he requested that his daguerreotype of " Greene," in his great character of Sir Harcourt Courtly, might be shown him. As I held before him the representation of that artist, a barrel organ in the street below struck up his favorite tune, " The Low-Backed Car." As the well-known sound struck on his ear, a light spread over his countenance. Sitting up in bed, he seized the miniature and clasped it to his breast. " Where is M. W.?" he screamed. " Give it me quick! quick!!" I hastily handed him yesterday's *Herald.* His eye fell on the lines. Gazing alternately on them and the miniature, and eagerly listening to the organ—" Poetry! Music! and the Drama!" he exclaimed—" Farewell! farewell, for ever!" The light passed from his visage, his eye glazed, and falling back upon his pillow, his gentle spirit passed away without a struggle.

*　　　*　　　*　　　*　　　*　　　*

I had left the room to give directions to the weeping Nancy, with reference to the disposal of the body, when returning, judge of my surprise at finding him sitting up in bed. " Look here, old fellow," said he, " By George! I quite forgot my last words—" *This is the last of earth!—I still live!!*—I WISH THE CONSTITUTION TO BE PRESERVED!!!—HERE'S LUCK!!!!" Then lying down, and closing one eye, with a wink, the intense meaning of which beggars all description, he expired—this time "positively without re serve."

P. S.—The funeral ceremonies will take place to-morrow, at 11 o'clock, at "Patty and Barren's," when the public generally are invited to attend (with rifles). The "Tangarees" (of which association the deceased was a member), and the "Moral Reform Society," will form around the bier (*lager*), and accompany the body to its last resting place.

Winn is now busily engaged in the melancholy duty of modelling his features in soft gingerbread. A copy of the bust in candy he promises shall be sent to the offices of the *Herald* and the *Evening Journal.*

A Spiritual Medium (one of the tipping ones) has just been experimenting in the room with the remains. The following questions were put, eliciting the following answers—

QUESTION.—"Is the spirit of Squibob present?"

ANSWER.—"Slightually."

QUESTION.—"Are you happy?"

ANSWER.—"Rather."

The Spirit here asked, through the Medium, the following question—

"Are the public generally glad I am dead?"

A regard for veracity compelled every person in the room to reply: "Very!"—when the table on which the experiments were being conducted was violently capsized, and the remains, sitting up in bed, threw a boot at the Medium, which broke up the meeting—the Medium very properly remarking, that "it would be bootless to prosecute the in-quiry farther."

Should any thing further of interest transpire, I will take much pleasure in informing you.

Yours respectfully,

SKEWBALL

RETURN OF THE COLLECTOR.

THRILLING AND FRANTIC EXCITEMENT AMONG OFFICE-
SEEKERS. PROCESSION AND SPEECH.

INTELLIGENCE having reached the city yesterday morning
that the new Collector might be expected by the Sophie
from Stockton, at an early hour in the afternoon the crowd
of office-seekers began to assemble, and by eight o'clock
last evening, every avenue of approach to Long Wharf was
entirely closed and the wharf itself so densely packed with
human beings, that the merchants and others compelled to
resort thither, were obliged to step from the corner of Montgomery and Commercial streets upon the heads of the
crowd, and proceed to their places of business over a living
pavement. Much suffering having been caused by the passage of loaded drays and other carriages over the shoulders
of the crowd, and many serious accidents having occurred
to individuals—among which we can only notice the unfor-

tunate case of a plethoric elderly gentleman, who, slipping
on a glazed hat, fell down and broke himself somewhere—
our worthy Mayor, ever alive to the calls of humanity,
throwing aside all political prejudice, caused plank to be
laid over the heads of the assembly from Sansome street to
the extremity of the wharf, which in a great measure allevi-
ated their suffering.

There was no fighting or disorder among the crowd, for
so closely were they packed that no man could move a
finger ; one unfortunate individual who at an early stage of
the proceedings had inadvertently raised his arm above his
head, remained with it immutably fixed in that position.
Like an East Indian Fakir, who had taken a vow to point
for ever toward heaven, that melancholy hand was seen for
hours directed towards the nearest bonded warehouse.
Some idea of the amiable feeling existing among the multitude may be gathered from the statement of Capt. J.——
B——, familiarly known as " Truthful James." He informs
me that early this morning the keeper of a restaurant on
the wharf picked up no less than seven hundred and eighty-
four ears and three peck baskets full of mutilated fragments!
To use the words of James, as with horror-stricken countenance he made me this communication, " they had been
chawed sir ! *actilly chawed off !* " Such horrible barbarity
makes humanity shudder ! But I forbear comment, the
business of your reporter is to state facts, not to indulge in
sentiment.

At half-past nine o'clock an electric shock ran through

the vast assemblage at the well-known sound of the Sophie's bell. All the agony and suffering of the past few hours was forgotten: for an instant Long Wharf quivered like an aspen leaf, and then rose to heaven a mighty shout, which shook every building in the city to its foundations. The Sophie approached the wharf, the Collector and her other passengers disembarked, and in a few moments a procession was formed and proceeded in the following order to the Oriental.

THE NEW COLLECTOR,

In a carriage drawn by two horses, lashed to their utmost speed, tearing along Battery street towards the Hotel.

All the male inhabitants of Stockton (except one reckless and despairing old Whig, who, knowing he had no chance, and being confined to his bed by sickness, remained behind to take charge of the city) running eight abreast, at the top of their speed.

THE POLICE OF SAN FRANCISCO,

On a dead run, and much blown.

Candidates for office in the Custom House who had known the Collector in his early youth, ten abreast, bearing a banner with the following motto: " Don't you remember the path where we met, long, long ago ? "

A fire company, who had inadvertently turned into

Battery street, were driven furiously along with the procession, and were wondering how the d—l they were ever to
get out of it.

Candidates for office who had lately become acquainted
with the Collector, twelve abreast.

Banner—"We saw him but a moment, but methinks
we've got him now."

Candidates who fervently wished to the Lord they could
get acquainted with him.

Candidates who had frequently heard of him—forty-five
abreast.

THE U. S. ARMY,

Consisting of a discharged sergeant of the 9th infantry
slightly inebriated, one abreast, desiring the Deputy Col
lectorship, or the Porterage, or that the Collector would give
him four bits—didn't care a d—n which.

MUSIC,

By an unhappy dog, trodden under foot by the crowd
and giving vent to the most unearthly yells.

All the members of the Democratic party in California
who did not wish for an office in the Custom House, consisting of a fortunate miner who had made his pile and was
going home on the first of the month.

Gentlemen who had the promise of appointments from
influential friends, and were sure of getting them, walking

arm in arm with gentlemen without distinction of party, who were confident of drawing the Diamond watch in Reeve's Lottery. This part of the procession was four hours in passing a given point.

M. L. WINN,

Bearing in his right hand a pole from which floated a Bill of Fare three hundred and twenty-six feet in length, and in his left, a buckwheat cake glittering with golden syrup.

MR. BRANCH,

Supporting the other extremity of the Bill of Fare.

CITIZENS GENERALLY,

The procession having moved with great rapidity, soon arrived at the Oriental, but not as soon as the Collector, who rushing hastily into his room, locked and barricaded the door, having previously instructed the Landlord to inform all persons who might inquire for him, that he was dead. Meanwhile the multitude had completely surrounded the hotel, and signified their impatience and disgust at finding the doors, closed by angry roars, uttered at half-second intervals. Finding their cries disregarded, a sudden movement took place among them, and for a few moments I feared the hotel was to be carried by storm, when a window on Bush street opened, and a gentleman, whom the darkness of the evening prevented my completely identifying, but who I religiously believe to have been the Collector, appeared, and amid the most profound silence, made the following beautiful and touching address: "Gentlemen—I wish to God you would all go to bed; you have worried and annoyed me beyond endurance. I am not to be caught by you as was General Scott, for I actually have no time to remove any portion of my clothing. I do not love brogue; I beseech you, therefore, to retire and allow me a little repose." The address here concluded with some allusion to the Deity and a reference to the eyes of the crowd, which being pronounced indistinctly, your reporter was not able entirely to comprehend, and with a sudden slam the window closed.

The scene without now beggared description: roars, yells, frantic cries for "ladders!" "ladders!" rent the air. Within the hotel all was alarm and confusion—the ladies screamed, children cried, the alarmed proprietor spoke of sending for the Mary Ann Rifles, when—the scene suddenly changed. Upon the piazza of the house appeared a gentleman, walking slowly with his hands in the pockets of a shawl dressing-gown; he wore a brown wig, and an enormous pair of false whiskers framed his well-rouged cheeks. In a word, he was dressed in the character of Sir Harcourt Courtly. Turning slowly towards the crowd, he withdrew one hand from the pocket of the shawl dressing-gown, and slowly and awkwardly extending it, said:—"Cool!" It was sufficient. For an instant, a shudder ran through the mob—then, with cries of "It's him! it's Greene!" they broke and dispersed in every direction—up Bush and down Battery, through Stockton street and over the sand-hills, they fled like fright-ened deer. The earth seemed to have opened and swallowed them up, so sudden and complete was the dispersion. In one moment, where stood a mob of fifteen thousand, re-mained but two individuals. Above, with a sidelong bow and melancholy smile, slowly retired Sir Harcourt, and on the earth below, with open mouth and distended eyes, his admiring gaze fixed upon that extraordinary man with reverential awe. stood

PHŒNIX.

SATURDAY MORNING.

P. S. " Truthful James " has just rushed up in a frantic state to inform me that the Collector did not arrive last night after all. When I made my report, I did not know whether he had or not, but I am inclined now to think he might have done so. I don't know that it makes any differ-ence. If he did arrive, my report is all true now—if he did not, why, when he *does* arrive, it will be all true then ; and those who read it this morning, and find it false, will have the pleasure of reading it again, when it becomes the history of an actual occurrence. Of course you won't publish this.

PHŒNIX.

PHŒNIX TAKES AN AFFECTIONATE
LEAVE OF SAN FRANCISCO.

SAN DIEGO, Aug. 10, 1853.

I₁ was about 7½ A. M., on the first day of this present month
of August, that I awaked from a very pleasant dream in the
great city of San Francisco, to the very unpleasant conviction
that it was a damp and disagreeable morning, and that my
presence was particularly required in the small city of San
Diego So, having shaken hands with Frink, taken an affectionate leave of the chaimbermaid, and, lastly, devoured a
beefsteak at the Branch of Alden, which viand, in perfect
keeping with the weather, was both cold and raw, I shouldered my cane with a carpet bag suspended at each end, " a la
Chinois," and left the Tehama House without " one lingering hope or fond regret." When a man is going down, every
body lends him a kick, an aphorism which I came very near
realizing in my own proper person, for as I went on my way
down Long Wharf, I accidentally grazed a mule, who being in

an evil frame of mind and harnessed to a dray might be considered as passionately attached to that conveyance. This interesting animal, fancying from my appearance that I was "going down," "lent me a kick," which, had his legs been two inches longer, would have put a stop to my correspondence for ever. As it was I escaped, and hurried on down the wharf, thinking with a shudder on the mysterious prophecy of my friend little Miss B., who had told me I was "sure to be kicked" before I left San Francisco, and wondering if she was really "among the prophets." The Northerner, like the steamboat runners, was *lying* at the end of the wharf, blowing off steam, and as usual when a steamer is about to leave for Panama, a great crowd surrounded her. What made them all get up so early? Out of the three or four hundred people on the end of that wharf I don't believe fifty had friends that were about to sail. No! they love to look upon a steamer leaving. It brings to their minds recollections of the dear ones at home to whom she is speeding with fond tidings, and they love to gaze and wish to Heaven they were going in her. The usual mob of noisy fruit venders encompassed the gangway plank; green pears they sold to greener purchasers; apples, also, whereof, every thing but the shape of an apple had long since departed, and oranges, the recollection of one of which, doth to this day abide by me and set my teeth on edge; but high above their din, the roar of the steamer and the murmuring of the crowd, rang the shrill cry of the newsboy in his unknown tongue, *Here's the Alteruldniguntimes Heup !* I stepped across the plank and

found myself in the presence of three fine bullocks. How fat
and sleek they looked; uneasy though, as if they smelled mischief in the wind.

A tall gaunt specimen of Pike County humanity stood regarding them approvingly, his head thrown slightly back, to
get their points to better advantage. It was the tomb gazing on its victim. As I paused for a moment to look on the
picture, Pike yawned fearfully, his head opening like the top
of an old-fashioned fall-back chaise. The nearest bullock,
turning, caught his eye. I thought the unhappy animal shuddered and nudged his companion, as who should say, " Ye living, come and view the grave where you shall shortly lie."
It was quite a touching little scene. On deck all was bustle
and excitement. The sailors, apparently in the last extremity
of physical suffering, judging by their agonized cries, were
heaving away at mysterious ropes. The mate, Mr. Dall, was
engaged in busy, not tender dalliance with the breast lines,
while Burns the Purser exhibited an activity and good nature only to be accounted for by the supposition that he had
eaten two boxes of Russia salve (which is good for Burns—
see your advertising columns) for his breakfast.

As the last line fell from the dock, and our noble steamer
with a mighty throb and deep sigh, at bidding adieu to San
Francisco, swung slowly round, the passengers crowded to the
side to exchange a farewell salutation with their friends and
acquaintances. " Good bye, Jones," " Good bye, Brown,"
' God bless you old fellow, take care of yourself! " they
shouted. Not seeing any one that I know, and fearing the

passengers might think I had no friends, I shouted " Good bye Muggins," and had the satisfaction of having a shabby man much inebriated, reply as he swung his rimless hat, "Good bye, my brother." Not particularly elated at this recognition, I tried it again, with, "Good bye, Colonel," whereat thirty-four respectable gentlemen took off their hats, and I got down from the position that I had occupied on a camp stool, with much dignity, inwardly wondering whether my friends were all aids to Bigler, in which case their elevated rank and affection for me would both be satisfactorily accounted for.

Away we sped down the bay, the captain standing on the wheel-house directing our course. "Port, Port a little, Port." he shouted. "What's he a calling for ?" inquired a youth of good-natured but unmistakable verdancy of appearance, of me. ' Port wine," said I, "and the storekeeper don't hear him ; you'd better take him up some." "I will," said Innocence ; "Iv'e got a bottle of first rate in my state room." And he did, but soon returned with a particularly crest-fallen and sheepish appearance. "Well, what did he say to you," inquired I. "Pointed at the notice on that tin," said the poor fellow "Passengers not allowed on the wheel-house." "*He* is, though, ain't he ?" added my friend with a faint attempt at a smile, as the captain in an awful voice shouted, "Starboard !" "Is what ?" said I, "*Loud on the wheel house !*" Good God ! I went below.

At 9 o'clock in the evening we arrived at Monterey, where our modest salute was answered by the thundering response of a 24-pounder from the fort. This useful defen sive work, which mounts some twenty heavy guns and con tains quarters for a regiment, was built in 1848, by Halleck, Peachy & Billings. It is now used as a hermitage by a lonely officer of the U. S. Army. The people of Monterey have a wild legend concerning this desolate recluse. I was told that he passes the whole of his time in sleep, never by any chance getting out of bed until he hears the gun of a steamer, when he rushes forth in his shirt, fires off a 24-pounder, sponges and reloads it, takes a drink and turns in again. They never have seen him; it's only by his *semi-monthly reports* they know of his existence. "Well," said I to my informant, a bustling little fellow named Bootjacks, who came off on board of us, " suppose, some day a steamer should arrive and he should not return her gun ? " " Well sir," replied Bootjacks, with a quaint smile, " we should conclude that he was either dead, *or out of powder.*" Logical deduction this, and a rather curious story, altogether; how I should like to see him! Bootjacks kindly presented me with the following state of the markets, &c. in Monterey, which will give you a better idea of the large business and commercial prosperity of that flourishing city, than any thing that I can write on those subjects.

MONTEREY MARKETS.

The arrival of a stranger by the Maj. Tompkins from San Francisco, during the past week, with specie to the amount of $4 87½, most of which has been put in circulation, has produced an unprecedented activity among our business men.   Confidence is in a great measure restored, and our merchants have had no reason to complain of want of occupation.   The following is the state of our market, for the principal articles of domestic con-sumption :

FLOUR—Twenty-five pounds, imported by Boston, & Co. per Major Tompkins, still in first hands; flour in small quantities is jobbing readily at 15 @ 18 cents ℔ ℔.   We notice sales of 10 ℔ by Boston, & Co., to Judge Merritt, on private terms.

PORK—The half bbl. imported by Col. Russell, in March last, is nearly all in the hands of jobbers ; sales of 4 ℔ at $1, half cash ; remainder in note at 4 months.   A half bbl. expected by Boot-jack & Co., early in September, will overstock the market.

CANDY—Sales of 6 sticks by Boston & Co. to purser of Maj. Tompkins, on private terms; the market has a downward ten-dency ; candy is jobbing in sticks at 6 @ 8 cents.

POTATOES—We notice arrival of 10 ℔ from the Santa Cruz ; no sales.

DRY GOODS—Sales of two cotton pocket hdkfs. by Mc Kinley & Co. at 62½ @ 75 cents ; indorsed note at 6 months.

Lively place this.   Thank Heaven my lot is not cast there—it was once, but the people sold it for taxes.   Having taken on board the U. S. mail, containing one letter (which I believe must have been the resignation of the Collector), our noble steamer bore away to the Southward.

Four bells tinkled from the little bell aft ; four bells chimed from its deep-toned brother forward, and being cf a retiring disposition, I retired.

9

PHŒNIX IS ON THE SEA.

Bright and beautiful rose the sun, from out the calm blue sea, its early rays gleaming on the snow-white decks of the *Northerner*, and " gilding refined gold " as they pene-trated the state-room "A," and lingering, played among the tresses of the slumbering McAuburn. It was a lovely morn-ing, " the winds were all hushed, and the waters at rest," and no sound was heard but the throbbing of the engine and the splash of the paddle wheels as the gallant old *Northerner* sped on her way, " tracking the trackless sea." Two sailors engaged in their morning devotions with the holy stones near my room, amused me not a little. One of them, either acci-dentally or with " malice prepense," threw a bucket of water against the bulwark, which *ricocheting*, struck the other on his dorsal extremity, as he leaned to his work, making that portion of his frame exceedingly damp and him exceedingly angry. " You just try that again, —— your soul," exclaimed the offended one, " and I'll slap your chops for you." " Oh, yes you will," sarcastically rejoined he of the water bucket " I've heerd of you afore ! *You're old chop-slapper's son,* *aint you? Father went round slapping people's chops,* *didn't he?* " Then followed a short fight, in which, as might have been expected, " Old chop-slapper's son " got rather the worst of it.

There was no excuse for being sick that morning, so our passengers, still pale, but with cheerful hope depicted in their countenances, soon began to throng the deck, segars were again brought into requisition, and we had an opportunity of ascertaining " whether there was any Bourbon among us." A capital set of fellows they were. There was Moore, and Parker, and Bowers (one of Joe Bowers' boys), and Sarsaparilla Meade, and Freeman, which last mentioned gentlemen, so amusing were they, appeared to be travelling *expressly* to entertain us. And there were no ladies, which to me was a blessed dispensation.

> " Oh, woman ! in our hours of ease
> Uncertain, coy, and hard to please ;
> When pain and anguish wring the brow,
> A ministering angel thou."

Certainly : but at sea, Woman, you are decidedly disagreeable. In the first place, you generally bring babies with you, which are a crying evil, and then you have to have the best state-room and the first seat at the table, and monopolize the captain's attention and his room, and you make remarks to one another about us, and our segars and profanity, and

ıccuse us of singing rowdy songs, nights; and you generally
wind up by doing some scandalous thing yourself, when half
of us take your part and the other half don't, and we get
ıll together by the ears, and a pretty state of affairs ensues.
No, woman! you are agreeable enough on shore, if taken
homœopathically, but on a steamer, you are a decided nuisance.

We had a glorious day aboard the old *Northerner;* we
played whist, and sang songs, and told stories, many of which
were coeval with our ancient school-lessons, and like them
came very easy, going over the second time, and many drank
strong waters, and becoming mopsed thereon, toasted " the
girls we'd left behind us," whereat one, who, being a temperance man, had guzzled soda-water until his eyes seemed
about to *pop* from his head, pondered deeply, sighed, and said
nothing. And so we laughed, and sang, and played, and
whiskied, and soda-watered through the day. And fast the
old *Northerner* rolled cn. And at night the Captain gave
us a grand game supper in his room, at which game we played
not, but went at it in sober earnest; and then there were
more songs (the same ones, though, and the same stories too,
over again), and some speechifying, and much fun, until at
eight bells we separated, some shouting, some laughing, some
crying (but not with sorrow), but all extremely happy, and so
we turned in. But before I sought state-room A that night,
I executed a small scheme, for insuring undisturbed repose,
which I had revolved in my mind during the day, and which
met with the most brilliant success, as you shall hear.

You remember the two snobs that every night, in the

pursuit of exercise under difficulties, walk up and down on
the deck, arm in arm, right over your state-room. You
remember how, when just as you are getting into your first
doze, they commence, tramp! tramp! tramp! right over
your head; then you " hear them fainter, fainter still; " you
listen in horrible dread of their return, nourishing the while
a feeble-minded hope that they may have gone below—when,
horror! here they come, louder, louder, till tramp! tramp!
tramp! they go over your head again, and with rage in your
heart, at the conviction that sleep is impossible, you sit up in
bed and despairingly light an unnecessary segar. They were
on board the *Northerner*, and the night before had aroused
my indignation to that strong pitch that I had determined on
their downfall. So, before retiring, I proceeded to the upper
deck, and there did I quietly attach a small cord to the
stanchions, which stretching across, about six inches from the
planking, formed what in maritime matters is known as a
" booby trap." This done, I repaired to my room, turned in
and calmly awaited the result. In ten minutes they came, I
heard them laughing together as they mounted the ladder.
Then commenced the exercise, louder, louder, tramp! tramp!
—thump! (a double-barrelled thump) down they came
together, " Oh, what a fall was there my countrymen." Two
deep groans were elicited, and then followed what, if published,
would make two closely printed royal octavo pages of profanity. I heard them d—n the soul of the man that did it.
It was *my* soul that they alluded to, but I cared not, I lay
there chuckling; " they called, but I answered not again,'

and when at length they limped away, their loud profanity, subdued to a blasphemous growl, I turned over in a sweet frame of mind and, falling instantaneously asleep, dreamed a dream, a happy dream of "home and thee"—Susan Ann Jane !

The next morning bright and early, the Coronados hove in sight, and at 10 o'clock we rounded Point Loma and ran alongside the coal hulk Clarissa Andrews, at the Playa of San Diego—just forty-nine hours from San Francisco.

The captain (he is the crew also) of the Clarissa Andrews, the gallant Bogart, stood on her rail ready to catch our flying line, and in a few moments we were secured alongside, our engine motionless and my journey ended.

It was with no small regret that I bade adieu to our merry passengers and our glorious captain.   Noble fellow !   I don't wonder enthusiastic passengers get up subscriptions and make speeches and present plate and trumpets, and what not to such men.   It's very natural.

A good captain is sure to have a good ship ; a voyage with him becomes an agreeable matter ; he makes his passengers happy and they very naturally fall in love with him, and seek some method of displaying their attachment and "trumpeting his praise abroad."   Our captain was one of this sort; kind, courteous and obliging, and "every inch a sailor," he is as much beloved and respected by his passengers as Dick Whiting of the *California* (who to my mind is the *ne plus ultra* of steamboat men), and when I say that the first letter of his name is Isham, I'm sure every body that ever travelled with him, will agree with me.

The *Northerner*, too, is a splendid and most comfortable ship, as which of the Pacific Mail boats are not? however. And this subject brings to my mind a little circumstance which took place the day before I left San Francisco.

A shabby-genteel individual, with a pale face, in the centre of which shone a purple nose that couldn't be beat (though it resembled the vegetable of that name), called on me, and drawing from his coat-tail pocket, with an air of mystery, a voluminous manuscript, spread it solemnly before me and requested my signature. It was a petition to Congress, or Mr. Pierce, or John Bigler, or somebody, to transfer the contract for carrying the mails, from the "Pacific Company" to "Vanderbilt's Line," and was signed by Brown & Co., Jones & Co., Smith & Brothers, Noakes, Stiles & Thompson, and ever so many more responsible firms, whereof I recognized but one, which deals in candy nightly at the corner of Commercial and Montgomery streets, and pays no taxes, and whose correspondence with the Eastern States I suspect is not large. I love to sign my name. It is a weakness that most modest men have. I love to write it, and cut it, and scratch it in steeples, and monuments, and other places of public resort. Most men do. It looks pretty, passes away the time, perpetuates their memory among posterity, and *costs nothing.* I frequently buy something that I don't want at all, just for the pleasure of signing my name to a check---(I bought a ridiculous buggy the other day for no other reason that I can imagine.) But I had no inclination to append my autograph to *that* petition, and I declined, positively and peremptorily—declined. My friend with the nose rolled up his eyes and rolled up his paper, pocketed it, and was about to withdraw. "Stop!" said I, as a vivid recollection flashed across my mind ; "what are you going about with that paper for ? Didn't I see you a few months ago marching down the street at the head of a long procession, bearing a big banner with "VANDERBILT'S DEATH LINE!" in great letters thereon, and giving vent to all sorts of scurrility against the Nicaragua route?" The red nose grew redder, as he muttered something about "a man's being obliged to get a living," and he retired. I saw him go and get his boots blacked by a Frenchman right opposite, give him a quarter, and get him to sign his name, which that exile did and thought it was a receipt for the money, and I laughed heartily. But it is no laughing matter.

Having taken leave of all on board the dear old *Northerner*, and shaken hands twice all round, during which process the mate sang out, "Bare a hand there," and I mechanically took off my glove, McAuburn and I were transported to the shore, where, while waiting for a wagon to take us to the old town of San Diego, we stopped at the little public house of the Playa, kept by a civil fellow named Donahoo, whom the Spaniards here, judging from his name (*Don't know who*), believe to be the son of old "*Quien sabe*" himself. What befell us there and thereafter I will shortly inform you.

THE Bay of San Diego is shaped like a boot, the leg forming the entrance from the sea, and the toe extending some twelve miles inland at right angles to it, as a matter of course, points southward to the latter end of Mexico, from which it is distant at present, precisely three miles!

The three villages then, which go to make up the great city of San Diego, are the "Playa," "Old Town," and "New Town," or "Davis's Folly." At the "Playa" there are but few buildings at present, and these not remarkable for size or architectural beauty of design. A long low, one-storied tenement, near the base of the hills, once occupied by rollicking Captain Magruder, and the officers under his command, is now the place where Judge Witherby, like Matthew, patiently "sits at the receipt of customs." But few *customers* appear, for with the exception of the mail steamers once a fortnight, and the *Goliah* and *Ohio*, two little coasting steamers that wheeze in and out once or twice a month, the

9*

calm waters of San Diego Bay remain unruffled by keel or
cutwater from one year's end to another. Such a thing as
a foreign bottom has never made its appearance to gladden
the Collector's heart; in this respect, the harbor has indeed
proved bottomless. Two crazy old hulks riding at anchor,
and the barque *Clarissa Andrews* (filled with coal for P. M.
S. S. Co.), wherein dwells Captain Bogart, like a second
Robinson Crusoe, with a man Friday, who is mate, cook,
steward and all hands, make up the amount of shipping at
the "Playa." Then there is the "Ocean House" (that's
Donahoe's), and a store marked Gardiner & Bleeker, than
the inside of which nothing could be bleaker, for "there's
nothing in it," and an odd-looking little building on stilts out
in the water, where a savan named Sabot, in the employ of
the U. S. Engineers, makes mysterious observations on the
tide ; and these with three other small buildings, unoccupied,
a fence and a grave-yard, constitute all the "improvements"
that have been made at the " Playa." The ruins of two old
hide-houses, immortalized by Dana in his " Two Years before
the Mast," are still standing, one bearing the weather-beaten
name of Tasso. We examined these and got well bitten by
fleas for our trouble. We also examined the other great
curiosity of the Playa—a natural one—being a cleft in the
adjacent hills, some hundred feet in depth, with a smooth,
hard floor of white sand, and its walls of indurated clay, per-
torated with cavities, wherein dwell countless numbers of
great white owls, from which circumstance, Captain Bogart
calls it " Owldom."

Through this cleft we marched into the bowels of the land without impediment, for nearly half a mile, when being brought to a stand still by a high, smooth wall, McAuburn did proceed to carve thereon a name. But as he laid out his work on too extensive a scale, the letters being about three feet in length—though he worked with amazing energy—he got no farther than this—JO, when his knife broke and the inscription remained incomplete. Whether, therefore, it was intended to perpetuate to posterity the memory of the great Joseph Bowers, or one of his girls, we may never know, as Mac showed no disposition to be communicative, and indeed requested me to "dry up," when I questioned him on the subject. From present appearances, one would be little disposed to imagine that the "Playa" in five or six years might become a city of the size of Louisville, with brick buildings, paved streets, gas lights, theatres, gambling houses, *and so forth*. It is not at all improbable, however, should the great Pacific Railroad terminate at San Diego, an event within the range of probability, the "Playa" must be the depot, and as such will become a point of great importance. The landholders about here are well aware of this fact, and consequently affix already incredible prices to very unprepossessing pieces of land. Lots of one hundred and fifty feet front, not situated in particularly eligible places either, have been sold within the last few weeks for five hundred dollars apiece. "*De gustibus*," &c. At present I confess I should prefer the money to the real estate. While at the Playa, I had the pleasure of forming an acquaintance with the Pilot, Captain

Wm. G. Oliver, as noble a specimen of a sailor as you would wish to see. He was a lieutenant in the Texas navy, under the celebrated Moore, and told me many yarns concerning that gallant commander. Great injustice, I think, has been done in not giving to these officers the rank to which they are entitled in our service. Captain Oliver would do honor to any navy in the world, for beside being a thorough seaman, he is an accomplished and agreeable gentleman. Leaving the Playa in a wagon drawn by two wild mules, driven at the top of their speed, by the intrepid Donaho, Mac and I were whirled over a hard road, smooth and even as a ball-room floor, on our way to "Old Town." Five miles from the " Playa" we passed the estate of the Hon. John Hays, County Judge of San Diego, an old Texian, and a most amiable gentleman. The judge has a fine farm of eighty or one hundred acres, under high cultivation, and what few gentlemen in California can boast of—a private fish pond! He has enclosed some twenty acres of the flats near his residence, having a small outlet, with a net attached, from which he daily makes a haul almost equalling the miraculous draught on the Lake Gennesaret.

The old town of San Diego is pleasantly situated on the left bank of the little river that bears its name. It contains, perhaps, a hundred houses, some of wood, but mostly of the " Adoban" or " Gresan" order of architecture. A small Plaza forms the centre of the town, one side of which is occu- pied by a little *adobe* building used as a court room, the " Colorado House," a wooden structure, whereof the second story is occupied by the San Diego *Herald*, as a vast sign bearing that legend informed us, and the Exchange, a hostelry, at which we stopped. This establishment is kept by Hoof (familiarly known as Johnny, but whom I once christened *Cloven*), and Tibbetts, who is also called *Two bitts*, in honorable distinction from an unworthy partner he once had, who obtained unenviable notoriety as "*Picayune Smith*." On entering, we found ourselves in a large bar and billiard room fitted up with customary pictures and mirrors. Here I saw Lieut. Derby, of the Topograpical Engineers, an elderly gentleman of emaciated appearance, and serious cast of features. Constant study and unremitting attention to his laborious duties have reduced him almost to a skeleton, but there are not wanting those who say that an unrequited attachment in his earlier days, is the cause of his care-worn appearance.

He was sent out from Washington some months since, " to dam the San Diego River," and he informed me with a deep sigh and melancholy smile, that he had done it (mentally) several times since his arrival. Here, also, I made the acquaintance of Squire Moon, a jovial, middle-aged gentleman from the State of Georgia, who replied to my inquiries concerning his health, that he was " as fine as silk, but not half so well beliked by the ladies." After partaking of supper, which meal was served up in the rear of the billiard room, *al fresco*, from a clothless table, upon an earthen floor, I fell in conversation with Judge Ames, the talented, good-hearted but eccentric editor of the San Diego Herald, of whom the poet Andrews, in his immortal work, "The Cocopa Maid," once profanely sang as follows:

> "There was a man whose name was Ames,
> His aims were aims of mystery;
> His story odd, I think by——
> Would make a famous history."

I found "the Judge" exceedingly agreeable, urbane and well informed, and obtained from him much valuable information regarding San Diego and its statistics. San Diego contains at present about seven hundred inhabitants, two-thirds of whom are "native and to the manor born," the remainder, a mixture of American, English, German, Hebrew and Pike County. There are seven stores or shops in the village, where any thing may be obtained from a fine-tooth comb to a horse rake, two public houses, a Catholic church which meets in a private residence, and a Protestant *ditto*, to which the Rev. Dr. Reynolds, chaplain of the military post six miles distant, communicates religious intelligence every Sunday afternoon.

San Diego is the residence of Don Juan Bandini, whose mansion fronts on one side of the Plaza. He is well known to the early settlers of California as a gentleman of distinguished politeness and hospitality. His wife and daughters are among the most beautiful and accomplished ladies of our State. One of the latter is married to Mr. Stearns, a very wealthy and distinguished resident of Los Angelos, another to Col. Couts, late a Lieutenant in the first regiment of U. S. dragoons, and another to Mr. Charles Johnson, who for a long time was the agent of the **P. M. S. S.** Company at this place. The whole family is highly connected and universally respected.

Having smoked the pipe of contemplation, and played a game of billiards with a young gentleman who remarked, "he could give me fifty and beat me," which he certainly did, with a celerity that led me to conclude "he couldn't do any thing else," I retired for the night, but not to sleep, as I fondly imagined. Fleas? rather! I say nothing at present; my feelings of indignation against those wretched insects are too deep for utterance. On another occasion, when in a milder mood, I intend to write a letter concerning and condemnatory of them, and publish it. Yes, by Heaven, if I have to pay for it as an advertisement!

The next morning, bright and early, I parted with my young military friend McAuburn, who was about to join his company at the Gila River. "Good bye, Phœnix," says he, "God bless you, old fellow! And look here, if you go to San Francisco, tell her—no, by George! you always make fun of every thing. Good bye." So he wrung my hand and galloped away, and I stood looking after him till his prancing horse and graceful figure were hid by the projecting hills of the old Presidio. "Blessings go with you my boy!" said I, "for a fine, honest, noble-hearted young chap, you haven't many superiors in the U. S. Army; and happy, in my opinion, is the woman who gets you."

How I went to a *Baile*, and visited "New Town," and rode forth to the Mission, and attended a *Fiesta*, and the ex-

traordinary adventures that befell me there, shall form the
subject of a future epistle; at present my time is too much
occupied, for lo, *I am an editor!* Hasn't Ames gone to San
Francisco (with this very letter in his pocket), leaving a notice
in his last edition, " that during his absence an able literary
friend will assume his position as editor of the Herald," and
am I not that able literary friend? (Heaven save the mark.)
" You'd better believe it." I've been writing a " leader " and
funny anecdotes all day (which will account for the dryness
of this production), and *such* a " leader," and *such* anecdotes.
I'll send you the paper next week, and if you don't allow that
there's been no such publication, weekly or serial, since the
days of the " Bunkum Flagstaff," I'll *craw fish*, and take to
reading Johnson's Dictionary.   Fraternally—ahem!

Yours.

CAMP REMINISCENCES.

Perhaps, you will not object to a few short military yarns which I have hastily twined for your edification. And if the interesting, fair-haired, blue-eyed (or otherwise) son of the reader, now sitting on his knee, on hearing them, should look confidingly into his parent's face, and inquire— "Is that true, Papa?" reply, oh reader, unhesitatingly— "My son, it is."

Many years since, during the height of the Florida war, a company of the Second Infantry made their camp for the night, after a rainy day's march, by the bank of a muddy stream that sluggishly meandered through a dense and unwholesome everglade. Dennis Mulligan, the red-haired Irish servant of the commanding officer, having seen his master's tent comfortably pitched, lit a small fire beneath a huge palmetto, and having cut several slices of fat pork from the daily ration, proceeded to fry that edible for the nightly repast

In the deep gloom of the evening, silence reigned unbroken but by the crackling of Dennis's small fire and the
frizzling of the pork as it crisped and curled in the mighty
mess-pan, when suddenly, with a tremendous "whoosh," the
leaves cf the palmetto were disturbed and a great barred
owl, five feet from tip to tip, settled in the foliage. Dennis
was superstitious, most Irishmen are, and startled by the
disturbance, he suspended for an instant his culinary operations, and frying-pan in hand, gazed slowly and fearfully
about him. Persuading himself that the noise was but the
effect of imagination, he again addressed himself to his task,
when the owl set up his fearful hoot, which sounded to the
horrified ears of Dennis, like, " *Who—cooks—for you—all?*
Again he suspended operations, again gazed fearfully forth into
the night, again persuaded himself that his imagination was at
fault, and was about to return to his task, when accidentally
glancing upward he beheld the awful countenance and glaring
eyes of the owl turned downward upon him, and from that
cavernous throat in hollow tones, again issued the question,
" *Who—who—cooks—for you—all?* " "God bless your
honor," said poor Dennis, while the mess-pan shook in his
quivering grasp, and the unheeded pork poured forth a molten
stream, which, falling upon the flames, caused a burst of illu-
mination that added to the terrors of the scene, "God bless
your honor, *I* cooks for Captain Eaton, but I don't know sir,
who cooks for the rest of the gintlemen." A burst of fiendish
'aughter followed—from those who had witnessed the in-

cident unseen, and "Dennis's Devil" became a favorite yarn in the Second Infantry from that time forth.

In New Mexico, at some time during the last two years, Capt. A. B. of the First Dragoons, commanding Company, had been stationed about forty miles from a small post commanded by Lieut. O. B. of the Infantry. One day Capt. B. concluded to ride over and give his neighbor a call; so throwing himself athwart a noble horse, he started, and after a hard gallop—forty miles *is* a respectable ride you know—he arrived at O. B.'s tent just as the drummer was performing that popular air, " Oh, the roast beef of Old England."

Reining in his horse and shaking hands with O. B., who came forth to greet him, "on hospitable thought inte t," he said, " Well, Lawrence, been to dinner ? " " No, I haven't," was the reply, "just going, come in, come in ; " " Devilish glad of it," said Capt. B. dismounting, " never was so hungry in all my life." " Well, come in," said O. B., and they went in accordingly, and took seats at a small uncovered pine table, on which a servant shortly placed a large tin pan full of boiled rice, and a broken bottle half full of mustard. The Captain looked despairingly around—there was nothing else. " Abe." said O. B., as he drew the tin pan towards him, "are you fond of boiled rice ? " " Well, no," said Abe, somewhat hesitatingly, " I can't say that I am—very—Lawrence." " Ah," replied Lawrence, coolly, " *well just help yourself to the mustard!* " " He was from South Carolina," said B., when he told this story, "and they eat rice down there some-what."

For the following, Lieut. W. of the Engineers is responsible. He told it to me in 1852, at the Café of Do minico, in Havana.

Old Col. Tom S. of the Infantry, a very large, burly, red-faced gentleman, with a snow-white head and a voice like a bass trombone, has an unfortunate habit of thinking out loud. While stationed temporarily in Washington, the old gentleman one Sunday morning, took it into his head to go to church, where he took a seat in a pew beneath the pulpit, and, prayer-book in hand, attentively followed the clergyman through the service. It happened to be the 17th day of the month; but in giving out the Psalms for the day, the Rev. Mr. P. made a mistake and announced—"The 16th day of the month, morning prayer, beginning at the 79th Psalm." When to the astonishment of the congregation, Old Col. Tom in the pew below, in a deep bass voice *thought* aloud—" *The 17th day of the month, by Jupiter !* " The clergyman immediately corrected himself—" Ah ! the 17th day of the month, morning prayer, beginning at the 86th Psalm." When the propriety of the assembly was immediately disturbed by another *thought* from Old Tom, who in the same deep tone remarked, " *Had him there !* " He had, certainly, and the congregation also.

Two years ago, when the gallant Col. Magruder, of convivial memory, commanded the U. S. forces at the Mission of San Diego, it entered into that officer's head to execute a serenade for the behoof of certain fair ladies then honoring New Town with their presence. Accordingly all the officers of the mess who could sing, play, or beat time, were pressed into the service, and one night about 12 o'clock, a jolly crowd left the Mission for New Town, in a large wagon plentifully furnished with guitars, flutes, and other arangements of a musical nature. Among the rest, a jovial young surgeon, attached to the command, had installed himself on the back seat, with *his* instrument; which happened on this occasion to be a bottle of whiskey, and on which he played during the ride with such effect as to have raised his spirits on the arrival at New Town, considerably above the fifth ledger line. You may remember a Bowery song, rather popular in those days, the chorus of which ran—

"Oh my name is Jake Keyser, I was born in Spring Garden,
  To make me a preacher, my father did try;
  But it's no use a blowing, for I am a hard one,
  And I am bound to be a butcher, by Heavens, or die."

This unfortunate song had somehow or other occurred to the Doctor, he couldn't get rid of it, he couldn't help singing it; and accordingly when the whole party were duly ranged beneath the window and with flutes and voices upraised, were solemnly bleating forth

"Oft in the stilly night,"

the entertainments were disagreeably varied ; for far louder

than the "stilly night," rang the wild medical chant, only
varied by an occasional hic,

> "Oh my name is Jake Keyser," &c.

This was not to be borne; so turning fiercely on the de-
linquent Esculapius, Col. Magruder commanded him to
desist from the interruption, and to "thenceforth hold his
peace."

With admirable strategy the Doctor backed up against
an adjacent fence, where he could deliver himself safely and
to advantage, and with most intense dignity replied—"Col.
Magrudger, I'm roflicer of the arry, when I'm ath' Mission,
I'm under your orrers; consider se'f so—and—obey 'im; *But*,
when I'm down here sir! serrerading—"*Oh, I'm bound to
be a butcher, by Heavens, or die !* whoop !" and after performing an extempore dance, of a frantic description, during
which he fell to the earth, the Doctor was borne by main
force to the wagon, where he slept at intervals during the remainder of the serenade, occasionally waking as some flourish
of extra shrillness or power occurred, to mutter incoherently,
that his "name was Jake Keyser."

My last sheet of paper is exhausted, so I presume is
your patience. I have glanced hastily over my work to see
if there is any thing that Miss Pecksniff may object to; I
see nothing. A little blank swearing, to be sure, but I
grieve to say that it is difficult to relate stories without, for
since the days of Uncle Toby and the Flanders campaign

there is no question but what the army *have* sworn terribly; but I really believe that " they don't mean any thing by it, it's just a way they've got," which is a remark made by an affectionate father, when told that his seven children had all been seized with the measles in one night.—Adieu.

" When other lips and other hearts," &c.

Yours respectively.

JONN PHŒNIX TO THE PIONEER.

San Diego, Cal., April 20th, 1854.

On receiving my long-promised file of *The Pioneer*, accom-panied by your affecting entreaty to " Come over into Mace-donia and help us," deeply impressed with the importance of the crisis, I rushed about this village as wildly as a fowl de-capitated, but with purpose more intent.

Hastily collecting our Improvisatori, including " the Squire," " his Reverence," and the funny " Schcherazade," I besought them in the name of humanity, and by the mem-ory of Miller, to tell me quickly their choicest anecdotes, their raciest puns, and newest conundrums, that I might collate them for your benefit, and San Diego assume its prop-er literary position at (not under) your editorial table. My success was encouraging, and I herewith present you a choice selection of the anecdotes accumulated, which have at least the merit claimed by the late Ben Jonson for an original piece of blank verse; for " Poetry or not poetry, they're *true* by

Heavens." In the course of my researches, I collected many quite new and particularly shocking sayings of blasphemous little children; but I shall not tell you these, for with all due deference to the taste of those who have rendered this style of literature fashionable of late, I cannot refrain from expressing the opinion that the subject has been rather " inserted in the earth;" and if that wicked old Clark, of the *Knickerbocker*, don't roast hereafter for starting it, we're going to have a much easier time in the next world than my knowledge of the Scriptures gives reason to believe. " De gustibus non est disputandum," as the old lady remarked with an affectionate simper, when she kissed her cow. Here are the stories—*mira*.

In 1849, " Jacks & Woodruff" kept on Clay street, just above Kearney, one of the largest jewelry establishments in San Francisco. Jacks (who, by the way, is one of the funniest men that ever lived), being well-known and universally popular, in order to let new arrivals among his home acquaintances know that he was *round*, had his name, Pulaski Jacks, painted in big capitals on a sheet of tin, and nailed up beside the door. One day a tall, yellow-haired, sun-burned Pike, in the butternut-colored hat, coat and so forths " of the period," entered and accosted Woodruff, who was behind the counter, with, " Say, stranger, I want to take a look of them new-fangled things of yourn." " What things, sir ? " " Why them *Pulaski* Jacks ! " " Why that," said Woodruff, laughing, " is my partner's name. Jacks & Woodruff; name's Pulaski—Pulaski Jacks—see ? " " No ! " said Pike, " is it ! "

10

Well, looks like; darned if I knowed it though; I swar I
didn't know as they was boot-jacks or jack-asses; ho! ho!"
And taking another good long look at the object of his curiosity, he travelled.   Jacks took *that* tin thing down.—Suggestive, this is, of a story told us not long since by Maj. E.
of the army, which we are not aware ever appeared before in
print; "least-ways," we never saw it.   A solemn-looking fellow, with a certain air of dry humor about the corners of his
rather sanctimonious mouth, stepped quietly one day, into
the tailoring establishment of " Call & Tuttle," Boston, Mass.,
and quietly remarked to the clerk in attendance, " I want to
tuttle."   " What do you mean, sir ?" inquired the astonished
official.   " Well," rejoined he, " I want to *tuttle*—noticed your
invitation over the door, so I *called*, and now I should like to
tuttle ! "   He was ordered to leave the establishment, which he
did, with a look of angry wonder, grumbling, *sotto voce*, that it
seemed devilish hard he couldn't be allowed to *tuttle* after an
express invitation.—And this again reminds us of a facetious
performance of the late J. P. Squibob, who, " once on a time,"
while walking down Pennsylvania Avenue, was sorely mystified by a modest little sign, standing in the window of a neat
little shop on the left-hand side as you go down.   The sign
bore, in gayly painted letters, the legend, " Washington Ladies'
Depository."   Flattening his nose against the window, Squibob descried two ladies, whom he describes as of exceeding
beauty, neatly dressed and busily engaged in sewing, behind
a little counter.   The fore-ground was filled with lace caps,
babies' stockings, compresses for the waist, capes, collars and

other articles of *still life*. Hat in hand. Squibob reverently entered, and with intense politeness, addressed one of the ladies as follows: " Madam, I perceive by your sign that this is the depository for *Washington* ladies; I am going to the North for a few days, and should be pleased to leave my wife in your charge—But I don't know, if by your rules you could receive her, as she is a *Baltimore* woman!" " One of the ladies," says Squibob, " a pretty little girl in a blue dress, sewing on a thing that looked like a pillow-case with arm-holes, turned very red, and holding down her head, made the remark ' *te he !* ' But the elder of the twain, after making as if she would laugh, but by a strong-minded effort holding in, replied, ' Sir, you have made a mistake ; this is the place where the society of Washington ladies deposit their work, to be sold for the benefit of the distressed natives of the Island of Fernando de Noronha,' or words to that effect." Gravely did the wicked Squibob bow, all solemnly begged her pardon, and putting on his hat, walked off, followed by a sound from that depository, as of an autumnal brook, gurgling and babbling gayly over its pebbly bed in a New England forest.

My stock is my no means exhausted, but " *Demasiado de una cosa buena es demasiado,*" as Don Juan remarked when he took twenty-four Brandreth's pills and his wife earnestly solicited him to swallow the box. Next month, *Deo volente,* you shall hear from me again ; till then adieu.

REVIEW OF NEW BOOKS.

PREPARED BY JOHN PHŒNIX.

*Life and Times of Joseph Bowers the Elder. Collated from
Unpublished Papers of the Late John P. Squibob.* By
J. BOWERS, JR. Vallecitos: Hyde & Seckim, 1854.

MANY of your readers will doubtless remember to have been
occasionally mystified, when, struck by the remarkable beauty
of some passing female stranger, or by the flashes of wit
sparkling from the lips of some gentlemanly unknown, on
making the inquiry, " Who is that ?' the reply has been given,
' Oh that is one of old Joe Bowers' girls " or boys, as the
case may have been ; and they will also remember that when
about to propound the naturally succeeding question, " Who
is Old Joe Bowers ? " they have been deterred from so doing,
by a peculiar smile, and an indefinable glance of the eye, ap-
proximating to what is vulgarly termed a wink, on the part
of their informant.

Such persons, and indeed all who seek to improve their minds by indulging a wholesome curiosity as to the private history of the good and great of earth, will be glad to hear that this question of "Who is Joseph Bowers?" is about to be definitely answered.

Through the kindness of Messrs. Hyde and Seekim of Vallecitos, we have been permitted to glance over the proof-sheets of their forthcoming work, the title of which is given above, and to make therefrom such selections as we may deem sufficient to interest the public in promoting the filial design of the younger Bowers, to transmit the name and virtues of his honored sire to posterity.

Joseph Bowers the elder (or as he is familiarly known, "Old Joe Bowers"), we learn from this history, was born in Ypsilanti, Washtenaw county, Michigan, on the first day of April, 1776, of "poor but honest parents." His father, during the troubles of the revolutionary struggle, was engaged in business as a malefactor in western New York, from which part of the country he was compelled to emigrate, by the prejudices and annoyances of the bigoted settlers among whom he had for many years conducted his operations. Emigrating suddenly, in fact "with such precipitation," says the narrator, "that my grandfather took nothing with him of his large property, but a single shirt, which he happened to have about him at the time he formed his resolution," he found himself after a journey of several days, of vicissitude and suffering, upon the summit of a hill overlooking a beautiful valley in the fertile State of Michigan. Struck by the beauty of the surrounding scenery, he leaped from the ground in his enthusiasm, and cracking his heels twice together while in the air ("by which" says the narrator, with much naïveté, "my grandfather didn't mean anything, it was just a way he'd got"), he uttered the stirring cry of "Yip !—silanti !" from which memorable circumstance the place thereafter took its name.   Here he finally settled, and marrying afterward a young lady whom the author somewhat obscurely speaks of as "one of 'em," had issue, the subject of this narrative, and finally ended his career of usefulness, by falling from a cart in which he had been standing, addressing a numerous audience, and in which fall he unfortunately broke his neck.

Our limits will not permit us at present to do more than glance hastily over the stirring incidents in the life of the elder Bowers.   He appears to have been connected in some way with almost every prominent event of the times in which he lived.   We find him a servant and afterwards a confidential friend and adviser of Gen. Cass; consulted on matters of religion by Gen. Jackson ; an admirer of one of Col. Dick Johnson's daughters (by the way it was Bowers who slew Tecumseh !), an ardent admirer and intimate friend of Mr. Tyler; Gen. Pillow's military adviser; special messenger from Mr. Polk to Santa Anna; professional adviser of Mr. Corwin in the matter of the Gardner Claim; the first to nominate Mr. Pierce for the Presidency, and after his arrival in California, the agent of Limantour ; friend and Secretary of Pio Pico ; adviser of Walker; amanuensis for Peck; owner of a great part of the extended Water Front of San

Francisco, and a partner in a celebrated Candy Manufactory on Long Wharf, with a Branch in Washington street. His literary labors and success have been great; few of your readers but have seen his signature (Anon.) in Newspapers, Magazines, the New Reader and First Class Books; he has edited several of our City papers, and we add it in a whisper, is

The author of Idealina.

We may hereafter revert to these incidents in his eventful life; at present, as we before remarked, our limits forbid our enlarging upon them, as we wish to make room for a few extracts from the work, which, exhibiting the great man's manner of thought and expression, will do more toward giving our readers an insight into his character, than would pages of his biography,—we quote from p. 45, vol. 1:

"My father had been much annoyed by reading certain letters from New York to the *Alta California*, signed ' W.' The plagiarisms and egotistic remarks of which they were made up disgusted him. They remind me, he said—expectorating upon the carpet, a habit he had when much offended—of the back of a lady's dress; they are all hooks and I's. I ventured to ask him, why he did not reply to them? Sir, said he, making a beautiful adaptation that I have never heard equalled, ' *Where impudence is wit, 'tis folly to reply!*' "

Comment is unnecessary; let us proceed, p. 47, vol. 1.

"On arriving at Nevada, we unsaddled and turned out our horses, and taking our saddles and blankets beneath our arms, repaired to the Inn. My father was exceedingly fatigued by the journey, and hastened to throw himself into the first chair that offered. As he did so, I thoughtlessly drew the chair from under him, and much to my sorrow and chagrin he fell with great vio lence upon the floor. The shock with which he came down dis composed him not a little, and a paper of pump tacks which had fallen from the table and scattered over the floor exactly where he was seated, materially increased his uneasiness.

"I shall not soon forget his indignant reproof. 'Joseph, my son,' said he, 'never, never again attempt a practical joke; it is a false, unfeeling, traitorous amusement. Remember, sir,' said he, as he painfully rose, and reached to the table for a small claw hammer to draw the tacks, 'remember the fate of the first practical joker and profit thereby;' I ventured humbly to ask him who this was; 'Judas Iscariot,' he replied with bitterness, 'he *sold* his master, and you know well what came of it.' I was overpowered with remorse."

This is very affecting. On p. 49, we find the following :

" We were much disturbed during the night by the hoarse braying of a donkey in the stable-yard. I remarked to my father that he (the donkey) was suffering with a bronchial complaint; and on his inquiring why, replied, that he had an *ass-ma*, subsequently explaining the intended play upon the word asthma. Upon comprehending with some difficulty my meaning, my father immediately rose, and taking his blanket, in indignant silence left the room and the house, passing the night, as I afterwards learned, in angry meditation beneath a tree in the Plaza."

Very properly we think. The following is rather amusing, p. 108, vol. 1:

" After his second interview with Senator Peck, I endeavored to learn from my father the result of his proposal. ' Peck talks

a great deal,' said he, 'but it is very difficult to tell what he is
going to do; or to what *side* he belongs. In fact I begin to believe he is *all talk and no cider!*' "

Precisely the opinion expressed by a number of others.
Turning back to page 82, vol. 1, we find the following:

"I turned to my father and asked him why it was that women
were so frequently robbed by pick-pockets, in public carriages;
'they must,' I observed, 'be conscious that the rogues are feeling
about them.' 'Yes,' he replied, 'but 'a fellow feeling makes
them wondrous kind.'' I was struck by the force of this remark."

Probably. Thus much for young Joe. On taking up the
second volume, we find it mainly filled with incidents in the
life of the elder Bowers, from the pen of the lamented J. P.
Squibob, who, it appears, during his life, contemplated getting
up, himself, the work which young Bowers has completed.
We make a few extracts in which the style of the lamented
S will be readily recognized.

"'No man,' said Bowers, sententiously, 'should indulge in
more than one bad habit at a time. If I am a drunkard, it is no
reason why I should ruin my character by gambling or licentious-
ness; or, if I love the ladies inordinately,' and here the old fellow looked indescribably waggish, 'why should I add to the
enormity by indulging also in cards and liquor? No,' added he,
'one bad habit is enough for any man to indulge in.'"
"'And why, Mr. Bowers,' said Jones, 'have you given up
smoking?'
"'Because I *chews*,' replied the old fellow, with a quiet
chuckle, 'and therein I carry out my principle.'"

10*

"Jones pondered a minute, but he couldn't 'see it,' and shaking his head musingly, he slowly dispersed."—p. 19.

Mr. Bowers mentioned to me as deserving the commisera-
tion of the charitable and benevolent, the distressing case of
a journeyman shoemaker *who had lost his little awl.*—p. 31,
vol. 2.

The following smacks, to us, slightly of "Jeems:"

"It was on a lovely morning in the sweet spring time, when
'two horsemen might have been seen' slowly descending one of
the gentle acclivities that environ the picturesque village of San
.Diego.   It was a bright and a sunny day, and the shrubbery and
trees around were alive with the harmonious warbling of the
feathered songsters of the grove.   'And oh!' sighed the younger
of the twain, 'would that my existence might be like that of
those fair birds—one constant, unwearying dream of love.'
'Aye,' responded the elder, a man of years and of experience,
known to the readers of this history as Joseph Bowers the elder,
'Aye, my brave youth, they are indeed a happy race, and the
spring is to them their happiest season, for they are now engaged
in pairing.'
"'And where, my father,' inquired the curious youth, 'do
they go to pair?'
"'*Up into the pear-trees, probably,*' rejoined old Joe, with a
quaint smile.
"The son, with the air of one who has acquired a curious and
useful piece of information, rode quietly on, and the silence that
ensued was unbroken, but by his asking his parent for the
tobacco, until they arrived at the village."—p. 47.

Young Bowers was reading to the author of his existence,
some passages from Lickspittle's life of General Pierce, of
whom (the general, not the author) old Joe is a great admirer

On arriving at that affecting anecdote of the liberality of the General in bestowing a cent upon a forlorn boy to enable him to purchase candy like his playmates, Bowers commanded his offspring to pause. Young Joe reverently obeyed.

" 'The General,' said Joseph dogmatically, ' should never have mentioned that circumstance, never."

" ' And why, my father? ' asked his son.

" ' Because,' replied the philosopher, ' *Silence gives a cent*, or I've read my Bible to very little purpose.'

• " And acknowledging the application of Scripture by a concurring nod, young Joe resumed his literary labors, and his father the pipe, which he had withdrawn for the enunciation of his sentiments."—p. 81, vol. 2.

With the following exquisite morçeau from the pen of old Joe Bowers himself, it being the commencement of a tale, which concludes the book, we must conclude our extracts.

The tale is entitled " The Dun Filly of Arkansas, or Thereby Hangs a Tail."

" Many a long year ago, when the ' Child's Own Book ' was all true—when fairies peopled every moonlit glen, and animals enjoyed the power of conversation, in a sequestered dell, beneath the shadow of a mighty oak, upon a carpet of the springiest and most verdant moss, disported a noble horse of Arabian blood, and his snow-white bride,' The Lily of the Prairie.'

" ' And oh ! my noble lover,' said the Lily, as in playful tenderness she seized and shook between her teeth, a lock of his coalblack mane, ' may I indeed believe thy vows? Hast thou forgotten for aye, the dun filly of Arkansas? And wilt thou ever, ever be faithless to me again ?'

" ' Nay. dearest,' he replied.

" *And she neighed.*"

From these extracts, the reader will get an idea of the nature of the forthcoming work, which we trust will find a place on their centre-tables, in their libraries and reading-rooms. We subjoin a few notices from the southern press, handed us by Mr. Bowers; the marks in the margin of each having been made with a pencil, probably by himself:

" The most elegant book of the season—with greater attrac-tions for the eye of taste and the enlightened mind than any other."—*Vallecitos Sentinel.* $1,25, *pd.*

" These volumes will have a permanent and increasing value, and will adorn the libraries and centre-tables of American fami-lies as long as American literature continues to be read."—*San Isabel Vaquero.* $3 *pd. for two insertions, and another notice for two bottles of whiskey."—J. B.*

" This superb and elegant affair is *the* book of the season un-questionably.—*Penasquitas Picaron.* 4*s. two drinks, and invited him to dinner."—J. B.*

" The typography of these volumes is all that could be de-sired. Nothing superior to it has been issued from the American Press. Bowers will be among American classics, what Goldsmith is among those of Fatherland. It is an elegant edition of the works of our foremost writer in the *belles lettres* department of literature."—*Soledad Filibuster.* $5, *drink, string of fish, and half-pig when I kill.—J B*

PHŒNIX AT BENICIA.

BENICIA, Cal., 10th June, 1855.

I OBSERVED your pathetic inquiry as to my whereabouts. I'm
all right, sir. I have been vegetating for two or three weeks
in this sweet (scented) place, enjoying myself, after a manner,
in " a tranquil cot, in a pleasant spot, with a distant view of
the changing sea." Howbeit, Benicia is not a Paradise. Indeed, I am inclined to think that had Adam and Eve been
originally placed here, the human race would never have been
propagated. It is my impression that the heat, and the wind,
and some other little Benician accidents, would have been too
much for them. It would have puzzled them, moreover, to
disobey their instructions; for there is no Tree of Knowledge,
or any other kind in Benicia; but if they had managed this,
what, in the absence of fig-leaves, would they have done for
clothing? Maybe tulé would have answered the purpose—
there's plenty of that. I remarked to my old friend, Miss
Wiggins, the other day, in a conversation on Benicia, its advantages and its drawbacks, that there was not much society

here. "Wal," replied the old lady, "thar's *two*, the Meth odists and Mr. Woodbridge's, but I don't belong to nuther. "I don't either," said I, and the conversation terminated.

I hardly know what to write to you; I remind myself of the old Methodist Elder, way down on the French Broad, in Tennessee, who was unexpectedly called upon to address a Camp-Meeting. He slowly rose and ejaculated, "Brutherin," —here an idea struck him—"Brutherin," said he, "the term *Brutherin* arose from an old custom of the Apostles, who used to go up to the tabernacle and *breathe therein!* Hence the term, Brutherin. But my brutherin," he went on, "I'm not a going to take my text from any particular part of the Bible to-night. I'll tell you," said he, with a pleasant smile, as he warmed to his work, "I'll tell you all about old brother Paul—who went down to Corinth and got into an all-fired scrape—and was knocked down—and drug out— and left thar for dead—all of which is written by Hellicar- nassus, up the Archipelago—bless-ed be the Lord!" Now, like this "ancient worthy," who by the way went on and made a very effective speech of it, I'm not going to take my text from any thing in particular, but I will commence this rambling epistle by an anecdote of "old Brother" Tush- maker, which I think extremely probable has never yet been published.

Dr. Tushmaker was never regularly bred as a physician, or surgeon, but he possessed naturally a strong mechanical genius and a fine appetite; and finding his teeth of great ser- vice in gratifying the latter propensity, he concluded that he

could do more good in the world and create more real happi
ness therein by putting the teeth of its inhabitants in good
order, than in any other way; so Tushmaker became a dentist. He was the man that first invented the method of
placing small cog-wheels in the back teeth for the more perfect mastication of food, and he claimed to be the original
discoverer of that method of filling cavities with a kind of
putty, which, becoming hard directly, causes the tooth to
ache so grievously that it has to be pulled, thereby giving
the dentist two successive fees for the same job. Tushmaker
was one day seated in his office, in the city of Boston, Massachusetts, when a stout old fellow named Byles presented himself to have a back tooth drawn. The dentist seated his
patient in the chair of torture, and opening his mouth, discovered there an enormous tooth, on the right-hand side,
about as large, as he afterwards expressed it, " as a small
Polyglot Bible." I shall have trouble with this tooth,
thought Tushmaker, but he clapped on his heaviest forceps,
and pulled. It didn't come. Then he tried the turn-screw,
exerting his utmost strength, but the tooth wouldn't stir.
" Get away from here," said Tushmaker to Byles, " and return
in a week, and I'll draw that tooth for you, or know the reason why." Byles got up, clapped a handkerchief to his jaw,
and put forth. Then the dentist went to work, and in three
days he invented an instrument which he was confident would
pull any thing. It was a combination of the lever, pulley,
wheel and axle, inclined plane, wedge and screw. The cast-
ings were made, and the machine put up in the office, over an

iron chair, rendered perfectly stationary by iron rods going down into the foundations of the granite building. In a week old Byles returned; he was clamped into the iron chair, the forceps connected with the machine attached firmly to the tooth, and Tushmaker stationing himself in the rear, took hold of a lever four feet in length. He turned it slightly Old Byles gave a groan, and lifted his right leg. Another turn; another groan, and up went the leg again. "What do you raise your leg for?" asked the doctor. "I can't help it," said the patient. "Well," rejoined Tushmaker, "that tooth is bound to come now." He turned the lever clear round, with a sudden jerk, and snapped old Byles' head clean and clear from his shoulders, leaving a space of four inches between the severed parts! They had a *post mortem* examination—the roots of the tooth were found extending down the right side, through the right leg, and turning up in two prongs under the sole of the right foot! "No wonder," said Tushmaker, "he raised his right leg." The jury thought so too, but they found the roots much decayed, and five surgeons swearing that mortification would have ensued in a few months, Tushmaker was cleared on a verdict of "justifiable homicide." He was a little shy of that instrument for some time afterward; but one day an old lady, feeble and flaccid, came in to have a tooth drawn, and thinking it would come out very easy, Tushmaker concluded, just by way of variety, to try the machine. He did so, and at the first turn drew the old lady's skeleton completely and entirely from her body eaving her a mass of quivering jelly in her chair! Tushmaker took her home in a pillow-case. She lived seven years after that, and they called her the " India-Rubber Woman.' She had suffered terribly with the rheumatism, but after this occurrence never had a pain in her bones. The dentist kept them in a glass case. After this, the machine was sold to the contractor of the Boston Custom-House, and it was found that a child of three years of age could, by a single turn of the screw, raise a stone weighing twenty-three tons. Smaller ones were made, on the same principle, and sold to the keepers of hotels and restaurants. They were used for boning tur- keys. There is no moral to this story whatever, and it is possible that the circumstances may have become slightly exaggerated. Of course, there can be no doubt of the truth of the main incidents.

The following maritime anecdote was related to me by a small man in a pea-jacket and sou'-wester hat, who had salt standing in crusts all over his face. When I asked him if it were true, he replied, " The jib-sheet's a rope, and the helm's a tiller." I guess it's all right.

Many years ago, on a stormy and inclement evening, " in the bleak December," old Miss Tarbox, accompanied by her niece, Mary Ann Stackpole, sailed from Holmes's Hole to Cotuit, in the topsail schooner *Two Susans*, Captain Black- ler. " The rains descended, and the floods came, and the winds blew and beat upon " that schooner, and great was the tossing and pitching thereof; while Captain Blackler, and his hardy crew, " kept her to it," and old Miss Tarbox and her niece rolled about in their uncomfortable bunks, wishing

themselves back in Holmes's Hole, or any other hole, on the
dry land.   The shouts of Captain Blackler as he trod the
deck, conveying orders for "tacking ship," were distinctly
audible to the afflicted females below; and "Oh!" groaned
old Miss Tarbox, during a tranquil interval of her internal
economy, as for the fifteenth time the schooner "went in
stays," "what a drefful time them pore creeturs of sailors is
a having on't.   Just listen to Jim Blackler, Mary Ann, and
hear how he is ordering about that pore fellow, *Hardy Lee*.
I've heerd that creetur hollered for twenty times this blessed
night, if I have onst."   "Yes," replied the wretched Mary
Ann, as she gave a fearful retch to starboard, "but he ain't
no worse off than poor *Taupsle Hall*—he seems to ketch it
as bad as Hardy."   "I wonder who they be," mused old Miss
Tarbox; "I knowed a Miss Hall, that lived at Seekonk Pint
onect—mebbe it's her son."   A tremendous sea taking the
"Two Susans" on her quarter at this instant, put a stop to
the old lady's cogitations; but they had an awful night of
it—and still above the roaring of the wind, the whistling and
clashing of the shrouds, the dash of the sea, and the tramp
of the sailors, was heard the voice of stout Captain Blackler,
as he shouted, "Stations! *Hard* a lee! *Top*'sle haul! Let
go and haul,"—and the "Two Susans" went about.   And,
as old Miss Tarbox remarked years afterward, when she and
Mary Ann had discovered their mistake, and laughed thereat,
"Anybody that's never been to sea, won't see no pint to this
story."

Circumstances over which I have no control, will soon

call me to a residence in Washington Territory, a beautiful and fertile field of usefulness, named for the "Father of his Country," who, I am led to understand, was "first in peace, first in war, and first in the hearts of his countrymen." As the Kentuckian remarked, "I may be heered on again, but I stand about as much chance as a bar going to —— the infernal regions (not to put too fine a point on it) without any claws." Before I go, however, I will endeavor to give you a little history of the rise, progress and decline of "*My San Diego Lawsuit*," which I think you and your readers will find curious, if not amusing. Adieu.

P. S.—You think this a stupid letter, perhaps? Think of my surroundings, young man! 'Tis not often you get a good thing out of Nazareth. Oh, Benicia, Benicia, "don't you cry for me," for I positively assure you, the feeling will not be reciprocated.

LECTURES ON ASTRONOMY

CORRESPONDENCE.

SAN FRANCISCO, OC.. 10, 185.

To PROFESSOR JOHN PHŒNIX, ESQ., San Diego Observatory.

Dear Sir:—Perceiving by perusal of your interesting article on Astronomy, that you have an organ which it is presumed you would like to dis-
pose of, I am instructed by the vestry of the meeting-house on ——— street,
to enter into a negotiation with you for its purchase. Please state by return of mail, whether or no the organ is for sale; if so, the price, and if
it is in good repair, and plays serious tunes.

Very truly yours,

A. SLEEK STIGGINS,

Ruling Elder and Agent for the sale of Stiggins' Elder Blow Tea.

PROF. PHŒNIX has the honor to acknowledge the receipt
of Mr. Stiggins' polite communication, and regrets to inform him that the organ alluded to has been disposed of to a
member of the Turn-verein Association. Owing to some
"fatuity or crookedness of mind," on the part of the manu
facturer, the organ never could be made to play but one

tune, "The Low Backed Car," which Prof. Phœnix con-
siders a most sad and plaintive melody, calculated to fill
the mind with serious and melancholy emotions. Prof. P.
takes occasion to inform Mr. S., that he has a bass trombone
in his possession, which, with a double convex lens fitted in
the mouth-piece, he has used in his observations on the stars.
This instrument will be for sale at the conclusion of this
course of lectures, and if adapted to Mr. Stiggins' purpose,
is very much at his service.

LECTURES ON ASTRONOMY—PART II.

MARS.

This planet may be easily recognized by its bright, ruddy
appearance, and its steady light. It resembles in size and
color the stars Arcturus, in Boötes, and Antares, in Scorpio;
but, as it is not like them, continually winking, we may consider it, in some respects, a body of superior gravity. Our
readers will be pleased to learn that Mars is an oblate
spheroid, with a diameter of 4,222 miles. It is seven times
smaller than the Earth; its day is forty-four minutes longer
than ours, and its year is equal to twenty-two and a half of
our months. It receives from the sun only one half as much
light and heat as the Earth, and has no moon; which, in
some respects, may be considered a blessing, as the poets of
Mars cannot be eternally writing sonnets on that subject.

Mars takes its name from the God of War, who was considered the patron of soldiers, usually termed sons of Mars,
though it was well remarked by some philosopher, that they
are generally sons of pa's also.   Macauley, however, in his
severe review of " Hanson's Life of the Rev Eleazer Williams," remarks with great originality, that " It is a wise
child that knows its own father."

Mars is also the tutelary divinity of Fillibusters, and we
are informed by several of the late troops of the late President William Walker, that this planet was of great use in
guiding that potentate during his late nocturnal rambles
through the late Republic of Sonora.   The ruddy appearance
of Mars is not attributed to his former bad habits, but to the
great height of his atmosphere, which must be very favorable
to the æronauts of that region, where, doubtless, ballooning
is the principal method of locomotion.   Upon the whole,
Mars is but a cold and ill-conditioned planet, and if, as
some persons believe, the souls of deceased soldiers are sent
thither, there can be little inducement to die in service, unless, indeed, larger supplies of commissary whiskey and tobacco are to be found there than the present telescopic observations would lead us to believe.

JUPITER.

This magnificent planet is the largest body, excepting
the Sun, in the Solar System.   " It may be readily distinguished from the fixed stars by its peculiar splendor and
magnitude, appearing to the unclothed eye, almost as re-

splendent as Venus, although it is more than seven times her distance from the Sun." Its day is but nine hours, fifty-five minutes and fifty seconds; but it has rather a lengthy year, equivalent to nearly twelve years of our time. It is about thirteen hundred times larger than the Earth.

In consequence of the rapid movement of Jupiter upon his axis, his form is that of an oblate spheroid, very considerably flattened at its poles, and the immense centrifugal force resulting from this movement (26,554 miles per hour), would, undoubtedly, have long since caused him to fly asunder, were it not for a wise provision of nature, which has caused enormous belts or hoops, to encircle his entire surface.

These hoops, usually termed belts, are plainly visible through the telescope. They are eight in number, and are supposed to be made of gutta percha, with an outer edge of No. 1 boiler iron. Owing to the great distance of Jupiter from the Sun, he receives but one twenty-seventh part of the light and heat that we do from that body. To preserve the great balance of Nature, it is therefore probable, that the whales of Jupiter are twenty-seven times larger than ours, and that twenty-seven times as much cord-wood is cut on that planet as on the Earth.

The axis of Jupiter is perpendicular to the plane of its orbit; hence its climate has no variation of seasons in the same latitude. It has four moons, three of which may be readily discerned with an ordinary spy-glass. By observation on the eclipses of these satellites, the velocity of light

has been measured, and we find that light is precisely eight
minutes and thirteen seconds in coming to us from the Sun.
According to the poet, " the light of other days " has a considerably slow motion.   Jupiter, in the Heathen Mythology,
was the King of the Gods.   As there can be no doubt that,
with the progress of time, advancement in liberal ideas, and
a knowledge of the immortal principles of democracy, has
obtained among these divinities, it is probable that he has
long since been deposed, and his kingdom converted into a
republic, over whose destinies, according to the well-known
principles of availability, some one-eyed Cyclops, unknown
to fame, has probably been elected to preside.   His repre-
sentative will, however, always remain King of the Planets,
while such things as kings exist; after which he will become
their undisputed president.   Jupiter is the patron of Mon-
archs, Presidents and Senators.   It is doubtful, however
whether he pays much attention to State Senators, or even
continues his patronage to him of the Congressional body
who fails to be re-elected, although bent on being notorious,
he may continue to vociferate that he " knows a hawk from
a hand-saw," and was " not educated at West *Pint*."

SATURN.

Whoever, during the present year, has had his attention
attracted by that beautiful group, the Pleiades, or Seven
Stars, may have noticed near them, in the constellation
Taurus, a star apparently of the first magnitude, shining with
a peculiarly white light, and beaming down with a gentle,

steady radiance upon the Earth. This is the beautiful planet Saturn, which, moving slowly at the rate of two minutes daily among the stars, may be readily traced from one constellation to another. Saturn is nearly nine hundred millions of miles from the Sun. His volume is eleven hundred times that of the Earth; and while his year is equivalent to twenty-nine and a half of ours, his day is shorter by more than one-half. Receiving but one-nineteenth part of the light from the Sun that we do, it follows that the inhabitants of Saturn are not equally enlightened with us; and supposing them to be phys- ically constituted as we are, stoves and cooking ranges un- doubtedly go off at a ready sale and pretty high figure among them. Saturn differs from all the other planets, in being surrounded by three rings, consecutive to each other, which shine by reflection from the Sun, with superior brilliancy to the planet itself. It is also attended by eight satellites. Many theories have been started to account for the rings of Saturn, but none of them are satisfactory. Our own opinion is that this planet was originally diversified, like the Earth, with continents of land and vast oceans of water. By the rapid motion of the planet upon its axis, the oceans were col- lected near the equatorial regions, whence by the immense centrifugal force, they were subsequently thrown clear from the surface, and remained revolving about the denser body, at that distance where the centrifugal force and the attraction of gravitation, from the other planets, were in equilibrio.

The ships floating on the surface of the waters at the time of this great convulsion, of course, went with them, and it is

11

a most painful reflection to the humane mind, that their crews have undoubtedly long since perished, after maintaining for a while their miserably isolated existence on a precarious supply of fish.

It is a curious and interesting fact, much dwelt on in popular treatises on Astronomy, that were a cannon ball fired from the Earth to Saturn, it would be one hundred and eighty years in getting there. The only useful deduction that we are able to make from this fact, however, is, that the inhabitants of Saturn, if warned of their danger by the sight of the flash or the sound of the explosion, would have ample opportunity in the course of the one hundred and eighty years, to dodge the shot!

Saturn was the father of all the Heathen Divinities, and we regret to say, was a most disreputable character. It will hardly be credited that he had a revolting habit of devouring his children shortly after their birth, and it was only by a pious deception of his wife, who furnished him with dogs, sheep, buffalo, and the like, on these occasions, with assurances that they were his offspring, that Jupiter and his brothers were preserved from their impending fate. A person of such a disposition could never be tolerated in a civilized community, and there is little doubt that if Saturn were a resident of the Earth at the present time, and should persist in his unpleasant practices, he would speedily be arrested and held to bail in a large amount.

HERSCHEL.

We know little of this planet, except that with its six moons, it was discovered by Dr. Herschel, a native of the island of England (situated on the north-west coast of Europe), in 1781. It was named by him the " Georgium Sidus," as a tribute of respect to a miserable, blind, old lunatic, who at that time happened to be king of the Island. Overlooking the sycophancy of the man, in their admiration for the services of the Astronomer, his philosophical contemporaries re-named the planet, Herschel, by which title it is still known. An attempt made by the courtiers of the English king to call it *Uranus* (a Latin expression, meaning " You reign over us "), happily failed to succeed. Herschel is supposed to be about eighty times larger than the Earth, and to have a period of revolution of about eighty-four years, but its diurnal motion has not yet been discovered.

NEPTUNE

Was discovered by a French gentleman, named Le Verrier, in 1846. It is supposed to be about forty thousand miles in diameter, and to have a period of one hundred and sixty-four years. But of this planet, and another still more remote from the Sun, lately discovered (to which the literati and *savans* of Europe propose to give the name of *Squibob*, a Hebrew word signifying, " *There you go with your eye out* "), we know little from actual observation. That they exist, there can be no doubt, and it is possible, to use the expressive language of a modern philosopher "There are a few more of the same sort left" beyond them.

Neptune is the God of the Sea, an unpleasant element, full of disagreeable fish, horrible sea-lions, and equivocal serpents, the reflection on which, or some other reasons, generally makes every one sick who ventures upon it. He married a Miss Amphitrite, who, unlike sailors' wives in general, usually accompanies her husband on all his voyages. Neptune is the tutelar deity of seamen, who generally allude to him as "Davy Jones," and speak of the ocean as his "locker" (a locker indeed, in which untold thousands of their worn-out bones are bleaching), and on crossing the Equinoctial line, it was formerly the custom among them to perform certain rites in his honor, which pagan ceremonial has gradually passed out of date.

THE ASTEROIDS.

These are ten small planets, revolving about the Sun in different orbits, situated between those of Mars and Jupiter. They can seldom be seen without a powerful telescope; and are of no great importance when you see them. Our friend, Dr. Olbers, who paid much attention to these little bodies, is of the opinion that they are fragments of a large celestial sphere, which formerly revolved between Mars and Jupiter, and which, by some mighty internal convulsion, burst into pieces. With this opinion we coincide. What caused the explosion, how many lives were lost, and whether blame could be attached to any one on account of it, are circum-

stances that we shall probably remain in as profound ignorance of as the unfortunate inhabitants of the planet found
themselves after the occurrence. What purpose the Asteroids now serve in the great economy of the Universe, it is
impossible to ascertain; it may be that they are reserved as
receptacles for the departed souls of ruined merchants and
broken brokers. As the Spaniard profoundly remarks,
" Quien Sabe ? "

CHAPTER II.

OF THE FIXED STARS.

For convenience of description, Astronomers have divided the entire surface of the Heavens into numerous small
tracts, called constellations, to which have been given names,
resulting from some real or fancied resemblance in the arrangement of the stars composing them, to the objects indicated. This resemblance is seldom very striking, but
nomenclature is arbitrary, and it is perhaps quite as well to
call a collection of stars that don't look at all like a scorpion,
" The Scorpion," as to name an insignificant village, with
two or three hundred inhabitants, a tavern, no church, and
twenty-seven grog shops, Rome, or Carthage. We once
knew a couple of honest people, who named their eldest
child (a singularly pug-nosed little girl), MADONNA, *Madonna* Smith—and that infant grew up and did well, and
was lately married to a highly respectable young butcher.

A zone 16° in breadth, extending quite around the
Heavens, 8° on each side of the Ecliptic, is called Zodiac.

This zone is divided into twelve equal parts or constellations, which are sometimes called the Signs of the Zodiac. The
following are the names of these constellations, in their regular order, and the number of visible stars contained in each ·

1. Aries . . .	*The Hydraulic Ram*, .	. . . . .	. 66
2. Taurus . .	*The Irish Bull*, .	. . . . .	. 141
3. Gemini , .	*The Siamese Twins* .	. . . .	. 85
4. Cancer . .	*The Soft Shelled Crab*,	. . . .	. 83
5. Leo . . .	*The Dandy Lion*,	. . . . .	. 95
6. Virgo . .	*The Virago*,	. . . . . .	. 110
7. Libra . . .	*The Hay Scales* .	. . . . .	51
8. Scorpio . .	*The N. Y. Herald* .	. . · . .	. 44
9. Sagittarius .	*The Sparrow*,	. . . . .	. 69
10. Capricornus .	*The Bishop*,	. . . . .	. 51
11. Aquarius . .	*The Decanter*,	. . . . .	. 108
12. Pisces . .	*The Sardines*, .	. . . . .	73

To discover the position of these several constellations
it is merely nesessary to have a starting point. On looking
at the Heavens during the month of April, and considering
the stars therein intently, the observer will at length find
six bright stars arranged exactly in the form of a sickle.
A very bright star is at the extremity of the handle. This
is the star Regulus in the constellation Leo. Then some
30° further to the east, he will observe a very brilliant
star, with no visible stars near it. This is Spica in the
Virgin.

Still further east, rises Libra, distinguished by two rather
bright stars forming a parallelogram, with two rather dim
ones, followed by Scorpio, whose stars resemble in their arrangement a kite, with a tail to it, and in which a brilliant
red star, named Antares, forms the centre. Then Sagit-

tarius and Capricornus separately span 30°; when rises Aquarius, in which the most careless observer will notice four stars, forming very plainly, the letter Y. Pisces, a loose straggling succession of stars, intervenes between this sign and that of Aries, which may be distinguished by two bright stars, about 4° apart, the brightest, to the N. E. of the other. Taurus cannot be mistaken—it contains two remarkable clusters, the Pleiades and the Hyades; the latter forming a well-marked letter V. with the bright red star Aldebaran at the upper left-hand corner. Gemini contains two remarkably bright stars, Castor and Pollux;—the former much the most brilliant and the more northerly of the pair; they are but 5° apart. Then follows 30° including Cancer, which contains no remarkably brilliant stars, and we return to our starting point. In the month of September, we would select as a starting point the star Antares, giving us the position of the Scorpion. Antares is of a remarkably red appearance, situated between, and equi-distant from, two other less brilliant stars with which it forms a curved line, which, extended by other stars, curve around at its extremity like the tail of a flying kite, or if you please, like the tail of a scorpion.

The fixed stars are classed according to their magnitude, first, second, third, fourth, fifth, etc.; the stars of the fifth magnitude being the smallest that can be seen by the unassisted eye. It is by no means our intention, in this course of lectures, to convey a complete, and thorough knowledge of Uranography (we assure you, madam, that this word is in the Dictionary); however great our ability or inclination, the limits prescribed us will not permit of it we shall, there- fore, confine ourselves to a brief description of the principal constellations, trusting that the interest awakened in the minds of our numerous readers on the subject, by our re- marks, may lead them to make it a study hereafter. For this purpose we would recommend as a suitable preparation a light course of reading, such, for instance, as " Church's Deferential and Integral Calculus," to be followed by " Bartlett's Optics,'' and Gummer's Elements of Astro- nomy." After this, by close and unremitting study of La Place, and other eminent writers, for twenty or thirty years, the reader, if of good natural ability, may acquire a super- ficial knowledge of the science.

" The Great Bear " (which is spelled—Bear—and has no reference whatever to Powers' Greek Slave) is one of the most remarkable constellations in the Heavens. We cannot imagine why it received its name, unless indeed, because it has not the slightest resemblance to a great Bear, or any other animal. It may be distinguished by means of a clus- ter of seven brilliant stars, arranged in the form of a dipper (not a *duck*, but a *tin* dipper). Of these, the two, forming the side of the dipper, furthest from the handle, are named, the lower *Merak*, the upper *Dubhe*, and are called the *Pointers*, from the fact, that in whatever position the con- stellation is observed, a line passing through these two stars and continued in the direction of *Dubhe* for 28° passes through *Cynosura*, the North or pole star. To this re-

markable star—it was discovered some years since— a mag-
netic needle will constantly point, a discovery which has
done more for commerce, made more sailors and caused
more fatigue to the legs of the author, than any other under
heaven, Colt's pistols not excepted.   It must not be understood that the needle points to the pole star, because the
star possesses any particular attraction for it.   Currents of
electricity passing constantly from W. to E. about the eartℓ,
cause the needle to point N. and S., and it is merely in consequence of the star Cynosura lying exactly in the N., that
it appears directed toward it.   Immediately opposite to the
Great Bear, beyond Cynosura, we observe the constellation
Cassiopeia, which, instead of representing as it should, a respectable looking old woman sitting on a throne, takes the
appearance of a chair, which, constantly revolving about the
North star, is thrown into as many different positions as the
chair used by the celebrated "India-rubber man," in his
wonderful feats of dexterity.

Near Cassiopeia, but further to the E., we find Andromeda, which constellation, representing a young lady, chained
to a rock, without a particle of clothing, we shall not attempt
to point out more definitely.   Perseus, near Andromeda,
holds in his hand the head of Medusa, a glance from whose
eyes turned the gazer into stone, which accounts for the origin of the Stones, a numerous and highly respectable family
in the United States.   If we prolong the handle of the dipper some 25°, we observe a brilliant star of the first magnitude, of a ruddy appearance, called Arcturus ; which many

years since, a person named Job, was asked if he could guide
and he acknowledged he couldn't do it. The star is in the
knee of the Boötes (which is pronounced Bootees; he was
the inventor and wearer of those articles), who, with two
greyhounds, Asterion and Chara, is apparently driving the
Bear forever around the pole. A beautiful star 30° E. of
Arcturus, named Lyra, distinguished by two small stars with
which it makes an equilateral triangle, points out the position
of the Harp; immediately beneath which is seen the Swan,
· distinguished by five stars forming a large and regular cross,
the foot of which being turned up, prevents its being noticed,
unless closely examined. The bright star in the head of the
cross is Deneb Cygni. Twenty degrees S. E. of Lyra, we
observe the brilliant star Altair in the Eagle, equidistant
from two other small stars, making with it a slight curve.

The beautiful constellation Orion (which takes its name
from the founder of the celebrated Irish family of O'Ryan)
may be easily distinguished by its belt, three bright stars,
forming a right line about 3° in length; with three smaller
stars immediately below (forming an angle with it), which
distinguish the handle of the sword. The brilliant star of
the first magnitude, in the left shoulder of Orion, is called
Betelguese, that in the right shoulder, Bellatrix; the star in
the right knee, is Saiph, that in the left foot, Rigel. Some
20° N. E. of the seven stars, the brilliant star Capella, in
the Wagoner, may be recognized by three small stars, forming an acute-angled triangle, immediately below it. A very
beautiful star, of peculiarly whitish lustre, named Formal·

haut, forms the eye of the Southern Fish; it is about 30° S.
E. of the Y in Aquarius and cannot be mistaken, as it is the
only brilliant star in that part of the Heavens. We have
now mentioned most of the principal constellations, but we
suspect that the ardent curiosity and love of research of our
readers will hardly allow them to rest contented with the
meagre information thus conveyed, but that they will hasten
to seek in the writings of standard authors, such a knowledge
of this interesting subject, as the scope of these lectures will
not permit us to attempt imparting. They will thus find the
truth of Hamlet's statement, "that more things exist in
Heaven and Earth, than are dreamed of" in their philosophy.
Dragons, Hydras, Serpents and Centaurs, Big Dogs and Little Dogs, Doves, Coons and Ladies' Hair, will be exhibited
to their admiring gaze, and they will also have their attention directed to the remarkable constellation Phœnix (named
for an ancestor of the present Johannes, but not in the least
resembling him, or the family portraits), to which the modesty
of the author has merely permitted him to make this brief
allusion. On the subject of Comets, we should have desired
to make a lengthy dissertation; but Professor Silliman in his
late efforts to throw light upon it, has decided that these
bodies are nothing but GAS; which sets the matter at rest
forever, and renders discussion useless.

The lecture now closes, with an exhibition of the " *Phan-
tasmagoria*" (which is the scientific name of a tin Magic
Lantern), showing the various Heavenly Bodies tranquilly
revolving round the Sun, perfectly undisturbed by the ex-

travagant motions of these rampant comets, continually crossing their paths in orbits of impossible eccentricity, while the
organ, slowly turned by the Professor with one hand (the
other imparting motion to the planets), emits in plaintive
tones that touching melody the " Low Backed Car," giving
an excruciating and probably correct idea of the " Music of
the Spheres," which nobody ever heard, and, therefore, the
correctness of the imitation cannot be disputed.   This portion of the entertainment should be continued as long as possible, as the author has observed, it never fails to give great
satisfaction to the audience; any exhibition requiring a
darkened room, being a " sure card " of attraction in a com
munity where there are many young people, which accounts
for the wonderful success of Banvard's Panorama.   Should
the Professor's arm become wearied before the audience are
entirely satisfied, it is easy to disperse them, by the simple
process of shutting down the slide, stopping the organ, and
inducing a small boy, by a trifling pecuniary compensation, to
holla *Fire!* in the vicinity of the lecture room.

The author acknowledges the receipt of " An Astronomi
cal Poem " from a " Young Observer," commencing

" Oh, if I had a telescope with fourteen slides,"

with the modest request that he would "introduce" it in his
second lecture; but the detestable attempt of the " Young
Observer" to make "slides" rhyme with " Pleiades " in the
second line, and the fearful pun in the thirty-seventh verse,
on " the Meteor by moonlight alone," compel him to decline

the introduction. The manuscript will be returned to the author, on making known his real name, and engaging to destroy it immediately

A LEGEND OF THE TEHAMA HOUSE.

CHAPTER I.

IT was evening at the Tehama. The apothecary, whose shop
formed the south-eastern corner of that edifice, had lighted
his lamps, which, shining through those large glass bottles
in the window, filled with red and blue liquors, once supposed
by this author, when young and innocent, to be medicine of
the most potent description, lit up the faces of the passers-by
with an unearthly glare, and exaggerated the general redness
and blueness of their noses. Within the office the hands of
the octagonal clock, which looked as though it had been
thrown against the wall in a moist state and stuck there,
pointed to the hour of eight. The apartment was nearly
deserted. Frink, " the courteous and gentlemanly manager,"
and the Major, had gone to the Theatre; having season tickets, they felt themselves forced to attend, and never missed
a performance. The coal fire in the office stove glowed with
a hospitable warmth, emitting a gentle murmur of welcome to

the expected wayfarers by the Sacramento boats, interrupted only by an occasional deprecatory hiss, when insulted by a stream of tobacco juice. Overcoats hung about the walls, still moist with recent showers; umbrellas reclined lazily in corners; spittoons stood about the floor, the whole diffusing that nameless odor so fascinating to the married man, who, cigar in mouth and hot whiskey punch at elbow, sits nightly until twelve o'clock in the enjoyment of it, while the wife of his bosom in their comfortable home on Powell street, wonders at his absence, and unjustly curses the Know Nothings or the Free and Accepted Masonic Fraternity.

Behind the office desk, perched on a high, three-legged stool, his head supported by both hands, the youthful but literary John Duncan was deeply engaged in the exciting perusal of the last yellow-covered novel, " Blood for Blood, or the Infatuated Dog." He knew that, in a few moments, eighty-four gentlemen " in hot haste," would call to inquire whether the Member of Congress had returned, and was anxious to find out what the " Robber Chieftain " did with the " Lady Maude Alleyne " before the arrival of the Sacramento boat. The only other occupant of the office, was a short, fleshy gentleman with a white hat, dark green coat with brass buttons, drab pantaloons, short punchy little boots and gaiters.

These circumstances might be noted as he stood with his back to the door, gazing intently upon one of those elaborate works of art with which the spirited proprietor has lately seen fit to adorn the walls of the Tehama. It represented a lady in a ball dress, seated on the back of a large dray-horse (at least eighteen hands high), and holding a parrot on her right forefinger, while at her horse's feet kneeled a man in the stage dress of Mercutio, doing something with five or six other parrots. The piece was called " Hawking," had a fine gilt frame and glass, and in certain lights, answered the purpose of a mirror, and was therefore a very pretty object to gaze upon. In fact, the short, stout gentleman was adjusting his shirt collar, which was of prodigious height, and had a perverse inclination to turn down on one side, by its reflection.

As he turned from this employment, he exhibited one of the most curious faces it is possible to conceive. Unlike most fat men, whose little eyes, round, red cheeks, wart-like noses and double chins, convey but little meaning or expression, this gentleman's face was all expression. He wore a constant look of the most intense curiosity. Inquisitiveness sat upon every lineament of his countenance. His small, green eyes protruding from his head, surmounted by thin but well-defined and very curvilinear eyebrows, looked like two notes of interrogation; his nose, though small, was sharp at the end like a gimlet, and his little round mouth was constantly pursed up into an expression of inquiring wonder, as though the most natural sound that could fall from it, should be, " O-o-o-o! come now, do tell." In fact he was one of those beings created by a wise but inscrutable Providence, for no other purpose apparently but " to meddle with other people's business," and ask questions.

His name was Bogle, and with Mrs. Bogle, whom he had married two years before, because, having exhausted all other subjects of inquiry in conversation with her, he had finally asked her if she would have him, and a little Bogle, who had made its appearance some three months since, and already " took notice " with an inquiring air painful to contemplate, he occupied, for the present, " Room No, 31."

Bogle would have made a fortune in no time, if he had lived in the blessed era when the promise " Ask and ye shall receive " was fulfilled ; and so well was his disposition understood by the frequenters of the Tehama, that they invariably left the vicinity when he looked askant at them; his presence cleared the room as quickly as a stream from a fire engine, or a mad dog could have done it. Brushing some remains of snuff from his snow white vest—Bogle took snuff inordinately —he said it sharpened up his faculties—he turned upon the hapless Duncan—who had just got the " Lady Maude " into the cave, where the skeleton hand dripped blood from the ceiling—" John, what time is it ? " John looked at the clock with a slight groan, " Five minutes past eight, Mr. Bogle."

" What time will the boat be in ? "

" In a few moments, Mr. Bogle."

" Will the General come down to-night ? "

" I don't know, Mr. Bogle."

" How old a man do you take him to be now ? "

" Fontaine she screamed !—that is, I don't know, Mr Bogle."

" How much does he weigh ? "

" The skeleton !—indeed, I don't know, sir."

The conversation was here suspended by the sudden arrival of a stranger. He was a large man, of stern and forbid
ding aspect, exceedingly dark complexion, with long, black
hair hanging in unkempt tangles about his shoulders, and
with a fierce and uncompromising moustache and beard,
blacker than the driven charcoal, completely concealing the
lower part of his face. His dress was singular; a brown hat,
brown coat, brown vest, brown neck cloth, brown pantaloons,
brown gaiter boots. In his hand he carried a brown carpet
bag, and beneath his arm a brown silk umbrella. Hastily he
inscribed his name upon the Register, " General Tecumseh
Brown, Brownsville," and, for an instant, seemed to fall into
a brown study. Bogle was on the *qui vive;* he looked over
the General's shoulder.

" From Sacramento, sir ? " said he.

The General gazed at Bogle, sternly, for a moment, and
replied, " I am, sir."

" I see, sir," said Bogle with a cordial smile, " you live in
Brownsville ; may I inquire if you are in business there ? "

The General gazed at Bogle more sternly than before,
and shortly answered, " You may, sir."

" Well," said Bogle, " are you ? "

" Yes, sir," replied General Brown in a stentorion voice,
at the same time advancing a step toward his fat little in-
quisitor, " I have lately made a fortune there."

" Oh ! " said Bogle, nimbly jumping back as the General
advanced, " How ? "

"*By minding my own business, sir !* " thundered the

General, and turning to Duncan, who had forgotten the "Lady Maude" in the charms of this conversation, said, "Give me my key, sir, and the moment a young man calls here to inquire for me, send him up to my room."

So saying, and grasping the key extended to him, General Brown turned away, and, casting a look of fierce malignity at little Bogle, who tried to conceal his confusion by taking a pinch of snuff, retired, taking with him as he went, the only brown japanned candlestick that stood among the numerous array of those articles, provided for the Tehama's guests."

"Well," said Bogle, "of all the Brown—where did you put him, John?"

"No. 32," replied that individual, returning to "the cave."

"Thirty-two!" exclaimed Bogle, "Goodness! Gracious! why that joins my room, and the partition is as thin as a wafer."

CHAPTER II.

Up stairs went Bogle, two steps at a time. The door of thirty-two slammed, as he reached the door of his apartment; it slammed on a brown coat-tail, about half a yard of which remained on the outside; there was a muttered ejaculation, then a deep growl, and—rip! went the coat-tail, the fragment remaining in the door.

"Gracious! Goodness!" said Bogle, "what a passionate man! he's torn it off! he's like Halley's comet; no! that never had a tail! he's like that fox,"—and Bogle entered his apartment.

Here sat his interesting wife, rocking their offspring, and instilling into its infant mind the first lesson of practical economy, by singing that popular nursery refrain,

"Buy low, Baby; buy low, buy low."

" Hush!" said Bogle, as he entered on tip-toe, and, carefully closing the door of thirty-one, held up a warning finger to the partner of his joys and sorrows. The lullaby ceased. It is said that all women become like their husbands after a certain time, both in appearance and disposition. Mrs. Bogle, who had been a Miss Artemesia Stackpole before marriage (Bogle said she was named for an elder sister, Mesia, who died, and she was called Arter-mesia), certainly did not at all resemble her husband in appearance. She was of the thread-paper order; one of those gaunt, bony females of no particular age, who always have two false eye-teeth, and wear brown merino dresses and muslin night-caps with a cotton lace border in the morning. But in disposition she was his very counterpart. Curious, meddling, inquisitive, fond of gossip and indefatigable in " the pursuit of knowledge under difficulties," she was an invaluable coadjutor to Bogle, whom she had materially assisted many times in obtaining information, that even his prying nature had failed to accomplish. Eagerly she listened to his tale about the mysterious Brown and *his* tail, and, like a good and dutiful wife, all quietly she nursed the olive branch, while Bogle, seated in close prox imity to the partition, listened with eager ear, intent, to the motions of their neighbor.

Three times in as many quarters of an hour did that mysterious General ring the bell; three times came up the waiter; three times he replied to the General's anxious question, "that no one had called for him," and three times he went down again. After each interview with the waiter, Bogle listening at the partition, heard the General mutter to himself a large word, a scriptural word, but not adapted to common conversation; it began with a capital D and ended with a small n. Each time that he heard it, Bogle said " Gracious ! Goodness !" At length his patient exertions were rewarded. As the clock struck ten, a step was heard upon the stairs; nearer and nearer it came. Bogle's heart beat heavily; it stopped in front of " thirty-two ; "—he held his breath ;—a knock ;—the General's voice, " Come in ; "— he heard the door open, and the stranger commence with " Good evening, General," but before he could say " Brown," that gentleman exclaimed, " Charles, *have* you seen Fanny ? "

Bogle, his ear glued to the wall, turned his eye toward his wife and beckoned. Artemesia approached, and seating herself on his knee, the infant clasped to her breast, listened with her husband

The stranger slowly replied, " I have."

" And who was she with ? "

" That Frenchman, as you supposed."

" Good God ! " exclaimed the stricken Brown, as in agony

he paced the room with fearful strides. There was a mo
ment's silence.

" Did you take her from him ? "

" Yes, I persuaded her to accompany me to my room at
' The Union.' "

" Why did you not bring her to me at once ? "

" I knew your passionate nature, General, and I feared
you would kill her."

" *I will !* " growled the General, " By Heaven, I will !—
but not so—not as you think; I'll poison her ! "

Bogle, his face pallid with apprehension, his teeth chat-
tering with fear, looked at Artemesia; "—she met his horror-
stricken gaze, and with a subdued shriek, clasped the baby;
—it awoke.

The General, in a low, deep voice of concentrated pas-
sion, continued;—" I'll poison her, Charles ! "

" Oh ! " he exclaimed with deep emotion, " how I have
loved that—"

Here the infant Bogle, who had been drawing in his
breath for a cry, broke forth;—" At once there rose so wild
a yell." Human nature could not stand it longer.

" Smother that little villain ! " said Bogle in a fierce
whisper; " I can't hear a word."

Artemesia, with the look of Lucretia Borgia, withdrew
with the child to the adjoining room, (No. 31, Tehama,
contains two rooms, a small parlor and a bed-chamber), and
administered a punishment that must have astonished it—

It was certainly *struck aback.* If babies remember any thing, that youthful Bogle has not forgotten that bastinado—applied a little higher up than is customary among the Turks—to this day. "At length the tumult dwindled to a calm," and again Bogle clapped his ear to the wall. He heard but the concluding words of the murderous General—

"Bring her up with you at ten o'clock to-morrow evening, and a sack; after it is over, we will put her body in it, and carry her to Meiggs' wharf, where there are plenty of brick; we can fill the sack with them and throw her off."

"Well, sir," replied the stranger, "if you are determined to do it, I will; but poor Fanny!"—here emotion choked his utterance.

"You do as I tell you, sir;" growled the General, "there's no weakness about me!" Here the door opened and closed.

Bogle rose from his knees, the perspiration was running down his fat face in streams.—"No weakness," said he, "Goodness Gracious! I should say not;—what an awful affair;—coming so close, too, upon the Meiggs' forgeries, and the loss of the Yankee Blade;—how providential that I happened to overhear it all! Gracious Goodness!"

That night, in a whispered consultation with his Artemesia, Bogle's plan of action was decided upon. But long after this, and long after the horror-stricken pair had sunk into a perturbed slumber, the footsteps of the intended murderer might have been heard, as hour after hour he paced the floor of his solitary chamber, and his deep voice might have been heard also, occasionally giving vent to his fell determination—"Yes, *sir!* I'll–mur–der ! ! ! !——! ! ! !—— ! ! !—!

CHAPTER III.

The next morning a great change might have been observed in our friend Bogle. He appeared unusually quiet and reserved—pallid and nervous;—starting when any one approached him, he stood alone near the door of the Tehama; he sought no companionship—he asked no questions. Men marvelled thereat.

"What has come over Bogle?" said the Judge to the Major. "I haven't heard him ask a question to-day."

"Well," was the unfeeling reply, "he's been asking questions for the last thirty years, and I reckon he has asked all there are."

But Bogle knew what he was about. At three P.M. precisely, General Brown came majestically down stairs; he passed Bogle so nearly that he could have touched him; but he noticed not the latter's shuddering withdrawal; he looked neither to the right or left, but, gloomy and foreboding, like an avenging genius, he passed into the apothecary's on the corner.

"Give me an ounce bottle of strychnine," said he.

"For rats, sir?" said the polite attendant.

The General started; he gave a fearful scowl. "Yes," he said, with a demoniac laugh, "for rats! ha! ha! oh yes— for—-rats!"

Bogle heard this;—he heard no more; he started for the Police Office.

*   *   *   *   *   *

Who was Fanny?—??—— ????l ——?——??——???

*   *   *   *   *   *

That evening about ten o clock, Bogle sat alone, or alone save his Artemesia, in No. 31. The baby had been put to bed; and silent and solemn in that dark apartment, for the lamp had been extinguished, sat listening that shuddering pair. A step was heard on the stairs, and closer drew the Bogles together, listening to that step, as it sounded fearfully distinct, from the beating of their own agitated hearts.

As it drew near, it was evident that two persons were approaching; for, accompanying the first distinct tread, was a light footfall like that of a young and tender female. "Poor thing!" said Artemesia, with a suppressed gasp. The heavy tread of General Brown could be heard distinctly in No. 32. The parties stopped at his door;--a knock, and they were silently admitted.

The voice of the General broke the silence—"Oh! Fanny," he exclaimed in bitter anguish, how could you desert me!" There was no articulate reply, but the Bogles heard from the unhappy female an expression of grief, which almost broke their hearts.

"Fanny," continued the General, "you have been faith-less to me—fickle and false as your sex invariably are! I
12

loved you, Fanny—I love you still!—but my heart can no more be made the sport of falsehood! You must die! Take this!"

"Hold—wretch!" shouted Bogle. "Let me go, Arte-mesia;" and throwing off his coat, the heroic little fellow threw open his own door, kicked down the door of thirty-two, and stood in the presence of the murderer and his victim—pistol in hand! At the same instant the bell of thirty-one was violently rung, the doors on each side opened, and the gallery was filled with men. But what caused Bogle to falter? Why did he not rush forward to snatch the victim from her destroyer? Near the centre-table, on which was burning an astral lamp, stood a remarkably fine looking young man, who gazed on Bogle's short, punchy figure with an inquiring smile.

On the other side of the table, but nearer the door, his brow blacker than a thunder-cloud, sat General Brown in one hand he held a small piece of meat, the other retained between his knees a small but exceedingly stanch-looking dog, of the true bull-terrier breed. Both the General and the dog showed their teeth;—both were epitomes of ferocity, but the snarl of the dog was as nothing to the snarl of the General, as, half-rising from his seat, but still holding the dog down by the collar, he shouted—"How's this, sir?"

Bogle staggered back—dashing back from his brow the perspiration, he dropped the pistol and leaning against the door, gasped rather than articulated—"It's a dog!"

"Yes, sir!" roared the infuriated General, rising from his chair—"*and a she dog at that!* what have *you* got to say about it?"

Bogle, almost fainting, stammered painfully forth, "Is her—name—Fanny?"

"D——n you sir," screamed the General, "I'll let you know! Sta-boy! bite him, Fan!"

Like an arrow from a bow, like lightning from the cloud, like shot off a shovel, like any thing that goes quick, sprang the female bull-terrier on the unhappy Bogle.

"Man is but mortal," and Bogle turned to flee. "It was too late!" Why did he take off his coat?—ah! why wear such tight pantaloons?

Shrieking like a demon, the ferocious beast clinging to one extremity, his hair on end with fright, and horror at the other, Bogle rushed frantically down the passage, overturning in his mad career police officers, chambermaids, housekeeper and boarders, who, alarmed at his outcries, thronged tumultuously into the hall. The first flight of stairs he took at a jump;—the second he rolled down from top to bottom, the bull-terrier clinging to him like a steel trap—first the dog on top, then Bogle;—arrived at the bottom, he sprang forth into Sansome street, and reckless of Frink's alarmed cry—"Stop that man—he hasn't paid his bill!" away he went on the wings of the wind. It was an awful sight to see that little figure, as, wild with horror, he ran adown the street, the staunch dog swinging from side to side, as he fled.

It was a fearful race! Never did a short pair of legs get

over an equal space in an equal time, than on that trying occasion. At length a sailor on Commercial street, taking the
dog for a portmanteau, with which he supposed Bogle was
making off, stretched out a friendly leg and tripped him up.
But his troubles were not ended. When a bull-terrier takes
a hold—a fair hold—to get it off, one of two alternatives
must obtain;—either the animal's teeth must be drawn, or
the piece must come out. They hadn't time to draw Fanny's
teeth—!

They brought Bogle home in a hand-cart, and put him
to bed. He hasn't sat down since. As they took him up
stairs to his room, surrounded by a clamorous throng, the
door of No. 10, at the foot of the first flight of stairs, opened,
and a gentleman of exceeding dignity, made his appearance
in a dressing gown of beautifully embroidered pattern.

" John," he said to Mr. Duncan, who, with an extensive
grin on his countenance, and " Blood for Blood " (somewhat
dilapidated in the scuffle) in his hand, was bringing up the rear
of the procession with a candle, " what's all this row about ? '

John briefly explained.

" I thought it a fire," said the gentleman, " but, ' *Partu-
riunt montes, nascetur—*' "

" A ridiculous muss," said the classic John Duncan.

The gentleman retired ; so did the chambermaid ; so did
the boarders generally ; so did General Brown, with his dog
under his arm, swearing he would not part with her for five
hundred dollars ; so did the policemen, somewhat scandalized
that nobody was murdered after all.

Bogle left the house next day in a baby-jumper, swung to a pole between two Chinamen. Artemesia and the infant followed.

I hear that he has lately increased his business, taken a partner, and attends to the examination of wills, marriage settlements, and other papers belonging entirely to other people's business. Sneak is the name of the partner; he or Bogle may be seen daily at the " Hall of Records," from ten until two o'clock, overhauling something or other, that is no concern of theirs. They furnish all sorts of information *gratis.* It is like the wine you get where they advertise " All sorts of liquors at 12½ cents a glass."

General Brown has settled in Grass Valley, Nevada County, and would have appointed every white male inhabitant of California a member of his staff with the rank of Lieutenant-colonel, had he not been anticipated.

Fanny killed forty-four rats in thirty seconds, only last week—so Tom says.

The Tehama House is still there.

INTERESTING CORRESPONDENCE.

[We have received for publication the following correspondence, which is more than rich; it is positively luscious.]

WASHINGTON, January 14, 1854.

Lieut. ——, U. S. A., San Diego, Cal.

SIR :—An effort having been made by me in connection with others, to obtain an act of Congress during its present session, by which army officers will receive the same allowances whilst they served in California and Oregon, as were granted to Navy officers, I beg to call your attention thereto, and especially ask your approval of the contemplated attempt.

You are aware that Congress, at its last session, granted in the Naval Appropriation bill, extra pay ($2 per diem), to the officers, and double pay to sailors and others, serving in the Pacific during the Mexican war, and up to the 28th of September, 1850. This allowance was based upon the supposition that the officers of the army serving in California *had* received the same allowance, by previous acts of Congress, when in fact this extra pay had only been granted them from the 1st July, 1850. There are a large number of army officers justly entitled to an additional allowance, and for precisely the same reasons which has induced Con-gress to grant it to the Navy, and especially those who served there subsequent to the 1st January, 1848; when they were compelled to pay the most exorbitant prices for the necessaries of life, having no other alternative, and no means of leaving the country like the officers of the Pacific squadron, who could have left the coast of California and gone to a cheaper station.

I have been requested by a number of officers stationed in Texas, to solicit your co-operation in carrying out this desirable object, by contributing, in the event of success, the proportionable per centum, agreed upon by them, namely five or ten per cent. on the amount that may accrue, to you, as a remuneration for services rendered. Your concurrence is therefore requested, and it is understood that if there should be a failure, which, however, is not anticipated, no charge of any kind shall be made.

Soliciting your immediate attention, and early reply,

I remain very respectfully,

Your ob'dt servant,

CHARLES D———.

———

SAN DIEGO, 20th March, 1854.

MY DEAR CHARLES :—I have received your modest request of the 4th of January, that I will give you five or ten per cent. of any sum that Congress may hereafter, in its infinite beneficence, appropriate to my relief; a request which you state you make to me at the instance of "a number of offi cers stationed in Texas."

For the benefit of those gentlemen, as well as yourself, I have asked Mr. Ames to print your letter, and my answer, in the world-renowned San Diego Herald—the only method I see of communicating with your advisers; as a letter directed to "a number of officers stationed in Texas," might possibly never reach them, through the ordinary channels.

Upon mature reflection, of nearly five minutes, I have come to the conclusion to decline acceding to your proposal. This decision has resulted from several considerations

In the first place, I don't know you, Charles. I never heard of you before, in all my life. To be sure, I see by your card, which you so kindly enclosed, and which my wife has just stuck up in the corner of the cracked looking-glass that adorns our humble chamber, that you are a General Agent (which may be a new military rank for all I know created with the Lieutenant-generalcy, and if it is, I beg your pardon and touch my hat, for I have a great respect for rank), and a Notary Public, and that you live on Seventh street, opposite the Odd Fellows' Hall, (why not move across the street?) But all this does not amount to friendship, intimacy, or even common acquaintance; and I declare, Charles, I do not even know now whether you may not be some designing person, who, seeing that a bill is likely to pass for the relief of certain distressed officers, seeks to levy a little black mail, say five or even ten per cent., on the scanty pittance, under the pretext of having influenced Congress in its humane decision; a thing that I believe all the General Agents, Notary Publics, U. S. Commissioners, and Commissioners of Deeds, that ever lived opposite or in Odd Fellows' Hall, would fail to accomplish, had not Congress made up its benevolent mind to do it without consulting them

2dly. Why should I promise to give you ten per cent. of that allowance? (Oh, *don't* you wish you might get it—I hope *I* shall.) You say you have made an effort to get it for us. Ah, Charles, I love and honor you for doing so, if you have; but how, when, and where—tell me where, did you make that effort. But if you did do so, what of it? Perhaps you made an effort, too, to get me the pay I now receive. Perhaps—startling thought!—you will be writing to me for "five or ten per cent." of that humble income! Don't try it, Charles; you wouldn't get it, I assure you.

As to your making an effort, that's all nonsense. Every body makes efforts now-a-days. Every body that ever I read of, except Mrs. Dombey, made an effort; and if my grandmother were to die and leave me a thousand dollars, you might, with equal propriety, inform me that you made an effort for that venerable person's decease, and claim "five or ten per cent." of that amount of property, as to humbug me with your making efforts to influence Congress, who, as I said before, I solemnly believe is independent of all the efforts of all the Notary Publics in all Washington.

From these two considerations, I conclude that you have

, no claim , shadow of a claim on me, but that your proposal state you me request for charity, to the amount of "five or ten per cent." on the small sum that you, living in Washington, and watching the signs of the times, begin to believe Congress is going to allow me. This charity I shall decline bestowing, for three good and sufficient reasons :

1st. I am very poor myself.

2d. I have a family to support on $89 83 a month, which isn't such a tremendous income, in a country where flour is $30 per barrel.

3d. I'll see you —— first, giving you full permission to fill the blank with any kind aspiration for your future well-fare and happiness, that may occur to you, and that you may deem appropriate.

Farewell, Charles—remember me kindly to "a number of officers stationed in Texas," when you write. Invest properly and judiciously, the "five or ten per cents" you get from them--in your future efforts forget me, and remember to

"Be virtuous and you will be happy."

Adieu,

Yours respectively,

—— —— ——, Lieut. U. S. A

To C. D. ESQUIRE, Opposite Odd Fellows' Hall, General Agent, Notary Public, Commissioner of Deeds, and U. S. Commissioner for all the States in the Union and Elsewhere!

THE EXTREMITY.

] JOHN PHŒNIX.

'irst of American Fun Makers.

ᵻnant Derby at San Diego.

ᵻnecdotes of the Famous Wit —His Bright Career in California.

are several old settlers left in the
ᵻ part of the State who knew
ᵻnt Derby, the engineer officer
ᵻned, under the pen name of
'hœnix," the reputation of being
humorist to appear in American
ᵻe. Grizzled old Phil Crosthwaite,
ᵻ of all he surveys on a 19,000-
ᵻch in Baja California, is one of
Crosthwaite, originally a collegian
ᵻilor, landed at San Diego in 1845
ᵻ the old town's first American
He has a budget of unpub-
'hœnixiana, some of which, owing
ᵻola-like realism of Derby's humor,
ᵻot bear publication.
ᵻyou ever hear about that row
ᵻad with a brother officer named
ᵻ over a young lady to whom
ᵻ was engaged? No? Well, as I
ᵻer it," said the veteran, "Derby

went to ca.. u... ᵻ I believe
his return he stopped at
ters and sat down with mᵻᵻn-
ment.
"'What's up, Derby?' was ᵻ
tion.
"Derby didn't want to tell, but fi
with many excuses and protestatio
said that he had h ppened into
——'s house accidentally and had ᵻ
found her out. He wanted to warn
tenant Williams about it and was sᵻ
in the hope that Williams wouldn'
it to heart.
"But Williams took it badly. H
deeply in love and a thing like thᵻ
more than he could stand. He demᵻ
the full particulars, and finally, altᵻ
humorist had tortured him for twᵻ
hours, learned that finding her oᵻ
equivalent to finding her away
home."
Phil Crosthwaite is not the only vᵻ
who can fish up a fresh Derby anᵻ
from the pool of personal reminisᵻ
Capt in George A. Johnson, who exᵻ
the Colorado river for the Governmᵻ
1851, is another. Dr. Winder who
manded the San Diego
post just before "Prince John"
gruder took it, and who was in
mᵻnd at Alcatraz during the
also knew the young Lieutenant.
Judge Witherby, who went to San
with the boundary commission aft
treaty of Guadalupe Hidalgo. Lil
Judge Thomas H. Bush and ex-Stat
ator McCoy.
One of these pioneers has had a gl
of some rare manu cripts which
bequeathed to his friend Mrs. H
and which are likely to be edited anᵻ
lished upon the return of that ladᵻ
Europe, where she is now traveliᵻg.
legacy consists of humorous sketch
drawings, with here and there ᵻ
chᵻracteristic verse.
Lieutenant Derby was given to
fornia by an act of jocose insubordiᵻ

avis was Secretary
sent the young
'ombigbee river
channel and
it would be
'ove it. — In an-
1 the department
gbee river ran up
eply, in which he
tioned the neigh-
ap and wandered
ld would venture
unce of a definite
bigbee river ran
o at all.
1 story about the
whether the Tom-
·by's designs : for
uniforms brought
xi ed him to San
h:.ve been enough
War Secretary to
to the most dis-
tour of duty that
· uniform designs
ixed to the seat of
or convenience in
o march, and with
n, which a soldier
ick" when he got
assio in the comic
Derby sent them
, gravely enough,
rity of the Cabinet
wed them about ·
have this man
the future Presi-
cy, "Now, don't
ary," urged the
venture to think
s and the public
ridiculous Better
ried. Commodore
d to Washington
Pacific coast and
bay of San Diego
less the waters of
:h their burden of
e diverted from it.
iated funds for the
ained was for the
an engineer to
his was Mr. Davis'
mon understand-
go, besides being
estern settlement,
sted with ideas and
Department took

the view that a t
more than any o
due Derby's hun:
bounds of officii
periment was tri
The young e
across the plait
went to San Die
erner. He foun
but the surround
The town of ti
pueblo, with 30
was yet far in to
guiltless of a fui
and the whirring
every sunbathed
place Sandy Ag
and then he sett
a few weeks be 1
dam the San Di
his full duty.
night and day ev
In the interva
engineer tried h
San Diego Heral
beyond the supp
annual bounties
central commit
around for the e
visit San Franci
A Gubernatoria
Waldo, the Wh
the Democratic
he went north, t
whose squibs sig
been read with
old San Diego w
asked him to tal
hot for Bigler sr
to the Democrat
next steamer.
story of what h
cal. Old settler
cratic managers
on the "Baldo
which ended w
for "Baldo," the
So did Ames, wt
Derby's account
ing with Ames,
prietor down ov
nose in the mou
ary for the purp
in n ended by t
the faces of th
affair a wholly d
best known bit
can be found 1
humor before tl

Ames and Derby grew reconciled and the humorist continued to work for the *Herald.* "The other day," he remarked in a pensive editorial paragraph, "we accidently threw a bucket of dirty water out of the window which struck a lone Mexican sitting on his horse. He said 'carrajo,' meaning that we were courageous, and when we observed his ferocious expression we thought we were."

Phœnix has the credit of introducing illustrations to the newspaper press, and this he did in a pictorial column which made the *Herald* nearly as famous as the political turn-about had done. Knocking around the office were a lot of small advertising cuts. Derby took these and ran them into the paper with annotations of his own. Four small frame houses were labeled "Abbotsford," "The capitol at Washington," "The residence of John Phœnix," and "The home of Governor Bigler at Benicia." They were all alike. A turtle stood for the steamer Goliah of the coast line. A cut of a Durham bull was labeled "Prince Albert," a royal personage whose German extraction was due, Derby said, to the fact that "his father was a Dutchman and his mother a Duchess." Two large coal cars, a small locomotive and a set of false teeth were put in line over the announcement of a fearful accident on the Princeton railroad. The crowning effect was produced, however, by a picture of two ballet dancers, labeled "An interview between Harriet Beecher Stowe and the Duchess of Sutherland."

When the engineering work on the river was completed Lieutenant Derby went East. He had married in San Francisco, but was divorced in a few years, his late wife going South, where Derby also found himself after the outbreak of the war. During the long fight he remained in the regular army, gaining the rank of captain, but before the end of hostilities he became insane. The last ever seen of him by his San Diego friends was when Captain Winder met him at the Astor House in 1864. He was smiling vacantly at the wall. He knew nobody, and soon afterward he was sent to the asylum, where he died. But his San Diego writings, collected in a volume of "Phœnixiana," remained as the sole literary example of American wit and humor until the rise of Mark Twain and his school of modern funmakers.

Sarah A. Wentz.

SMILES AND FROWNS. A Novel. 1 vol., 12mo. Cloth. $1.25.

Anonymous.

COMETH UP AS A FLOWER. An Autobiography. 1 vol., 8vo. Paper covers. 60 cents.

NOT WISELY, BUT TOO WELL. By the Author of "Cometh up as a Flower." 1 vol., 8vo. Paper covers. 60 cents.

The name of the author of the above is still buried in obscurity. The sensation which was created by the publication of "Cometh up as a Flower" remains unabated, as the daily increasing demand abundantly testifies. No work, since the appearance of "Jane Eyre," has met with greater success.

LADY ALICE; or, The New Una. A Novel. New edition. Paper. 60 cents.

MADGE; or, Night and Morning. A Novel. 1 vol., 12mo. Cloth. $1.25.

SHERBROOKE. By H. B. G., author of "Madge." 1 vol., 12mo. Cloth. $1.25.

MARY STAUNTON: or, The Pupils of Marvel Hall. By the Author of "Portraits of My Married Friends." 1 vol., 12mo. Cloth. $1.

MINISTRY OF LIFE. By the Author of "Ministering Children." Illustrated. 1 vol., 12mo. Cloth. $1.25.

THE VIRGINIA COMEDIANS; or, Old Days in the Old Dominion. 2 vols., 12mo. Cloth. $2.50.

WIFE'S STRATAGEM. A Story for Fireside and Wayside. By Aunt Fanny. Illustrated. 1 vol., 12mo. Cloth. $1.

Captain Marryatt.

Marryatt's Popular Novels and Tales. A new and beautiful edition. 12 vols., 12mo. Cloth. $12.

Or, separately:

PETER SIMPLE. 12mo. Cloth. $1.

JACOB FAITHFUL. 12mo. Cloth. $1.

NAVAL OFFICER. 12mo. Cloth. $1.

KING'S OWN. 12mo. Cloth. $1.

JAPHET IN SEARCH OF A FATHER. 12mo. Cloth. $1.

NEWTON FORSTER. 12mo. Cloth. $1.

MIDSHIPMAN EASY. 12mo. Cloth. $1

PACHA OF MANY TALES. 12mo. Cloth. $1.

THE POACHER. 12mo. Cloth. $1.

THE PHANTOM SHIP. 12mo. Cloth. $1.

SNARLEYOW. 12mo. Cloth. $1.75.

PERCIVAL KEENE. 12mo. Cloth. $1.

Fine edition, printed on tinted paper. 12 vols., large 12mo. Cloth, $18.00; Half Calf, extra, $36.00.

THE CHEAP POPULAR EDITION OF MARRYATT'S NOVELS. To be completed in 12 volumes. Printed from new stereotype plates, in clear type, on good paper. **Price per volume, 50 cents.**

"Capt. Marryatt is a classic among novel-writers. A better idea may be had of the sea, of ship-life, especially in the navy, from these enchanting books, than from any other source. They will continue to be read as long as the language exists."

Miss Jane Porter.

SCOTTISH CHIEFS. A Romance. New and handsome edition. With Engravings. 1 vol., large 8vo. Cloth. $2.50; Half Calf, extra, $4.

The great popularity of this novel has rendered it necessary to furnish this handsome edition in large, readable type, with appropriate embellishments, for the domestic library.

Sir Walter Scott.

WAVERLEY NOVELS. The Cheap Popular Edition of the Waverley Novels. To be completed in Twenty-five Volumes, from New Stereotype Plates, uniform with the New Edition of Dickens, containing all the Notes of the Author, and printed from the latest edition of the Authorized Text, on fine white paper, in clear type, and convenient in size. Each volume illustrated with a Frontispiece. Pronounced "A Miracle of Cheapness."

Order of Issue.

1. WAVERLEY 25
2. IVANHOE... 25
3. KENILWORTH..........25
4. GUY MANN-RING...25
5. ANTIQUARY 25
6. ROB ROY...... 25
7. OLD MORTALITY.....25
8. THE BLACK DWARF, and A LEGEND OF MONTROSE 25
9. BRIDE OF LAMMER-MOOR....................25
10. HEART OF MID-LO-THIAN...................25
11. THE MONASTERY...25
12. THE ABBOT.... 25
13. THE PIRATE 25
14. FORTUNES OF NI-GEL......................25

15. PEVERIL OF THE PEAK...... 25
16. QUENTIN DUR-WARD..................25
17. ST. RONAN'S WELL..25
18. REDGAUNTLET........25
19. THE BETROTHED, and HIGHLAND WI-DOW.................... 25
20. THE TALISMAN......25
21. WOODSTOCK...........25
22. FAIR MAID OF PERTH........... 25
23. ANNE OF GEIER-STEIN...................25
24. COUNT ROBERT OF PARIS............. 25
25. THE SURGEON'S DAUGHTER...........25

The Complete Popular Library Edition of the Waverley Novels. Handsomely printed, in good clear type. Illustrated with numerous Engravings, and a Steel-plate Portrait of the Author. 6 vols., small 8vo. (Uniform with the "Popular Library Edition of Dickens.") Cloth, extra, $10.50.

WAVERLEY NOVELS. Black's Edition. Illustrated with 204 Steel Engravings. 25 vols., 8vo. Full Calf, extra, gilt edges, $125.00. Morocco, antique, $175.00.

E. M. Sewell.

AMY HERBERT. A Tale.
12mo. Cloth. $1.

CLEVE HALL. A Tale. 12mo.
Cloth. $1.

THE EARL'S DAUGHTER.
12mo. Cloth. $1.

EXPERIENCE OF LIFE.
12mo. Cloth. $1.

A GLIMPSE OF THE WORLD. 12mo. Cloth. $:.

GERTRUDE. A Tale. 12mo
Cloth. $1.

IVORS. A Story of English Country Life. 2 vols. Cloth. $2.00.

KATHARINE ASHTON. 2 vols., 12mo. Cloth. $2.00.

MARGARET PERCIVAL. 2 vols., 12mo. Cloth. $2.00.

URSULA. A Tale of Country Life. 2 vols., 12mo. Cloth. $2.00.

LANETON PARSONAGE. A Tale. 3 vols., 12mo. Cloth. $3.00.

HOME LIFE. A Journal. 1 vol., 12mo. Cloth. $1.25.

"Scarcely any modern English authoress stands so high as Miss Sewell; and so long as the English language exists, such books as 'Amy Herbert,' 'Gertrude,' etc., will continually be sought for."

Thackeray.

The popular Novels of W. M. THACKERAY, comprising:

THE LUCK OF BARRY LYNDON.

CONFESSIONS OF FITZ-BOODLE.

MR. BROWN'S LETTERS.

JEAMES'S DIARY.

MEN'S WIVES.

PARIS SKETCH-BOOK.

PUNCH'S PRIZE NOVEL-ISTS.

A SHABBY GENTEEL STORY.

THE YELLOWPLUSH PA-PERS.

BOOK OF SNOBS.

12 vols. in 6, 12mo. Cloth, $9.00 : Half Calf, extra, $18.00.